SONGS OF STARS AND SHADOWS

There is a girl who goes between the worlds.

She is grey-eyed and pale of skin, or so the story goes, and her hair is a coal-black waterfall with half-seen hints of red. She wears about her brow a circlet of burnished metal, a dark crown that holds her hair in place and sometimes puts shadows in her eyes. Her name is Sharra.

The beginning of her story is lost to us, with the memory of the world from which she sprang. The end?
The end is not yet, and when it comes we shall not know it.

We have only the middle, or rather a piece of that middle, the smallest part of the legend, a mere fragment of the quest...

Songs of Stars and Shadows

George R. R. Martin

CORONET BOOKS
Hodder and Stoughton

Copyright © 1977 by George R. R. Martin

First published in the United States 1977
by Pocket Books, New York

Coronet edition 1981

British Library C.I.P.

Martin, George R R
    Songs of stars and shadows.
    I. Title
    823'.9'1FS

ISBN 0-340-25095-X

---

*The characters and situations in this book are
entirely imaginary and bear no relation to any real
person or actual happening*

This book is sold subject to the condition that
it shall not, by way of trade or otherwise, be
lent, re-sold, hired out or otherwise circulated
without the publisher's prior consent in any
form of binding or cover other than that in
which this is published and without a similar
condition including this condition being
imposed on the subsequent purchaser.

Printed and bound in Great Britain for
Hodder and Stoughton Paperbacks, a
division of Hodder and Stoughton Ltd.,
Mill Road, Dunton Green, Sevenoaks,
Kent (Editorial Office: 47 Bedford
Square, London, WC1 3DP) by
Richard Clay (The Chaucer Press) Ltd.,
Bungay, Suffolk

ACKNOWLEDGMENTS

"This Tower of Ashes" copyright, ©, 1976, by the Condé Nast Publications, Inc. From *Analog Annual* (Pyramid, 1976).

"Patrick Henry, Jupiter, and the Little Red Brick Spaceship" copyright, ©, 1976, by Ultimate Publishing Company, Inc. From *Amazing Science Fiction*, December 1976.

"Men of Greywater Station" copyright, ©, 1976, by Ultimate Publishing Company, Inc. From *Amazing Science Fiction*, March 1976.

"The Lonely Songs of Laren Dorr" copyright, ©, 1976, by Ultimate Publishing Company, Inc. From *Fantastic Stories*, May 1976.

"Night of the Vampyres" copyright, ©, 1975, by Ultimate Publishing Company, Inc. From *Amazing Science Fiction*, May 1975.

"The Runners" copyright, ©, 1975, by Mercury Press, Inc. From *The Magazine of Fantasy and Science Fiction*, September 1975.

"Night Shift" copyright, ©, 1973, by Ultimate Publishing Company, Inc. From *Amazing Science Fiction*, January 1973.

"... for a single yesterday" copyright, ©, 1975, by Roger Elwood and Robert Silverberg. From *Epoch* (Berkley-Putnam, 1975).

"And Seven Times Never Kill Man" copyright, ©, 1975, by The Condé Nast Publications, Inc. From *Analog Science Fiction/Fact*, July 1975.

For Dolly,
a friend whenever I needed one:

All your dreams are on their way.

CONTENTS

INTRODUCTION	11
THIS TOWER OF ASHES	17
PATRICK HENRY, JUPITER, AND THE LITTLE RED BRICK SPACESHIP	37
MEN OF GREYWATER STATION *with Howard Waldrop*	55
THE LONELY SONGS OF LAREN DORR	93
NIGHT OF THE VAMPYRES	114
THE RUNNERS	147
NIGHT SHIFT	154
"... FOR A SINGLE YESTERDAY"	173
AND SEVEN TIMES NEVER KILL MAN	200

INTRODUCTION

Here are some stories that I've written.

According to an ancient and honored cliché, a writer's stories are his children. Most writers I know are boastful, doting parents. I am no less vulnerable to this disease of the trade than others.

Some readers, of course, are terribly bored by all this. They feel that the story, or the child, should stand on its own feet and speak for itself, and they'd rather not hear about it before- and after-the-fact, if you don't mind. I don't. If you are of that persuasion, please do go right on to the stories.

If, however, you're more like me, and don't mind background detail and talk of inspiration and influences and headaches, then you might be interested in a few words about these stories, what they are and how they came to be and what they mean to me as a writer.

The oldest story in the collection is "Night Shift," written early in the summer of 1971, just at the start of the most prolific few months I've ever had (I turned out a story every two weeks throughout that summer; I've never again worked that fast). The youngest story is the one that closes the book, "And Seven Times Never Kill Man," which I completed late in the fall of 1974. The rest fall in between, but by and large they're of a more recent vintage than the stories in my first collection, *A Song for Lya and Other Stories*.

"Night Shift," which should be discussed first by simple historical right, grew out of a summer I'd spent working on a truck dock, and my father's experiences as a longshoreman. I thought it was a damned ambitious story when I started it—an attempt to write a gritty, realistic, slice-of-life SF story—and by the time I had finished I was convinced it was the best thing I'd ever done. Visions of sugarplums and awards danced in my head. Needless to say, the story vanished without a trace on publication, but I'm still fond of it. In many ways a very atypical story for me, "Night Shift" was the first of my stories to focus on the clash between romance and reality, a clash that I find endlessly fascinating. I've always thought that "Night Shift" was a sort of flip-side companion piece to my better-known "With Morning Comes Mistfall," which I wrote about a month later.

My prolific period ended when summer did in 1971, and was followed by a dry spell that was twice as long as the productive interlude that had preceded it. I moved to Chicago in September, and in January began work as a VISTA volunteer attached to Cook County Legal Assistance; meanwhile, my stories began to sell like hell. But I'd stopped working, except to make minor revisions on already completed stories to meet editorial demands.

"Night of the Vampyres" was the story that finally broke the slump. Ben Bova, who had recently taken over the reins of *Analog* and bought a brace of stories from me, provided me with the basic idea of a dogfight between laser-armed war-planes, as well as an envelope full of materials about lasers. I dutifully tried to digest it all, and finally wound up combining that plot with one that I'd been mulling for some time, and to my relief I discovered that I could still write after all. As it turned out, Ben didn't like the story when I finally completed it and shipped it off to him. But that was almost all right. By the time I got the rejection, I was deep into a new story.

"Men of Greywater Station" was the first collaboration I ever tried. Texas writer Howard Waldrop and I had been corresponding since 1963, when we were both in high school and I mailed him a quarter to buy a *Justice League of America* comic book, but we never actually met in the flesh until 1972, when we finally got together at an SF convention in Kansas City, Missouri. There was a Playboy Club on top of the convention hotel. Most of the folks Howard and I were hanging around with had never been in a Playboy Club, so one night a big party went up to swill expensive drinks and ogle the Bunnies. In the middle of all that decadence Howard and I sat nursing our beers, and suddenly a furtive look came into our eyes, and we got feverish and began to talk story, and from there it wasn't terribly long until we snuck down to the hotel room where we were sleeping on the floor (I was using my boots as a pillow) and Howard got out his portable typewriter. One of us wrote while the other partied, and by the time the weekend was over we had half the story. Howard took the manuscript down to Texas with him, finished the rough draft, and shipped it up to me. I revised, expanded, polished, and finally marketed the thing, by then the longest story either of us had ever done.

That was August, 1972. Howard Waldrop is a frighteningly fertile writer, capable of tossing off more good story ideas on a single afternoon than I can produce in a month. I'm really afraid that one of these days Howard is going to take over the world. Luckily, the little fellow is slow. I sent him a large chunk of our second collaboration in October of 72. He keeps telling me that he's going to get to it real soon now.

About the same time that I was mailing that manuscript to Howard, I was also writing " . . . for a single yesterday," a story that I love. Now, writers are always getting asked to name people who've influenced them. You're expected to name other writers, SF or otherwise. Well, lots of writers, SF and otherwise, have influenced me. But not all of them write books. Songwriters influence me, sometimes quite a lot, and Kris Kristofferson has probably influenced me most of all, especially his earlier, hungrier work. That's one of the things that " . . . for a single yesterday" is all about, though not the only thing. I thought, and still think, that it's one of my first-rank top-of-his-alleged-form stories. A number of people agree. A number of other people disagree rather vehemently. The 1973 Milford Writers' Conference almost came to blows when I threw the story into the hopper. Sometimes it seems to me that the people who love the story and the people who hate the story are both missing three-quarters of what I tried to put into it, but that may be my fault, not theirs. It is often called a love story, and it is partly that, of course, but mostly it's about time, and the way we deal with time. I still like it quite a lot.

"The Runners" had been rattling around inside my head for years, but it took me only an hour to set it down on paper. I did it during lunch while I was still with Cook County Legal Assistance, and for dessert I wrote another little short-short. It was astonishing, writing two stories in a single day. It seemed to open immense new vistas for me. Of course, I've never been able to do it again, but . . .

"Patrick Henry, Jupiter, and the Little Red Brick Spaceship" was done slightly later in 1973. It too had been inside my head for a long time. The seed for the story had been planted when a World Science Fiction Convention presented a special award to Apollo XI for "Best Moon Landing Ever," a utterly unwarranted accolade. From time to time critics have said that my favorite themes are love and loneliness. That shows how much critics know. Love and loneliness may be *among* my favorite themes, but the all-time champion to date has got to be reality's repeated search-and-destroy missions against romance, a subject that I've turned to again and again. "Patrick Henry, Jupiter, and the Little Red Brick Spaceship" is one of Those.

In between "Patrick Henry, et al." and "The Lonely Songs of Laren Dorr," I wrote a number of other stories which are not included in this collection for one reason or another. I also completed my two-year stint in VISTA, and began life as a starving full-time writer. Well, almost full-time; I supplemented my income by directing chess tournaments on weekends. The theory was that once I no longer had to put in hours at a Real Job, my production would go way up. Somehow that didn't work out.

I wrote "The Lonely Songs of Laren Dorr" in May of 1974. It's fantasy, not SF, and it's romantic as hell. I admit to being an unabashed romantic (I will not say "incurable"—romanticism is a literary/philosophic tradition with a long and honorable history, not a disease, thank you), but my philosophy and my psyche had both been sorely battered by various personal trials in 1973-74, and from time to time the corners of my mouth would tremble and I would begin to mutter surly, cynical things. So I sat myself down and tried to write the most romantic vision I could set to paper, to restore myself. It worked, sort of, although I suppose you can't ever put Humpty Dumpty together precisely as he was before, which is why the stories I've written after that period seem a bit darker than those I wrote earlier. At least to me.

I can find precious little to say about "This Tower of Ashes," save that it is in my estimation the best short story I have ever written.

Shortly after it was completed and off in the mails, I flew to a World SF Convention in Washington, D.C., and flew back to Chicago several days later in love. The woman was Gale Burnick; oddly enough, we had met at several previous conventions, but somehow never noticed each other before. But we became fast friends on the night I lost my first Hugo (a bit like losing your virginity, that), and she joined me in Chicago a month later, and in November of 1975 we were married (despite which her name remains Gale Burnick, thank you). But that's getting ahead...

"And Seven Times Never Kill Man" is the last story in the book, and the most recent. The title came first. I encountered it in Rudyard Kipling's *Jungle Books,* and instantly knew that I had to write a story to go with it. The people and the planet and the plot came sometime later. Oddly enough, although the title is taken from a fine lithe line of poetry, people seem to have an irresistible penchant for mucking it up. The story appeared on the 1976 Hugo ballot, as a contender in the novelette category, and even there it was called, "And Seven Times Never Kill a Man." I frothed a bit and wrote letters. After the story was published, one reader wrote to congratulate me on the extensive knowledge of Boer history I'd displayed. You learn something every day in this business.

Now, go read the stories.

Dubuque, Iowa
February, 1977

THIS TOWER OF ASHES

My tower is built of bricks, small soot-gray bricks mortared together with a shiny black substance that looks strangely like obsidian to my untrained eye, though it clearly cannot be obsidian. It sits by an arm of the Skinny Sea, twenty feet tall and sagging, the edge of the forest only a few feet away.

I found the tower nearly four years ago, when Squirrel and I left Port Jamison in the silver aircar that now lies gutted and overgrown in the weeds outside my doorstep. To this day I know almost nothing about the structure, but I have my theories.

I do not think it was built by men, for one. It clearly pre-dates Port Jamison, and I often suspect it pre-dates human spaceflight. The bricks (which are curiously small, less than a quarter the size of normal bricks) are tired and weathered and old, and they crumble visibly beneath my feet. Dust is everywhere and I know its source, for more than once I have pried loose a brick from the parapet on the roof and crushed it idly to fine dark powder in my naked fist. When the salt wind blows from the east, the tower flies a plume of ashes.

Inside, the bricks are in better condition, since the wind and the rain have not touched them quite so much, but the tower is still far from pleasant. The interior is a single room full of dust and echoes, without windows; the only light comes from the circular opening in the center of the roof. A spiral stair, built of the same ancient brick as the rest, is part of the wall; around and around it circles, like the threading on a screw, before it reaches roof level. Squirrel, who is quite small as cats go, finds the stairs easy climbing, but for human feet they are narrow and awkward.

But I still climb them. Each night I return from the cool forests, my arrows black with the caked blood of the dream-spiders and my bag heavy with their poison sacs, and I set aside my bow and wash my hands and then climb up to the roof to spend the last few hours before dawn. Across the narrow salt channel, the lights of Port Jamison burn on the island, and from up there it is not the city I remember. The square black buildings wear a bright romantic glow at night; the lights, all smoky orange and muted blue, speak of mystery and silent song and more than a little loneliness, while the starships rise and fall against the stars like the tireless wandering fireflies of my boyhood on Old Earth.

"There are stories over there," I told Korbec once, before I had learned better. "There are people behind every light, and each person has a life, a story. Only they lead those lives without ever touching us, so we'll never know the stories." I think I gestured then; I was, of course, quite drunk.

Korbec answered with a toothy smile and a shake of his head. He was a great dark fleshy man, with a beard like knotted wire. Each month he came out from the city in his pitted black aircar, to drop off my supplies and take the venom I had collected, and each month we went up to the roof and got drunk together. A truck driver, that was all Korbec was; a seller of cut-rate dreams and second-hand rainbows. But he fancied himself a philosopher and a student of man.

"Don't fool yourself," he said to me then, his face flush with wine and darkness, "you're not missing nothin'. Lives are rotten stories, y'know. Real stories, now, they usually got a plot to 'em. They start and they go on a bit and when they end they're over, unless the guy's got a series goin'. People's lives don't do that nohow, they just kinda wander around and ramble and go on and on. Nothin' ever finishes."

"People die," I said. "That's enough of a finish, I'd think."

Korbec made a loud noise. "Sure, but have you ever known anybody to die at the right time? No, don't happen that way. Some guys fall over before their lives have properly gotten started, some right in the middle of the best part. Others kinda linger on after everything is really over."

Often when I sit up there alone, with Squirrel warm in my lap and a glass of wine by my side, I remember Korbec's words and the heavy way he said them, his coarse voice oddly gentle. He is not a smart man, Korbec, but that night I think he spoke the truth, maybe never realizing it himself. But the weary realism that he offered me then is the only antidote there is for the dreams that spiders weave.

But I am not Korbec, nor can I be, and while I recognize his truth, I cannot live it.

I was outside taking target practice in the late afternoon, wearing nothing but my quiver and a pair of cut-offs, when they came. It was closing on dusk and I was loosening up for my nightly foray into the forest—even in those early days I lived from twilight to dawn, as the dream-spiders do. The grass felt good under my bare feet, the double-curved silverwood bow felt even better in my hand, and I was shooting well.

Then I heard them coming. I glanced over my shoulder toward the beach, and saw the dark blue aircar swelling rapidly against the eastern sky. Gerry, of course, I knew that from the sound; his aircar had been making noises as long as I had known him.

I turned my back on them, drew another arrow— quite steady—and notched my first bull's-eye of the day.

Gerry set his aircar down in the weeds near the base of the tower, just a few feet from my own. Crystal was with him, slim and grave, her long gold hair full of red glints from the afternoon sun. They climbed out and started toward me.

"Don't stand near the target," I told them, as I slipped another arrow into place and bent the bow.

"How did you find me?" The twang of the arrow vibrating in the target punctuated my question.

They circled well around my line of fire. "You'd mentioned spotting this place from the air once," Gerry said, "and we knew you weren't anywhere in Port Jamison. Figured it was worth a chance." He stopped a few feet from me, with his hands on his hips, looking just as I remembered him; big, dark-haired and very fit. Crystal came up beside him and put one hand lightly on his arm.

I lowered my bow and turned to face them. "So. Well, you found me. Why?"

"I was worried about you, Johnny," Crystal said softly. But she avoided my eyes when I looked at her.

Gerry put a hand around her waist, very possessively, and something flared within me. "Running away never solves anything," he told me, his voice full of the strange mixture of friendly concern and patronizing arrogance he had been using on me for months.

"I did *not* run away," I said, my voice strained. "Damn it. You should never have come."

Crystal glanced at Gerry, looking very sad, and it was clear that suddenly she was thinking the same thing. Gerry just frowned. I don't think he ever once understood why I said the things I said, or did the things I did; whenever we discussed the subject, which was infrequently, he would only tell me with vague puzzlement what *he* would have done if our roles had been reversed. It seemed infinitely strange to him that anyone could possibly do anything differently in the same position.

His frown did not touch me, but he'd already done his damage. For the month I'd been in my self-imposed exile at the tower, I had been trying to come to terms with my actions and my moods, and it had been far from easy. Crystal and I had been together for a long time—nearly four years—when we came to Jamison's World, trying to track down some unique silver and obsidian artifacts that we'd picked up on Baldur. I had loved her all that time, and I still loved her, even now, after she had left me for Gerry. When I was feeling good about myself, it seemed to me that the impulse that had driven me out of Port Jamison was a noble and unselfish one. I wanted Crys to be happy, simply, and she could not be happy with me there. My wounds were too deep, and I wasn't good at hiding them; my presence put the damper of guilt on the new-born joy she'd found with Gerry. And since she could not bear to cut me off completely, I felt compelled to cut myself off. For them. For her.

Or so I liked to tell myself. But there were hours when that bright rationalization broke down, dark hours of self-loathing. Were those the real reasons? Or was I simply out to hurt myself in a fit of angry immaturity, and by doing so, punish them—like a willful child who plays with thoughts of suicide as a form of revenge?

I honestly didn't know. For a month I'd fluctuated from one belief to the other while I tried to understand myself and decide what I'd do next. I wanted to think myself a hero, willing to make a sacrifice for the happiness of the woman I loved. But Gerry's words made it clear that he didn't see it that way at all.

"Why do you have to be so damned dramatic about everything?" he said, looking stubborn. He had been determined all along to be very civilized, and seemed perpetually annoyed at me because I wouldn't shape up and heal my wounds so that everybody could be friends. Nothing annoyed me quite so much as his annoyance; *I* thought I was handling the situation pretty well, all things considered, and I resented the inference that I wasn't.

But Gerry was determined to convert me, and my best withering look was wasted on him. 'We're going to stay here and talk things out until you agree to fly back to Port Jamison with us," he told me, in his most forceful now-I'm-getting-tough tone.

"Like shit," I said, turning sharply away from them and yanking an arrow from my quiver. I slid it into place, pulled, and released, all too quickly. The arrow missed the target by a good foot and buried itself in the soft dark brick of my crumbling tower.

"What *is* this place, anyway?" Crys asked, looking at

the tower as if she'd just seen it for the first time. It's possible that she had—that it took the incongruous sight of my arrow lodging in stone to make her notice the ancient structure. More likely, though, it was a premeditated change of subject, designed to cool the argument that was building between Gerry and me.

I lowered my bow again and walked up to the target to recover the arrows I'd expended. "I'm really not sure," I said, somewhat mollified and anxious to pick up the cue she'd thrown me. "A watchtower, I think, of nonhuman origin. Jamison's World has never been thoroughly explored. It may have had a sentient race once." I walked around the target to the tower, and yanked loose the final arrow from the crumbling brick. "It still may, actually. We know very little of what goes on on the mainland."

"A damn gloomy place to live, if you ask me," Gerry put in, looking over the tower. "Could fall in any moment, from the way it looks."

I gave him a bemused smile. "The thought had occurred to me. But when I first came out here, I was past caring." As soon as the words were out, I regretted saying them; Crys winced visibly. That had been the whole story of my final weeks in Port Jamison. Try as I might, it had seemed that I had only two choices; I could lie, or I could hurt her. Neither appealed to me, so here I was. But here they were too, so the whole impossible situation was back.

Gerry had another comment ready, but he never got to say it. Just then Squirrel came bounding out from between the weeds, straight at Crystal.

She smiled at him and knelt, and an instant later he was at her feet, licking her hand and chewing on her fingers. Squirrel was in a good mood, clearly. He liked life near the tower. Back in Port Jamison, his life had been constrained by Crystal's fears that he'd be eaten by alleysnarls or chased by dogs or strung up by local children. Out here I let him run free, which was much more to his liking. The brush around the tower was overrun by whipping-mice, a native rodent with a hairless tail three times its own body length. The tail packed a mild sting, but Squirrel didn't care, even though he swelled up and got grouchy every time a tail connected. He *liked* stalking whipping-mice all day. Squirrel always fancied himself a great hunter, and there's no skill involved in chasing down a bowl of catfood.

He'd been with me even longer than Crys had, but she'd become suitably fond of him during our time together. I often suspected that Crystal would have gone with Gerry even sooner than she did, except that she was upset at the idea of leaving Squirrel. Not that he was any great beauty. He was a small, thin, scuffy-looking cat, with ears like a fox and fur a scroungy gray-brown color, and a big bushy tail two sizes too big for him. The friend who gave him to me back on Avalon informed me gravely that Squirrel was the illegitimate offspring of a genetically-engineered psicat and a mangy alley tom. But if Squirrel could read his owner's mind, he didn't pay much attention. When he wanted affection, he'd do things like climb right up on the book I was reading and knock it away and begin biting my chin; when he wanted to be let alone, it was dangerous folly to try to pet him.

As Crystal knelt by him and stroked him and Squirrel nuzzled up to her hand, she seemed very much the woman I'd traveled with and loved and talked to at endless length and slept with every night, and I suddenly realized how I'd missed her. I think I smiled; the sight of her, even under these conditions, still gave me a cloud-shadowed joy. Maybe I was being silly and stupid and vindictive to send them away, I thought, after they had come so far to see me. Crys was still Crys, and Gerry could hardly be so bad, since she loved him.

Watching her, wordless, I made a sudden decision; I would let them stay. And we could see what happened. "It's close to dusk," I heard myself saying. "Are you folks hungry?"

Crys looked up, still petting Squirrel, and smiled. Gerry nodded. "Sure."

"All right," I said. I walked past them, turned and paused in the doorway, and gestured them inside. "Welcome to my ruin."

I turned on the electric torches and set about making dinner. My lockers were well stocked back in those days; I had not yet started living off the forests. I unthawed three big sandragons, the silver-shelled crustacean that Jamie fishermen dragged for relentlessly, and served them up with bread and cheese and white wine.

Mealtime conversation was polite and guarded. We talked of mutual friends in Port Jamison, Crystal told me about a letter she'd received from a couple we had known on Baldur, Gerry held forth on politics and the efforts of the Port police to crack down on the traffic in dreaming venom. "The Council is sponsoring research on some sort of super-pesticide that would wipe out the dream-spiders," he told me. "A saturation spraying of the near coast would cut off most of the supply, I'd think."

"Certainly," I said, a bit high on the wine and a bit piqued at Gerry's stupidity. Once again, listening to him, I had found myself questioning Crystal's taste. "Never mind what other effects it might have on the ecology, right?"

Gerry shrugged, "Mainland," he said simply. He was Jamie through-and-through, and the comment translated to, "Who cares?" The accidents of history had given the residents of Jamison's World a singularly cavalier attitude toward their planet's one large continent. Most of the original settlers had come from Old Poseidon, where the sea had been a way of life for generations. The rich, teeming oceans and peaceful archipelagoes of their new world had attracted them far more than the dark forests of the mainland. Their children grew up to the same attitudes, except for a handful who found an illegal profit selling dreams.

"Don't shrug it all off so easy," I said.

"Be realistic," he replied. "The mainland's no use to anyone, except the spider-men. Who would it hurt?"

"Damn it, Gerry, look at this tower! Where did it come from, tell me that! I tell *you*, there might be intelligence out there, in those forests. The Jamies have never even been bothered to look."

Crystal was nodding over her wine. "Johnny could be

right," she said, glancing at Gerry. "That was why I came here, remember. The artifacts. The shop on Baldur said they were shipped out of Port Jamison. He couldn't trace them back any farther than that. And the workmanship—I've handled alien art for years, Gerry. I know Fyndii work, and Damoosh, and I've seen all the others. This was *different*."

Gerry only smiled. "Proves nothing. There are other races, millions of them, farther in toward the core. The distances are too great, so we don't hear of them very often, except maybe third-hand, but it isn't impossible that every so often a piece of their art would trickle through." He shook his head. "No, I'd bet this tower was put up by some early settler. Who knows? Could be there was another discoverer, before Jamison, who never reported his find. Maybe he built the place. But I'm not going to buy mainland sentients."

"At least not until you fumigate the damned forests and they all come out waving their spears," I said sourly. Gerry laughed and Crystal smiled at me. And suddenly, suddenly, I had an overpowering desire to *win* this argument. My thoughts had the hazy clarity that only wine can give, and it seemed so logical. I was so clearly *right,* and here was my chance to show up Gerry like the provincial he was and make points with Crys.

I leaned forward. "If you Jamies would ever look, you might find sentients," I said. "I've only been on the mainland a month, and already I've found a great deal. You've no damned concept of the kind of beauty you talk so blithely of wiping out. A whole ecology is out there, different from the islands, species upon species, a lot probably not even discovered yet. But what do you know about it? Any of you?"

Gerry nodded. "So, show me." He stood up suddenly. "I'm always willing to learn, Bowen. Why don't you take us out and show us all the wonders of the mainland?"

I think Gerry was trying to make points, too. He probably never thought I'd take up his offer, but it was exactly what I'd wanted. It was dark outside now, and we had been talking by the light of my torches. Above, stars shone through the hole in my roof. The forest would be alive now, eerie and beautiful, and I was suddenly eager to be out there, bow in hand, in a world where I was a force and a friend, Gerry a bumbling tourist.

"Crystal?" I said.

She looked interested. "Sounds like fun. If it's safe."

"It will be," I said. "I'll take my bow." We both rose, and Crys looked happy. I remembered the times we tackled Baldurian wilderness together, and suddenly I felt very happy, certain that everything would work out well. Gerry was just part of a bad dream. She couldn't possibly be in love with him.

First I found the sober-ups; I was feeling good, but not good enough to head out into the forest when I was still dizzy from wine. Crystal and I flipped ours down immediately, and seconds later my alcoholic glow began to fade. Gerry, however, waved away the pill I offered him. "I haven't had that much," he insisted. "Don't need it."

I shrugged, thinking that things were getting better and better. If Gerry went crashing drunkenly through the woods, it couldn't help but turn Crys away from him. "Suit yourself," I said.

Neither of them was really dressed for wilderness, but I hoped that wouldn't be a problem, since I didn't really plan on taking them very deep in the forest. It would be a quick trip, I thought; wander down my trail a bit, show them the dust pile and the spider-chasm, maybe nail a dream-spider for them. Nothing to it, out and back again.

I put on a dark coverall, heavy trail boots, and my quiver, handed Crystal a flash in case we wandered away from the bluemoss regions, and picked up my bow. "You really need that?" Gerry asked, with sarcasm.

"Protection," I said.

"Can't be that dangerous."

It isn't, if you know what you're doing, but I didn't

tell him that. "Then why do you Jamies stay on your islands?"

He smiled. "I'd rather trust a laser."

"I'm cultivating a deathwish. A bow gives the prey a chance, of sorts."

Crys gave me a smile of shared memories. "He only hunts predators," she told Gerry. I bowed.

Squirrel agreed to guard my castle. Steady and very sure of myself, I belted on a knife and led my ex-wife and her lover out into the forests of Jamison's World.

We walked in single file, close together, me up front with the bow, Crys following, Gerry behind her. Crys used the flashlight when we first set out, playing it over the trail as we wound our way through the thick grove of spikearrows that stood like a wall against the sea. Tall and very straight, crusty gray of bark and some as big around as my tower, they climbed to a ridiculous height before sprouting their meager load of branches. Here and there they crowded together and squeezed the path between them, and more than one seemingly-impassable fence of wood confronted us suddenly in the dark. But Crys could always pick out the way, with me a foot ahead of her to point her flash when it paused.

Ten minutes out from the tower, the character of the forest began to change. The ground and the very air were drier here, the wind cool but without the snap of salt; the water-hungry spikearrows had drained most of the moisture from the air. They began to grow smaller and less frequent, the spaces between them larger and easier to find. Other species of plant began to appear; stunted little goblin trees, sprawling mockoaks, graceful ebonfires whose red veins pulsed brilliantly in the dark wood when caught by Crystal's wandering flash.

And bluemoss.

Just a little at first; here a ropy web dangling from a goblin's arm, there a small patch on the ground, frequently chewing its way up the back of an ebonfire or a withering solitary spikearrow. Then more and more; thick carpets underfoot, mossy blankets on the leaves above, heavy trailers that dangled from the branches and danced around in the wind. Crystal sent the flash darting about, finding bigger and better bunches of the soft blue fungus, and peripherally I began to see the glow.

"Enough," I said, and Crys turned off the light.

Darkness lasted only for a moment, till our eyes adjusted to a dimmer light. Around us, the forest was suffused by a gentle radiance, as the bluemoss drenched us in its ghostly phosphorescence. We were standing near one side of a small clearing, below a shiny black ebonfire, but even the flames of its red-veined wood seemed cool in the faint blue light. The moss had taken over the undergrowth, supplanting all the local grasses and making nearby shrubs into fuzzy blue beachballs. It climbed the sides of most of the trees, and when we looked up through the branches at the stars, we saw that other colonies had set upon the woods a glowing crown.

I laid my bow carefully against the dark flank of the ebonfire, bent, and offered a handful of light to Crystal. When I held it under her chin, she smiled at me again, her features softened by the cool magic in my hand. I remember feeling very good, to have led them to this beauty.

But Gerry only grinned at me. "Is this what we're going to endanger, Bowen?" he asked. "A forest full of bluemoss?"

I dropped the moss. "You don't think it's pretty?"

Gerry shrugged. "Sure, it's pretty. It is also a fungus, a parasite with a dangerous tendency to overrun and crowd out all other forms of plant-life. Bluemoss was very thick on Jolostar and the Barbis Archipelago once, you know. We rooted it all out; it can eat its way through a good corn crop in a month." He shook his head.

And Crystal nodded. "He's right, you know," she said.

I looked at her for a long time, suddenly feeling very sober indeed, the last memory of the wine long gone. Abruptly it dawned on me that I had, all unthinking, built myself another fantasy. Out here, in a world I had started to make my own, a world of dream-spiders and magic moss, somehow I had thought that I could recapture my own dream long fled, my smiling crystalline soulmate. In the timeless wilderness of the mainland, she would see us both in fresh light and would realize once again that it was me she loved.

So I'd spun a pretty web, bright and alluring as the trap of any dream-spider, and Crys had shattered the flimsy filaments with a word. She was his; mine no longer, not now, not ever. And if Gerry seemed to me stupid or insensitive or overpractical, well, perhaps it was those very qualities that made Crys choose him. And perhaps not—I had no right to second-guess her love, and possibly I would never understand it.

I brushed the last flakes of glowing moss from my hands, while Gerry took the heavy flash from Crystal and flicked it on again. My blue fairyland dissolved, burned away by the bright white reality of his flashlight beam. "What now?" he asked, smiling. He was not so very drunk after all.

I lifted my bow from where I'd set it down. "Follow me," I said, quickly, curtly. Both of them looked eager and interested, but my own mood had shifted dramatically. Suddenly the whole trip seemed pointless. I wished that they were gone, that I was back at my tower with Squirrel. I was down...

... and sinking. Deeper in the moss-heavy woods, we came upon a dark swift stream, and the brilliance of the flashlight speared a solitary ironhorn that had come to drink. It looked up quickly, pale and startled, then bounded away through the trees, for a fleeting instant looking a bit like the unicorn of Old Earth legend. Long habit made me glance at Crystal, but her eyes sought Gerry's when she laughed.

Later, as we climbed a rocky incline, a cave loomed near at hand; from the smell, a woodsnarl lair.

I turned to warn them around it, only to discover that I'd lost my audience. They were ten steps behind me, at the bottom of the rocks, walking very slowly and talking quietly, holding hands.

Dark and angry, wordless, I turned away again and continued on over the hill. We did not speak again until I'd found the dust pile.

I paused on its edge, my boots an inch deep in the fine gray powder, and they came straggling up behind me. "Go ahead, Gerry," I said. "Use your flash here."

The light roamed. The hill was at our back, rocky and lit here and there with the blurred cold fire of bluemoss-choked vegetation. But in front of us was only desolation; a wide vacant plain, black and blasted and lifeless, open to the stars. Back and forth Gerry moved the flashlight, pushing at the borders of the dust nearby, fading as he shone it straight out into the gray distance. The only sound was the wind.

"So?" he said at last.

"Feel the dust," I told him. I was not going to stoop this time. "And when you're back at the tower, crush one of my bricks and feel that. It's the same thing, a sort of powdery ash." I made an expansive gesture. "I'd guess there was a city here once, but now it's all crumbled into dust. Maybe my tower was an outpost of the people who built it, you see?"

"The vanished sentients of the forests," Gerry said, still smiling. "Well, I'll admit there's nothing like this on the islands. For a good reason. We don't let forest fires rage unchecked."

"*Forest fire!* Don't give me that. Forest fires don't reduce everything to a fine powder, you always get a few blackened stumps or something."

"Oh? You're probably right. But all the ruined cities I know have at least a few bricks still piled on top of each other for the tourists to take pictures of," Gerry said. The flash beam flicked to and fro over the dust pile, dismissing it. "All you have is a mound of rubbish."

Crystal said nothing.

I began walking back, while they followed in silence. I was losing points every minute; it had been idiocy to bring them out here. At that moment nothing more was on my mind than getting back to my tower as quickly as possible, packing them off to Port Jamison together, and resuming my exile.

Crystal stopped me, after we'd come back over the hill into the bluemoss forest. "Johnny," she said. I stopped, they caught up, Crys pointed.

"Turn off the light," I told Gerry. In the fainter illumination of the moss, it was easier to spot; the intricate iridescent web of a dream-spider, slanting groundward from the low branches of a mockoak. The patches of moss that shone softly all around us were nothing to this; each web strand was as thick as my little finger, oily and brilliant, running with the colors of the rainbow.

Crys took a step toward it, but I took her by the arm and stopped her. "The spiders are around someplace," I said. "Don't go too close. Papa spider never leaves the web, and mama ranges around in the trees at night."

Gerry glanced upward a little apprehensively. His flash was dark, and suddenly he didn't seem to have all the answers. The dream-spiders are dangerous predators, and I suppose he'd never seen one outside of a display case. They weren't native to the islands. "Pretty big web," he said. "Spiders must be a fair size."

"Fair," I said, and at once I was inspired. I could discomfort him a lot more if an ordinary web like this got to him. And he had been discomforting me all night. "Follow me. I'll show you a real dream-spider."

We circled around the web carefully, never seeing either of its guardians. I led them to the spider-chasm.

It was a great V in the sandy earth, once a creekbed perhaps, but dry and overgrown now. The chasm is hardly very deep by daylight, but at night it looks formidable enough, as you stare down into it from the wooded hills on either side. The bottom is a dark tangle of shrubbery, alive with little flickering phantom lights; higher up, trees of all kinds lean into the chasm, almost meeting in the center. One of them, in fact, does cross the gap. An ancient, rotting spikearrow, withered by lack of moisture, had fallen long ago to provide a natural bridge. The bridge hangs with bluemoss, and glows.

The three of us walked out on that dim-lit, curving trunk, and I gestured down.

Yards below us, a glittering multihued net hung from hill to hill, each strand of the web thick as a cable and aglisten with sticky oils. It tied all the lower trees together in a twisting intricate embrace, and it was a shining fairy-roof above the chasm. Very pretty; it made you want to reach out and touch it.

That, of course, was why the dream-spiders spun it. They were nocturnal predators, and the bright colors of their webs afire in the night made a potent lure.

"Look," Crystal said, "the spider." She pointed. In one of the darker corners of the web, half-hidden by the tangle of a goblin tree that grew out of the rock, it was sitting. I could see it dimly, by the webfire and moss light, a great eight-legged white thing the size of a large pumpkin. Unmoving. Waiting.

Gerry glanced around uneasily again, up into the branches of a crooked mockoak that hung partially above us. "The mate's around somewhere, isn't it?"

I nodded. The dream-spiders of Jamison's World are not quite twins to the arachnids of Old Earth. The female is indeed the deadlier of the species, but far from eating the male, she takes him for life in a permanent specialized partnership. For it is the sluggish, great-bodied male who wears the spinnerets, who weaves the shining-fire web and makes it sticky with his oils, who binds and ties the prey snared by light and color. Meanwhile, the smaller female roams the dark branches, her poison sac full of the viscous dreaming-venom that grants bright visions and ecstasy and final blackness. Creatures many times her own size she stings, and drags limp back to the web to add to the larder.

The dream-spiders are soft, merciful hunters for all that. If they prefer live food, no matter; the captive probably enjoys being eaten. Popular Jamie wisdom says a spider's prey moans with joy as it is consumed. Like all popular wisdoms, it is vastly exaggerated. But the truth is, the captives never struggle.

Except that night, something was struggling in the web below us.

"What's that?" I said, blinking. The iridescent web was not even close to empty—the half-eaten corpse of an ironhorn lay close at hand below us, and some great dark bat was bound in bright strands just slightly farther away—but these were not what I watched. In the corner opposite the male spider, near the western trees, something was caught and fluttering. I remember a brief glimpse of thrashing pale limbs, wide luminous eyes, and something like wings. But I did not see it clearly.

That was when Gerry slipped.

Maybe it was the wine that made him unsteady, or maybe the moss under our feet, or the curve of the trunk on which we stood. Maybe he was just trying to step around me to see whatever it was I was staring at. But, in any case, he slipped and lost his balance, let out a yelp, and suddenly he was five yards below us, caught in the web. The whole thing shook to the impact of his fall, but it didn't come close to breaking—dream-spider webs are strong enough to catch ironhorns and woodsnarls, after all.

"Damn," Gerry yelled. He looked ridiculous; one leg plunged right down through the fibers of the web, his arms half-sunk and tangled hopelessly, only his head and shoulders really free of the mess. "This stuff is sticky. I can hardly move."

"Don't try," I told him. "It'll just get worse. I'll figure out a way to climb down and cut you loose. I've got my knife." I looked around, searching for a tree limb to shimmy out on.

"*John.*" Crystal's voice was tense, on edge.

The male spider had left his lurking place behind the goblin tree. He was moving toward Gerry with a heavy deliberate gait; a gross white shape clamoring over the preternatural beauty of his web.

"Damn," I said. I wasn't seriously alarmed, but it was a bother. The great male was the biggest spider I'd ever seen, and it seemed a shame to kill him. But I didn't see that I had much choice. The male dreamspider has no venom, but he *is* a carnivore, and his bite can be most final, especially when he's the size of this one. I couldn't let him get within biting distance of Gerry.

Steadily, carefully, I drew a long gray arrow out of my quiver and fitted it to my bowstring. It was night, of course, but I wasn't really worried. I was a good shot, and my target was outlined clearly by the glowing strands of his web.

Crystal screamed.

I stopped briefly, annoyed that she'd panic when everything was under control. But I knew all along that she would not, of course. It was something else. For an instant I couldn't imagine what it could be.

Then I saw, as I followed Crys' eyes with my own. A fat white spider the size of a big man's fist had dropped down from the mockoak to the bridge we were standing on, not ten feet away. Crystal, thank God, was safe behind me.

I stood there—how long? I don't know. If I had just acted, without stopping, without thought, I could have handled everything. I should have taken care of the male first, with the arrow I had ready. There would have been plenty of time to pull a second arrow for the female.

But I froze instead, caught in that dark bright moment, for an instant timeless, my bow in my hand yet unable to act.

It was all so complicated, suddenly. The female was scuttling toward me, faster than I would have believed, and it seemed so much quicker and deadlier than the slow white thing below. Perhaps I should take *it* out first. I might miss, and then I would need time to go for my knife or a second arrow.

Except that would leave Gerry tangled and helpless under the jaws of the male that moved toward him inexorably. He could die. He could die. Crystal could never blame me. I had to save myself, and her, she would understand that. And I'd have her back again.

Yes.

NO!

Crystal was screaming, screaming, and suddenly everything was clear and I knew what it had all meant and why I was here in this forest and what I had to do. There was a moment of glorious transcendence. I had lost the gift of making her happy, my Crystal, but now for a moment suspended in time that power had returned to me, and I could give or withhold happiness forever. With an arrow, I could prove a love that Gerry would never match.

I think I smiled. I'm sure I did.

And my arrow flew darkly through the cool night, and found its mark in the bloated white spider that raced across a web of light.

The female was on me, and I made no move to kick it away or crush it beneath my heel. There was a sharp stabbing pain in my ankle.

Bright and many-colored are the webs the dreamspiders weave.

At night, when I return from the forests, I clean my arrows carefully and open my great knife, with its slim barbed blade, to cut apart the poison sacs I've collected. I slit them open, each in turn, as I have earlier cut them from the still white bodies of the dreamspiders, and then I drain the venom off into a bottle, to wait for the day when Korbec flies out to collect it.

Afterwards I set out the miniature goblet, exquisitely wrought in silver and obsidian and bright with spider motifs, and pour it full of the heavy black wine they bring me from the city. I stir the cup with my knife, around and around until the blade is shiny clean again and the wine a trifle darker than before. And I ascend to the roof.

Often Korbec's words will return to me then, and with them my story. Crystal my love, and Gerry, and a night of lights and spiders. It all seemed so very right for that brief moment, when I stood upon the moss-covered bridge with an arrow in my hand, and decided. And it has all gone so very very *wrong*...

... from the moment I awoke, after a month of fever and visions, to find myself in the tower where Crys and Gerry had taken me to nurse me back to health. My decision, my transcendent choice, was not so final as I would have thought.

At times I wonder if it *was* a choice. We talked about it, often, while I regained my strength, and the tale that

Crystal tells me is not the one that I remember. She says that we never saw the female at all, until it was too late, that it dropped silently onto my neck just as I released the arrow that killed the male. Then, she says, she smashed it with the flashlight that Gerry had given her to hold, and I went tumbling into the web.

In fact, there *is* a wound on my neck, and none on my ankle. And her story has a ring of truth. For I have come to know the dream-spiders in the slow-flowing years since that night, and I know that the females are stealthy killers that drop down on their prey unawares. They do not charge across fallen trees like berserk ironhorns; it is not the spiders' way.

And neither Crystal nor Gerry has any memory of a pale winged thing flapping in the web.

Yet *I* remember it clearly . . . as I remember the female spider that scuttled toward me during the endless years that I stood frozen . . . but then . . . they say the bite of a dream-spider does strange things to your mind.

That could be it, of course.

Sometimes when Squirrel comes behind me up the stairs, scraping the sooty bricks with his eight white legs, the wrongness of it all hits me, and I know I've dwelt with dreams too long.

Yet the dreams are often better than the waking, the stories so much finer than the lives.

Crystal did not come back to me, then or ever. They left when I was healthy. And the happiness I'd brought her with the choice that was not a choice and the sacrifice not a sacrifice, my gift to her forever—it lasted less than a year. Korbec tells me that she and Gerry broke up violently, and that she has since left Jamison's World.

I suppose that's truth enough, if you can believe a man like Korbec. I don't worry about it overmuch.

I just kill dream-spiders, drink wine, pet Squirrel. And each night I climb this tower of ashes to gaze at distant lights.

—*Chicago, August 1974*

PATRICK HENRY, JUPITER, AND THE LITTLE RED BRICK SPACESHIP

—◦≼ ⋅⋅⋅ ≽◦—

The *Flycaster* looked like nothing so much as the remains of a fish, after everything edible had been removed. The head was left; the small, enclosed life cabin. And the cluster of fusion engines looked something like a tail. Between was only the long skeleton, a tangled grid of duralloy girders and instrument paks open to the cold of space.

Plus Vito, strapped atop the skeleton near the harpoon gun so he wouldn't float away while Jan adjusted their orbit to match that of the old satellite below.

He studied it through his helmet visor while she moved them. Dark against the blue-green backdrop of Earth, it looked, Vito thought, like a metal bird, its twin solar panels spread like silvered wings.

This bird was flying dead, though. Jan had taken an energy readout as soon as they'd gotten close enough. Nil.

"We're matched," she said, over the helmet radio. "It's all yours."

"Check," Vito said. He ran through the figures quickly on the wrist computer built into his spacesuit. Then, nodding satisfaction, he swung the gun around. Slow and careful in weightlessness, he inched it down until the figures on the sight matched those the computer had given him. The satellite was lined up in the cross-hairs.

As always, he hesitated as he wrapped his gloved

hand around the trigger. He had faith in the computer, but the harpoon gun he wasn't so sure about. It was salvage from a derelict whaler, boosted up from Earth on his order and welded into place atop the *Flycaster* by Jan. Vito thought it was even more ramshackle than the rest of the ship.

So he closed his eyes, and squeezed.

When he opened them again, the 'poon was halfway there, trailing a cloud of wire so fine that Vito saw only glints when it caught the sun and winked at him. A brief instant later, one of the wings on the dead bird crumpled soundlessly.

Vito let out a noisy breath. "Got it," he said.

Then he waited patiently while Jan reeled it in. When the satellite bumped up against the far girder, he was ready. He floated over to it with a couple of magnetic clamps, and secured it to the girder beside the other catches. Four now, but the new one was the biggest of the lot; the instrument package alone was man-sized, the wings far bigger. But still small compared to the *Flycaster*.

He pulled himself back to the cabin when the catch was locked down, moving hand over hand down the girders with the ease of one long accustomed to weightlessness. Their quarters were the least impressive part of the *Flycaster*. Most of the space was filled with lockers and instrument panels and computer consoles. That left room for a small toilet cubicle, two chairs that reclined into couches, and Jan.

She was strapped into one of the chairs, checking something on the computer, when he entered. He kicked free of the airlock and floated over to her, dodging underwear and dirty socks. The door to the laundry locker was broken, and it popped open every time Jan moved the ship.

"That catch paid off the last of our expenses for the run," she told him. "And we won't even have to move back to hunting orbit. I've got a new prospect on the screens."

Vito grinned and kissed the back of her neck. "Great," he said. He started to strip off his spacesuit.

"It's an odd one, though," Jan said, still looking at the console. "Too big to be a satellite. Strap down and I'll boost us towards it."

Vito jammed his suit into a locker and started to gather socks, then thought better of it. He let them float free again and pulled himself down into the couch while Jan adjusted their orbit.

"Be there in an hour or so," she told him.

"Uh-huh," Vito said. "How big is big?"

"*Very* big," she said. "The reading I get says it's as big as us. What do you think it is?"

Vito shrugged. "Late twentieth century booster, maybe. They turned out real monsters back when they were using chemical fuels."

Jan shook her head. "I thought of that. But they were stage rockets, and the lower stages fell back into the atmosphere. This is as big as they were intact."

"An abandoned space lab, then," Vito suggested. "One of the Chinese mystery ships from thirty years ago. A dead cosmonaut the Russians never told us about. A flying saucer. I dunno. Could be anything. We'll see when we get there. At least we know one thing. It's money for us." He grinned at her, unstrapped, and starting hunting down socks.

An hour later, with the laundry secure, he was less blase. They'd blown the target up on the cabin viewscreen, and Vito was staring at it. "What," he said, "in the name of hell—is—*that?*"

"I thought you knew," Jan said. "Money, remember?"

Vito was not amused. "Goddamn," he said. "Look at it. Just *look* at it."

They looked.

It was big, slightly bigger than the *Flycaster*. But where the *Flycaster* was mostly girders and vacuum, this thing was solid. It was long and sleek and mirror-bright, and the sun flashed and danced along its silvered flanks as it hung in the cold of space. It looked like a needle, and its lines shrieked speed.

"It's beautiful," Vito said, "but it doesn't make sense."

"It's utterly dysfunctional is what it is," Jan replied.

"It can't be a spaceship. Looks like it was designed for atmosphere flight. But what's it doing up here?"

Vito was already at the locker. "Get in as close as you can," he said. "I'm going to take an air gun, shoot over, and find out."

His name was Peter Van Dellinore, but no one ever used the whole clumsy thing. He was Van Junior to his father's business associates, Van to his society friends, and Pete to the people he really cared about. When it was all over, one of the commentators called him the last romantic. That was a telling comment. In an earlier age, he might have been Byron. He was tall and graceful, lean and athletic, with sandy blond hair and blue eyes. He had an easy smile and a volcanic temper, plus lots and lots of money.

He was the heir to the Van Dellinore fortune. His father, Clifford Van Dellinore, had founded CVD Holosystems Inc, and helped to initiate Continental Broadcasting, the first of the holo networks and still the biggest. And then there was Delnor Lasers, Lightway Computers, Douglas-Dellinore Aerospace, and New Era Duralloy. The Van Dellinore family owned huge blocs of stock in each.

The father, who'd grown up only moderately rich, was a brilliant, ruthless businessman. The son grew up utterly rich and utterly unlike his father. Pete was talented, no one questioned that, but in the eyes of Van Senior he lent his talents to the oddest things.

Ray Lizak, who'd known him since college, understood Pete best. Lizak was a short, dark, colorless guy, who'd always dreamed of leading an exciting life but never seemed to find the time or the opportunity. Then he came to college, and wound up with Pete for a roommate. Within a year he'd raced sports cars, tried skindiving and skydiving, taken a weekend jaunt around the world, lost his virginity, and gotten arrested six times for taking part in all manner of strange demonstrations. Pete was a born leader of lost causes, and Lizak was a born right arm.

There was, for example, the incident of the Business

Building. It was one of the oldest buildings on campus, but not old enough to rate as a landmark. Until Pete came along, everyone agreed that it was a monstrosity. It was huge and dark, built of crumbling red brick, and no two sides of it looked the same. On one side the roof was flat, on the other it slanted; here there was a square belfry without bells, there a thin steeple, here a rickety spiraling fire escape that curled half around the structure like a metal cobweb. Inside the lighting was poor, the floors slanted, and the acoustics terrible. Everyone hated the building.

But when the university announced plans to tear it down, and build a new modern building in its place, Pete shrieked. "Look at that building," he said to Lizak. "That building wasn't designed by an architect. It's utterly assymetrical, almost like it just grew there. Everything's stuck together random. There's no building like it anywhere in the world, and there never will be again. It's so ugly it's beautiful. We can't let them tear it down and put up another shoebox."

On the day the wreckers came, six months later, nearly five hundred students were blocking their way, wearing buttons that said SAVE THE LITTLE RED BRICK SCHOOLHOUSE. They linked arms in a human barricade, and the university had to call the police to disperse them before the demolition could proceed.

That was Pete, at nineteen.

His movements got steadily more serious in his later college years. He led antiwar marches and ecology drives and sexual freedom celebrations, sometimes all three at once. He sat in for a month in front of the Biology Building to protest biowar research. He led a thousand people into the main plant of Douglas-Dellinore to disrupt the production of ABMs. His father didn't speak to him for almost a year, although he did stop making ABMs. The family rift was finally healed when Pete spearheaded a drive that got ten thousand signatures on a petition to protest cuts in the NASA budget. Douglas-Dellinore needed NASA.

Lizak liked to explain him to people who thought he was crazy. In fact, Lizak made a career of explaining

Pete. "You just have to understand him," Lizak would say. "He's not insane, he just thinks he's St. George." But he'd only say that when he thought Pete had a fair-to-middlin chance of winning whatever particular fight he was leading. If Lizak figured the venture was doomed, the line would change to "... he just thinks he's Don Quixote."

Pete loved wine, beer, fast cars, flying, girls, poetry, pizza, french bread, fog, a good fight or a good thunderstorm, and interesting people who did interesting things. He hated war, liver, cold weather, and dull people who wore coats and ties. The thing he loved most, and hated most, was space.

He loved the idea of the space program, and hated the reality of it. Once, in his college days, the university film society had run an odd double feature, an old science-fiction film about the first moon landing, followed by videotape highlights of the real thing. The film and the landing had both been before his time, but space travel was high on his list of things-to-do.

He attended, and preferred the film.

"The real thing was *dull*," he told Lizak afterwards. "They're doing it all wrong. Earth is bland and homogenized enough, they ought to leave space wild. Those damned astronauts act more like accountants than explorers. And dammit, that first-line-after-landing was the worst one I've ever heard. Armstrong had obviously been rehearsing it. Hell, it was probably written for him by a NASA PR man."

He went heavy into the space thing after that, and disliked most of it. He was very upset with the Soviet landing on Mars, when their first statement was a string of instrument readings. Still, he supported the space program. He figured they might get it right later on, Lizak explained.

Pete went to graduate school at his father's request, and mellowed a bit, but he always remained Pete. He spent some time in the offices atop the CBC Tower, being groomed as his father's assistant, and even scored a few minor business coups before he got bored. Then he started looking around for more interesting things to do.

Pete had just turned twenty-six when the Soviets announced their Jupiter mission. The *Jupiter* (Pete always said the Russian space program was utterly without imagination) was being built at their orbital docks, for a launch date nearly a year off.

The NASA announcement about the construction of the *Patrick Henry* came less than a week later, and stirred a considerable amount of interest. The Jupiter flyby would be the first real race in the fifty-year history of the space race, it seemed; two ships, leaving almost at the same time, for the same target.

Pete was one of the people who was interested. He applied for a berth on the *Patrick Henry*.

"Why not?" he told a reporter when the story got leaked to the press. "I'm young, I know lasers and computers and fusion engines, I've flown enough. The trip's a great adventure, and I'd be a definite asset to the crew."

NASA was not amused. Someone asked them about Pete at the press conference when they announced Donaldson's appointment as commander of the *Patrick Henry*. The mission chief just shook his head. "This is a scientific research mission, not an adventure. We don't need any adventurers. They tend to be unstable."

Pete probably would have answered them, but the timing was all wrong. Only hours after that conference, Clifford Van Dellinore died. There was a funeral and a period of mourning and a power struggle, and Pete didn't say anything publicly for months.

He'd inherited thirty-seven per cent of the stock of Van Dellinore Enterprises. His younger sister owned ten per cent, and other relatives shared another ten. The two big blocs were in the hands of his father's friends. Pete got on the phone, and came out chairman of the board. His father's business associates were a little shocked that Van Junior wanted the job, but they were glad to give him a chance. It would have made old Van Senior happy, they thought.

Hah.

43

By then, NASA had announced the crew roster for the *Patrick Henry*. Pete was not on it. The ship was half-complete up in orbit near Shepard Station. It was a dull black skeleton with most of its guts open to space for easy EVA repair. Only the forward section would be rigged with life-support systems. Some commentators said it looked like an unfinished skyscraper.

That was all right. Soviet news holos from the Komarov Wheel made the *Jupiter* look like a giant gray tomato.

Both ships were to leave in February.

In July, Pete called a press conference atop the CBC Tower. All the networks and the papers were there, most of them represented by crack financial reporters. They were already nicknaming Pete the Boy Wonder of Upper Wall, although he hadn't done anything more wondrous than assuming a title.

Until then.

"I suppose you're all wondering why I called you here today," he began, grinning. Lizak, Pete's communications aide, was the only one to laugh. They were financial reporters. "I'll keep it brief and to the point. Van Dellinore Enterprises is sending a ship a Jupiter. To safeguard our investment, I'll go along."

There was a confused silence. Someone laughed. "You're kidding," someone else shouted.

"Hardly," Pete said.

"You mean you're really building a ship? Where?"

Pete grinned. "In my backyard. Where else?"

Vito landed on the silver ship just a few feet away from the airlock. Almost immediately Jan's voice came crackling over the helmet radio. "What is it?"

"I don't know yet," Vito said patiently. His boots kept him clamped to the hull. He unlocked the metalyst from his leg, bent, and took a quick reading. "The hull is duralloy," he reported. "That tell you anything?"

"It can't be more than sixty years old, then," she said. "Duralloy didn't crowd out steel until early Twenty-One."

Vito locked the metalyst back into place and headed

for the airlock. He'd have no problem getting in. The outer door was wide open. He reached the portal, bent and grabbed, pulled himself down. The lock chamber was large, bigger than its counterpart on the *Flycaster*. And the inner door was open too.

"Everything's wide," Vito reported. "The thing's airless, whatever else it is." He pushed himself down through the lock with a burst from his airgun, into what should have been the control cabin.

It was dark in there, but not completely black. The forward wall was half transparent plastic, a thick curved window on the stars. Vito could see Earth turning far below, and the *Flycaster* outlined against its bulk. Jan had parked in a parallel orbit three hundred yards away.

In the reflected Earthlight that filtered through the plastic, Vito studied the cabin.

"Why so quiet?" Jan asked. "Is everything all right?"

"Yeah," he said. "Just looking around."

"What's it like in there?"

"Gutted," Vito said. "It is a ship, or it was, but there's nothing here. Just an empty cabin. Mountings for a couple of couches, but no couches. Control panels, but no controls. Just holes where the buttons and keyboards should be. Lots of garbage floating around the cabin too. Tools and squeeze tubes and bundles of wire, that kind of stuff."

He pushed off a bulkhead and floated over to a bank of lockers. "No provisions," he said after pulling several open. "No spacesuits in the suit locker either." For long minutes he rummaged around the cabin, pulling open whatever door would pull, prying apart panels, and keeping up a running account for Jan. "No power at all, the circuit boards are gone, or were never installed. Life-support system isn't here. There is a computer console, but no computer that I can see."

"Sounds like somebody got here before us," Jan suggested. "Everything valuable has already been removed."

"Not everything," Vito said, as he kicked himself

towards the airlock. "There's still the hull. Duralloy, remember. *Solid* duralloy."

He stopped inside the airlock chamber. There was something he had missed. Clipped to the wall; four old-style oxygen bottles, their gauges all down to empty. And a name, stenciled lengthwise down each of them.

"Challenger," read Vito.

You can't really build a spaceship in your backyard, of course, and Pete never intended to. His plan was to assemble the *Challenger* in orbit beside the *Patrick Henry*. Van Dellinore Enterprises was prepared to pay NASA a handsome rental for the use of the shuttle facilities at the Cape and the orbital construction yards of Shepard Station.

He hadn't convinced NASA to go along with that when he announced it at the press conference, but he was fairly confident he could. After all, NASA always needed money, and he had money. Besides, he had already accomplished a more impressive miracle; he'd sold the *Challenger* to his own board of directors.

As the ultimate advertising gimmick.

It all tied in beautifully. He'd command the ship, and that would put the Van Dellinore name on millions of lips. The *Challenger* would be designed and built by Douglas-Dellinore, its hull made of solid New Era duralloy. The shipboard computer would be a Lightway 999, Delnor Lasers would provide the comm link to Earth. And CBC would have exclusive rights to the holocasts of the first ship to orbit Jupiter.

The price tag was around a half-billion, but Pete could be very eloquent when he wanted to. And it didn't hurt to own thirty-seven per cent of the stock either.

So Van Dellinore Enterprises was to have a spaceship. What kind of a spaceship didn't become clear until about a week later.

That was when the engineering team from Douglas-Dellinore visited Pete in the CBC Tower. It was the same team that had designed the *Patrick Henry* for NASA, and they were proud of their work. The blueprints they gave him were refinements of the same design.

Pete shook his head. "I don't want a box kite," he said. "NASA has a box kite. I want to do this right."

"But this is the optimal design," one of the engineers insisted. "The *Jupiter* is much less efficient, I assure you. I'd stake my—"

"I don't want the *Jupiter* either," Pete interrupted. "I want a spaceship that looks like a spaceship should look, dammit."

The project chief scratched his head. "What exactly should a spaceship look like, Mr. Van Dellinore?"

Pete told them.

Afterwards, one of them stood in the outer office, mumbling and shaking his head. "It doesn't make any sense," he told anyone who would listen. "He wants something out of an old movie, not a real ship. He even wants a window. It took us a half hour to talk him out of tail fins. It's a joke. The man is crazy."

Ray Lizak stopped to talk to him. "Pete's not crazy," Lizak said. "You just have to understand him. He thinks he's St. George, and he can't go riding off to Jupiter on a plow horse, can he?"

As it turned out, the initial design wasn't all that much different than the *Patrick Henry*. They just pressed the parts together a little more tightly, took out a few backup systems, and sheathed the works in a slim silver hull.

Meanwhile, trouble was stirring on other fronts. Although the CBC commentators were hailing the *Challenger* as "a bold step that will open space to the common man," everyone else was taking potshots at the venture. Particularly NASA.

"My only reaction is amusement," Commander Donaldson of the *Patrick Henry* told the press. "Space exploration is not a game, but no one appears to have told Van Dellinore. We're going to Jupiter on a scientific mission. He's going on a lark."

"This is a new height in recklessness," another NASA spokesman said. "Space travel is far too dangerous for anyone but the most highly trained personnel. When the time comes for private citizens to travel to other worlds, commercial service will be opened in safe, government-inspected ships. But that time is not yet. No, of course Van Dellinore will not be permitted to use our facilities. We will have no part in helping him to kill himself."

For a long time, the Senate Space Committee had been sitting on a bill that would ban private citizens from space unless they had a NASA-stamped "space visa." Now the bill was finally reported out onto the floor. Favorably.

Pete sat back through most of this. Then he responded.

"All right," he said in an August press conference. "If we can't use their facilities we'll build our own. And we *will* beat them to Jupiter."

Denied use of the Cape as a launch point, Pete bought the abandoned Woomera facilities of the defunct British space program, for conversion into a modern spaceport.

Denied the NASA shuttles, Pete had Douglas-Dellinore build him two of his own. The *Pogo Stick* and the *Leapfrog* were twins to the NASA craft in every way, until Pete had racing stripes painted down their sides.

Denied use of Shepard Station, Pete announced plans for the construction of a private space station. The press promptly nicknamed it the Dellinore Doughnut.

By September, the *Patrick Henry* was complete and testing was about to begin. The thirty-man crew was just starting to ferry up on NASA shuttles. Reports from the Soviets indicated that the *Jupiter* was in its final stages. But Pete was still in the process of hiring his construction workers and the rest of his six-man crew.

By October, initial tests had been completed on the *Patrick Henry*, and Commander Donaldson announced that the ship was the finest he had ever served on. The Soviets named Colonel Tahl to command the newly-completed *Jupiter*. And at Woomera the final touches were being put on Pete's spaceport.

Public interest was running at a fever pitch, and bets were being made freely. From Las Vegas, the word went out that Tony the Croat had cited the odds as *Patrick Henry* 5-2, *Jupiter* 3-1, *Challenger* 50-1.

During the first week of November, the NASA shuttles began to provision the *Patrick Henry* for the long voyage. The *Jupiter* was just back from a test run around Luna, and the first load of parts for the Dellinore Doughnut had been lofted into orbit by the *Pogo Stick*. And Douglas-Dellinore had sent its best men to the CBC Tower to tell Pete that he'd lost.

"I'm sorry, Van," the project chief told him. "We just can't make it. We have to launch by February so Jupiter will be in the right position when we get there. And we can't. We just can't. Even with two crews up there, we'll be lucky if we have the Doughnut finished by then, let alone the *Challenger*."

"All right," Pete said. "Forget the Doughnut. Just build the *Challenger*."

"The construction crew needs some place to stay, Van. They can't just live in their spacesuits."

Pete considered that. "Do it this way. Send the crew up. Keep the *Pogo Stick* up there with them. The *Leapfrog* can haul up fresh supplies each trip, with the components. We'll run on one shuttle."

The project chief looked around for support. One of his assistants was scribbling on a legal pad. "Still won't work," the man said finally. "With only one shuttle, we'll barely be able to get the parts up there by February. We can't do it."

"Dammit!" Pete shouted. "Quit telling me why it can't be done. If we can't launch February, then we'll launch in March. You'll just have to make the *Challenger* faster than the others!"

The chief sighed. He was getting very tired of this. "It isn't that simple, Van. If we launch at the wrong time, it makes the whole operation very inefficient. We'd need a lot more fuel, a lot more thrust. That'd mean bigger engines, more powerful. Which gives the ship more mass. It'd mean redesigning the whole thing."

"No. Just juggle what you've got. *Cut* some mass. Figure on a crew of one instead of six, that gets rid of a lot of provisions and life-support gear. Cut out the probe bank and the sensors and you cut the mass by a third. Junk all the backup systems. Double the engine size, give me twice the potential thrust and the fuel to match. Then figure how long it'd take to get there."

There were mouths open all over the room.

"But—but the waste—" one man blurted.

"No sensors," another said in shock. "You won't be able to run the experiments. How can you find out anything about Jupiter?"

Pete stood up. "I'll land," he said. And left them open mouthed.

There is a verified report that at least two of them actually believed him.

The crew of the *Patrick Henry* celebrated Christmas aboard their ship, on a shakedown cruise around Luna. The Soviets announced that they were moving their launch date up a week to late January. And Pete did an interview show on CBC.

"This is the way it should have been done all along," he said, grinning. "With style. Space is the last refuge of romance, the only home left for the dreamers and the wildmen who are out of place on Earth. I'm going to take the stars away from the bureaucrats and the technicians, and give them back to the people who can appreciate them."

Above, the first hull sections of the *Challenger* were being fitted around her giant fusion motors by a crew on Christmas tripletime.

Outside again, between the sun and stars, Vito made his way along the hull and listened to Jan.

"I wish we had a library computer," she was saying. "The name sounds vaguely familiar, but I can't place it. I'm sure it'd be in the books somewhere. In any case, it was quite a while ago. Early Twenty-One at least, maybe late twentieth."

The sun was behind Vito's shoulder. Its reflections were long silver sabres flashing between his feet. He looked down and smiled, thinking of the dull black of the *Flycaster*. "She's pretty, whatever she was," he said. "I wonder who built her."

"A mad man," Jan said. "It's totally out of place up here. That ship has no excuse for existing."

Vito didn't reply. He'd found the emergency repair panel to the engine compartment. Just a panel, not an airlock. He unclipped the laser, sheared off the steel bolts that held it in place, and pulled the panel up. Then he slowly pulled himself down inside.

There was no window here, only the starlight that shone in from the empty space where the panel had been. Vito turned on his suit light. He stood in a clearing amid a forest of gleaming black machinery.

"Well?" Jan asked.

"The engines are here," he said. "Fusion-powered, and plenty big. Old, of course. We could get as much thrust from a third the size." He grinned. "I'll bet they had a hell of a kick, though. The *Challenger* was no orbital tug, I'll tell you that."

Jan was suddenly excited. "Excellent," she said. "Do you think they're still functional? Maybe we could rig it to move under its own power?"

"Uh-uh," Vito said. His lights prowled restlessly through the cold, hard dark between the engines. "There are no controls here, either. And no fuel, of course. And I'll bet the engines aren't hooked up to anything. The big components are here, but none of the fine work has been done."

He looked around again. "You know," he said, "I don't think this ship ever went anywhere."

In the end, of course, they crushed him. They always do.

The Space Visa Bill was signed into law during the first week of January. "In a way, the Van Dellinore incident was a good thing," its sponsor said. "It woke us up to the need for firmer regulation of space travel. And I'm proud to say we woke up pretty fast."

During the second week of January, the Douglas-Dellinore work crew returned to Earth under threat of indictment. They had just finished fitting together the hull of the *Challenger*.

During the third week of January, Pete's board of directors revolted and kicked him out.

"This project has gotten entirely out of hand," the leader of the opposition said at the meeting. "We voted to support a half-billion dollar ad campaign to generate a lot of favorable publicity. We were supposed to come out looking like benefactors of mankind, and the ship was going to work beautifully and give all of our products a boost. The holo documentary was going to be a sensation.

"Well, it hasn't worked out that way. Costs have tripled, and all the publicity has been bad. Instead of responsible men doing serious research, we've been painted as reckless fools engaged in a cheap stunt. Safety margins have been cut to the point where a disaster is very possible, and I don't have to tell you what a black eye that would give us. And who's going to go to see a holo about the third ship to Jupiter? Meanwhile, our chairman tells the nation that we're doing it all to make space safe for spaceheads.

"And now, *now,* he comes before us and asks us to defy the law. Well, I've had it. I say we cut our losses, abandon the Jupiter project, and replace Mr. Van Dellinore as our chairman."

He called for a vote. Pete still had thirty-seven per cent of the stock. His sister stood by him. But the opposition had everyone else.

He resigned with singular ill grace. "Fuck you," he told the directors as he handed over the gavel. "If you won't back me, I'll do it without you." Then he stalked out.

The new chairman watched him leave and shook his head. "Mr. Van Dellinore's selection was a sad mistake," he commented. "He's not made of the same stuff as his father. I almost think he's deranged."

Lizak, who'd been left behind with Pete's proxies, sighed. "No, no," he told them. "You just have to understand him. Pete's not crazy, Mr. Chairman, he just thinks he's Don Quixote."

Pete, meanwhile, still had a considerable personal fortune. He tried to use it. He liquidated most of his assets overnight, and tried to get the crew back on the job. "I'll pay you myself," he told them. "I'll double your salaries. I'll pay for attorneys if you're arrested. This is not a time to quit. We can't let the bastards beat us. The whole world is watching to see if we can do it. You men are part of history."

They applauded when he finished. And that was all. They were practical men, and Pete's dream was just a job to them.

During the final week of January, the *Jupiter* left, and the *Patrick Henry* conducted its last tests. Pete, still unable to get a crew into orbit, offered to hire the Russian workers who had pieced together the *Jupiter*. The Soviets ignored him.

During the first week of February, the *Patrick Henry* set out. Pete announced plans to lift into orbit and complete the *Challenger* with a space-green crew of unemployed aerospace workers. But when he tried to leave for Woomera, they arrested him for attempting to exit Earth without a visa.

No sooner had he bailed himself out than the new chairman of Van Dellinore Enterprises announced the impending sale of the *Pogo Stick,* the *Leapfrog,* and the Woomera facilities to NASA. Pete offered to up the price. The company refused to sell to him. He filed suit.

By the time the case got to court, the *Jupiter* had crossed the orbit of Mars, with the *Patrick Henry* close behind. It was around that time that Pete finally gave up.

Needless to say, he never got anywhere near Jupiter. In fact, he only got to Shepard Station once. And that was twenty years later. As Senator Van Dellinore, chairman of the Space Committee, they insisted on him giving a speech to the first boat of colonists for Ganymede.

"Will it work?" Vito asked, on his way across the gulf between the *Challenger* and the *Flycaster.*

"Just a sec," came Jan's voice, "I'm checking." Then, "Well, I think we can handle it, though the mass is really a little more than we're equipped for. It's too bad we don't have more power. This'll be slow, but we'll get there eventually. I figure we'll have to bring it in real tight, practically tie the two ships together."

"The hull is duralloy," Vito reminded her. "We can't punch through that as easily as steel. We'll have to shoot for the airlock and the engine panel."

"And the window," Jan said. "Don't forget the window."

"Yeah. We can smash through that easy enough."

He swung by the skeleton of the *Flycaster*, reached out, and pulled himself in. Then, swiftly, he began to move toward the harpoon gun.

Jupiter has thirteen moons now. One of them is an unfinished skyscraper called the *Patrick Henry*. Tour ships lift off every day from the hotels on Ganymede and Callisto and circle it, while the guides tell the old tale of her narrow two-day victory and later disaster.

The *Jupiter*, brought down to Earth and reassembled part by part, fills an entire wing of the Moscow Institute. The plaque on her hull brags of how she rescued the crew of the distressed *Patrick Henry*, and returned to Earth triumphant.

They've pierced her four times with their cruel harpoons, and now the *Challenger* is being reeled in. Vito stands in the skeleton of the *Flycaster*, watching, and wondering what sort of price she'll bring.

—*Chicago, July 1973*

MEN OF GREYWATER STATION

with Howard Waldrop

The men of Greywater Station watched the shooting star descend and knew it for an omen.

They watched it in silence from the laser turret atop the central tower. The streak grew bright in the northeast sky, divided the night through the thin haze of the spore dust. It went through the zenith, sank, fell below the western horizon.

Sheridan, the bullet-headed zoologist, was the first to speak. "There they went," he said, unnecessarily.

Delvecchio shook his head. "There they are," he said, turning towards the others. There were only five there, of the seven who were left. Sanderpay and Miterz were still outside collecting samples.

"They'll make it," Delvecchio said firmly. "Took too long crossing the sky to burn up like a meteor. I hope we got a triangulation on them with the radar. They came in slow enough to maybe make it through the crash."

Reyn, the youngest of the men at Greywater, looked up from the radar console, and nodded. "I got them, alright. Though it's a wonder they slowed enough before hitting the atmosphere. From the little that got through jamming, they must have been hit pretty hard out there."

"If they live, it puts us in a difficult position," said Delvecchio. "I'm not quite sure what comes next."

"I am," said Sheridan. "We get ready to fight. If anybody lives through the landing, we've got to get ready to take them on. They'll be crawling with fungus before they get here. And you know they'll come. We'll have to kill them."

Delvecchio eyed Sheridan with new distaste. The zoologist was always very vocal with his ideas. That didn't make it any easier for Delvecchio, who then had to end the arguments that Sheridan's ideas usually started. "Any other suggestions?" he asked, looking to the others.

Reyn looked hopeful. "We might try rescuing them before the fungus takes over." He gestured towards the window, and the swampy, fungus-clotted landscape beyond. "We could maybe take one of the flyers to them, shuttle them back to the station, put them in the sterilization ward . . ." Then his words trailed off, and he ran a hand nervously through his thick black hair. "No. There'd be too many of them. We'd have to make so many trips. And the swampbats . . . I don't know."

"The vaccine," suggested Granowicz, the wiry extee psychologist. "Bring them some vaccine in a flyer. Then they might be able to walk it."

"The vaccine doesn't work right," Sheridan said. "People build up an immunity, the protection wears off. Besides, who's going to take it to them? You? Remember the last time we took a flyer out? The damn swampbats knocked it to bits. We lost Blatt and Ryerson. The fungus has kept us out of the air for nearly eight months now. So what makes you think it's all of a sudden going to give us a free pass to fly away into the sunset?"

"We've got to try," Reyn said hotly. From his tone, Delvecchio could see there was going to be a hell of an argument. Put Sheridan on one side of a fight and immediately Reyn was on the other.

"Those are men out there, you know," Reyn continued. "I think Ike's right—we can get them some vaccine. At least there's a chance. We can fight the swampbats. But those poor bastards out there don't have a chance against the fungus."

"They don't have a chance whatever we do," Sheridan said. "It's us we should worry about. They're finished. By now the fungus knows they're there. It's probably already attacking them. If any survived."

"That seems to be the problem," said Delvecchio quickly, before Reyn could jump in again. "We have to assume the fungus won't miss a chance to take them over. And that it will send them against us."

"Right!" said Sheridan, shaking his head vigorously. "And don't forget, these aren't ordinary people we're dealing with. That was a troop transport up there. The survivors will be armed to the teeth. What do we have besides the turret laser? Hunting rifles and specimen guns. And knives. Against screechers and 75 mikemikes and God knows what else. We're finished if we're not ready. Finished."

"Well, Jim?" Granowicz asked. "What do you think? Is he right? What do you think our chances are?"

Delvecchio sighed. Being the leader wasn't always a very comfortable position. "I know how you feel, Bill," he said with a nod to Reyn. "But I'm afraid I have to agree with Sheridan. Your scheme doesn't have much of a chance. And there are bigger stakes. If the survivors have screechers and heavy armament, they'll be able to breach the station walls. You all know what that would mean. Our supply ship is due in a month. If the fungus gets into Greywater, then Earth won't have to worry about the Fyndii anymore. The fungus would put a permanent stop to the war—it doesn't like its hosts to fight each other."

Sheridan was nodding again. "Yes. So we have to destroy the survivors. It's the only way."

Andrews, the quiet little mycologist, spoke up for the first time. "We might try to capture them," he suggested. "I've been experimenting with methods of killing the fungus without damaging the hosts. We could keep them under sedation until I got somewhere."

"How many years would that take?" Sheridan snapped.

Delvecchio cut in. "No. We've got no reason to think we'll even be able to fight them, successfully. All the odds are with them. Capture would be clearly impossible."

"But rescue isn't." Reyn was still insistent. "We should gamble," he said, pounding the radar console with his fist. "It's worth it."

"We settled that, Bill," Delvecchio said. "No rescue. We've got only seven men to fight off maybe hundreds —I can't afford to throw any away on a useless dramatic gesture."

"Seven men trying to fight off hundreds sounds like a useless dramatic gesture to me," Reyn said. "Especially since there may be only a few survivors who could be rescued."

"But what if *all* of them are left?," said Sheridan. "And all of them have already been taken over by the fungus? Be serious, Reyn. The spore dust is everywhere. As soon as they breathe unfiltered air they'll take it in. And in 72 hours they'll be like the rest of the animal life on this planet. Then the fungus will send them against us."

"Goddammit, Sheridan!" yelled Reyn. "They could still be in their pods. Maybe they don't even know what happened. Maybe they're still asleep. How the hell do I know? If we get there before they come out, we can save them. Or something. We've got to try!"

"No. Look. The crash is sure to have shut the ship down. They'll be awake. First thing they'll do is check their charts. Only the fungus is classified, so they won't know what a hell of a place they've landed on. All they *will* know is that Greywater is the only human settlement here. They'll head towards us. And they'll get infected. And possessed."

"That's why we have to work fast," Reyn said. "We should arm three or four of the flyers and leave at once. Now."

Delvecchio decided to put an end to the argument. The last one like this had gone on all night. "This is getting us nowhere," he said sharply, fixing both Sheridan and Reyn with hard stares. "It's useless to discuss it any longer. All we're doing is getting mad at each other. Besides, it's late." He looked at his watch. "Let's break for six hours or so, and resume at dawn. When we're cooler and less tired. We'll be able to think more clearly. And Sanderpay and Miterz will be back then, too. They deserve a voice in this."

There were three rumbles of agreement. And one sharp note of dissent.

"No," said Reyn. Loudly. He stood up, towering over the others in their seats. "That's too late. There's no time to lose."

"Bill, you—" Delvecchio started.

"Those men might be grabbed while we sleep," Reyn went on, ploughing right over his superior. "We've got to *do* something."

"No," said Delvecchio. "And that's an order. We'll talk about it in the morning. Get some sleep, Bill."

Reyn looked around for support. He got none. He glared at Delvecchio briefly. Then he turned and left the tower.

Delvecchio had trouble sleeping. He woke up at least twice, between sheets that were cold and sticky with sweat. In his nightmare, he was out beyond Greywater, knee-deep in the greygreen slime, collecting samples for analysis. While he worked, he watched a big amphibious mud-tractor in the distance, wallowing towards him. On top was another human, his features invisible behind filtermask and skinthins. The dream Delvecchio waved to the tractor as it neared, and the driver waved back. Then he pulled up nearby, climbed down from the cab, and grasped Delvecchio in a firm handshake.

Only by that time Delvecchio could see through the transparent filtermask. It was Ryerson, the dead geologist, his friend Ryerson. But his head was swollen grossly and there were trails of fungus hanging from each ear.

After the second nightmare he gave it up as a bad show. They had never found Ryerson or Blatt after the crash. Though they knew from the impact that there wouldn't be much to find. But Delvecchio dreamed of them often, and he suspected that some of the others did, too.

He dressed in darkness, and made his way to the central tower. Sanderpay, the telecom man, was on watch. He was asleep in the small ready bunk near the laser turret, where the station monitors could awaken him quickly if anything big approached the walls. Reinforced duralloy was tough stuff, but the fungus had some pretty wicked creatures at its call. And there were the airlocks to consider.

Delvecchio decided to let Sanderpay sleep, and went to the window. The big spotlights mounted on the wall flooded the perimeter around Greywater with bright white lights that made the mud glisten sickly. He could see drifting spores reflected briefly in the beams. They seemed unusually thick, especially toward the west, but that was probably his imagination.

Then again, it might be a sign that the fungus was uneasy. The spores had always been ten times as thick around Greywater as elsewhere on the planet's surface. That had been one of the first pieces of evidence that the damned fungus was intelligent. And hostile.

They still weren't sure just how intelligent. But of the hostility there was no more doubt. The parasitic fungus infected every animal on the planet. And had used most of them to attack the station at one point or another. It wanted them. So they had the blizzard of spores that rained on Greywater for more than a year now. The overhead force screens kept them out, though, and the sterilization chambers killed any that clung to mudtractors or skinthins or drifted into the airlocks. But the fungus kept trying.

Across the room, Sanderpay yawned and sat up in his bunk. Delvecchio turned towards him. "Morning, Otis."

Sanderpay yawned again, and stifled it with a big, red hand. "Morning," he replied, untangling himself from the bunk in a gangle of long arms and legs. "What's going on? You taking Bill's shift?"

Delvecchio stiffened. "What? Was Reyn supposed to relieve you?"

"Uh-huh," said Sanderpay, looking at the clock. "Hour ago. The bastard. I get cramps sleeping in this thing. Why can't we make it a little more comfortable, I ask you?"

Delvecchio was hardly listening. He ignored Sanderpay and moved swiftly to the intercom panel against one wall. Granowicz was closest to the motor pool. He rang him.

A sleepy voice answered. "Ike," Delvecchio said. "This is Jim. Check the motor pool, quick. Count the flyers."

Granowicz acknowledged the order. He was back in less than two minutes, but it seemed longer. "Flyer five is missing," he said. He sounded awake all of a sudden.

"Shit," said Delvecchio. He slammed down the intercom, and whirled towards Sanderpay. "Get on the radio, fast. There's a flyer missing. Raise it."

Sanderpay looked baffled, but complied. Delvecchio stood over him, muttering obscenities and thinking worse ones, while he searched through the static.

Finally an answer. "I read you, Otis," Reyn's voice, of course.

Delvecchio leaned towards the transmitter. "I told you no rescue."

The reply was equal parts laughter and static. "Did you? Hell! I guess I wasn't paying attention, Jim. You know how long conferences always bored me."

"I don't want a dead hero on my hands. Turn back."

"I intend to. After I deliver the vaccine. I'll bring as many of the soldiers with me as I can. The rest can walk. The immunity wears off, but it should last long enough if they landed where we predict."

Delvecchio swore. "Dammit, Bill. Turn back. Remember Ryerson?"

"Sure I do. He was a geologist. Little guy with a pot belly, wasn't he?"

"Reyn!" There was an edge to Delvecchio's voice.

Laughter. "Oh, take it easy, Jim. I'll make it. Ryerson was careless, and it killed him. And Blatt too. I won't be. I've rigged some lasers up. Already got two big swampbats that came at me. Huge fuckers, easy to burn down."

"Two! The fungus can send hundreds if it gets an itch. Dammit, listen to me. Come back."

"Will do," said Reyn. "With my guests." Then he signed off with a laugh.

Delvecchio straightened, and frowned. Sanderpay seemed to think a comment was called for, and managed a limp, "Well . . ." Delvecchio never heard him. "Keep on the frequency, Otis," he said. "There's a chance the damn fool might make it. I want to know the minute he comes back on." He started across the room. "Look. Try to raise him every five minutes or so. He probably won't answer. He's in for a world of shit if that jury-rigged laser fails him."

Delvecchio was at the intercom. He punched Granowicz' station. "Jim again, Ike. What kind of laser's missing from the shop? I'll hold on."

"No need to," came the reply. "Saw it just after I found the flyer gone. I think one of the standard tabletop cutters, low power job. He's done some spot-welding, left the stat on the powerbox. Ned found that, and places where he'd done some bracketing. Also, one of the vacutainers is gone."

"Okay. Thanks, Ike. I want everybody up here in ten minutes. War council."

"Oh, Sheridan will be so glad."

"No. Yes. Maybe he will." He clicked off, punched for Andrews.

The mycologist took a while to answer. "Arnold?" Delvecchio snapped when the acknowledgement finally came. "Can you tell me what's gone from stores?"

There were a few minutes of silence. Then Andrews was back. "Yeah, Jim. A lot of medical supplies. Syringes, bandages, vaccine, plastisplints, even some body bags. What's going on?"

"Reyn. And from what you say, it sounds like he's on a real mercy mission there. How much did he take?"

"Enough, I guess. Nothing we can't replace, however."

"Okay. Meeting up here in ten . . . five minutes."

"Well, all right." Andrews clicked off.

Delvecchio hit the master control, opening all the

bitch boxes. For the first time in four months, since the slinkers had massed near the station walls. That had been a false alarm. This, he knew, wasn't.

"Meeting in five minutes in the turret," he said.

The words rang through the station, echoing off the cool humming walls.

". . . that if we don't make plans now, it'll be way too late." Delvecchio paused and looked at the four men lounging on the chairs. Sanderpay was still at the radio, his long legs spilling into the center of the room. But the other four were clustered around the table, clutching coffee cups.

None of them seemed to be paying close attention. Granowicz was staring absently out the window, as usual, his eyes and forebrain mulling the fungus that grew on the trees around Greywater. Andrews was scribbling in a notepad, very slowly. Doodling. Ned Miterz, big and blond and blocky, was a bundle of nervous tension; Bill Reyn was his closest friend. He alternated between drumming his fingers on the tabletop, swilling his coffee, and tugging nervously at his drooping blond mustache. Sheridan's bullet-shaped head stared at the floor.

But they were all listening, in their way. Even Sanderpay, at the radio. When Delvecchio paused, he pulled his long legs back under him, and began to speak. "I'm sorry it's come to this, Jim," he said, rubbing his ear to restore circulation. "It's bad enough those soldiers are out there. Now Bill is gone after them, and he's in the same spot. I think, well, we have to forget him. And worry about attacks."

Delvecchio sighed. "It's hard to take, I know. If he makes it, he makes it. If he finds them, he finds them. If they've been exposed, in three days they'll be part of the fungus. Whether they take the vaccine or not. If he brings them back, we watch them three days to see if symptoms develop. If they do, we have to kill them. If not, then nobody's hurt, and when the rest walk in we watch for symptoms in them. But those are iffy things. If he doesn't make it, he's dead. Chances are, the troopers are dead. Or exposed. Either way, we prepare for the worst and forget Reyn until we see him. So what I'm asking for now are practical suggestions as to how we defend ourselves against well-armed soldiers. Controlled by some intelligence we do not understand."

He looked at the men again.

Sanderpay whooped. He grabbed the console mike as they jumped and looked at him.

"Go ahead, Bill," he said, twisting the volume knob over to the wall speaker. The others winced as the roar of frequency noise swept the room.

". . . right. The damn thing's sending insects into the ship. Smear . . . ing . . . smear windscreen . . . on instruments." Reyn's voice. There was a sound in the background like heavy rain.

". . . swampbats just before they came . . . probably coming at me now. Goddamn laser mount loosened . . ." There was a dull thud in the background. "No lateral control . . . got that bastard . . . ohmigoddd . . ." Two more dull thuds. A sound like metal eating itself.

". . . in the trees. Altitude . . . going down . . . swampbats . . . something just got sucked in the engine . . . Damn, no power . . . nothing . . . if . . ."

Followed by frequency noise.

Sanderpay, his thin face blank and white, waited a few seconds to see if more transmission came through, then tried to raise Reyn on the frequency. He turned the volume down again after a while.

"I think that's about what we can expect will happen to us in a couple of days," said Delvecchio. "That fungus will stop at nothing to get intelligent life. Once it has the soldiers who survive, they'll come after the station. With their weapons."

"Well," snapped Sheridan. "He knew not to go out there in that flyer."

Miterz slammed down his coffee cup, and rose. "Goddamn you, Sheridan. Can't you hold it even a minute? Bill's probably dead out there. And all you want to do is say I-told-you so."

Sheridan jumped to his feet too. "You think I like listening to someone get killed on the radio? Just because I didn't like him? You think it's fun? Huh? You think I want to fight somebody who's been trained to do it? Huh?" He looked at them, all of them, and wiped the sweat from his brow with the back of his hand. "I don't. I'm scared. I don't like making plans for war when men could be out there wounded and dying with no help coming."

He paused. His voice, stretched thin, began to waver. "Reyn was a fool to go out there. But maybe he was the only one who let his humanity come through. I made myself ignore them. I tried to get you all to plan for war in case any of the soldiers made it. Damn you. I'm afraid to go out there. I'm afraid to go near the stuff, even inside the station. I'm a zoologist, but I can't even work. Every animal on the planet has that— that *stuff* on it. I can't bear to touch it. I don't want to fight either. But we're going to have to. Sooner or later."

He wiped his head again, looked at Delvecchio. "I— I'm sorry, Jim. Ned, too. The rest of you. I'm—I have —I just don't like it any more than you. But we have to." He sat down, very tiredly.

Delvecchio rubbed his nose, and reflected again that being the nominal leader was more trouble than it was worth. Sheridan had never opened up like this before. He wasn't quite sure how to deal with it.

"Look," he finally said. "It's okay, Eldon." It was the first time he could remember that he—or any of them —had used Sheridan's first name. "This isn't going to be easy on any of us. You may be right about our humanity. Sometimes you have to put humanity aside to think about . . . well, I don't know.

"The fungus has finally found a way to get to us. It will attack us with the soldiers, like it has with the slinkers and the swampbats and the rest. Like it's trying to do now, while we're talking, with the burrowing worms and the insects and the arthropodia. The station's defenses will take care of those. All we have to worry about are the soldiers."

"All?" said Granowicz, sharply.

"That, and what we'll do if they breach the wall or the field. The field wasn't built to take screechers or lasers or explosives. Just to keep out insects and flying animals. I think one of the first things we've got to do is find a way to beef up the field. Like running in the mains from the other power sources. But that still leaves the wall. And the entry chambers. Our weakest links. Ten or twenty good rounds of high explosives will bring it right down. How do we fight back?"

"Maybe we don't," said Miterz. His face was still hard and angry. But now the anger was turned against the fungus, instead of Sheridan. "Maybe we take the fight to them."

The suggestions flew thick and fast from there on. Half of them were impossible, a quarter improbable, the most of what were left were crazy. At the end of an hour, they had gotten past the points of mining, pitfalls, electrocution. To Delvecchio's ears, it was the strangest conversation he had ever heard. It was full of the madnesses men plan against each other, made more strange by the nature of the men themselves. They were all scientists and technicians, not soldiers, not killers. They talked and planned without enthusiasm, with the quiet talk of men who must talk before being pallbearers at a friend's funeral, or the pace of men who must take their turns as members of a firing squad the next morning.

In a way, they were.

An hour later, Delvecchio was standing up to his ankles in graygreen mud, wrestling with a powersaw and sweating freely under his skinthins. The saw was hooked up to the power supply on his mud-tractor. And Miterz was sitting atop the tractor, with a hunting laser resting across his knee, occasionally lifting it to burn down one of the slinkers slithering through the underbrush.

Delvecchio had already cut through the bases of four of the biggest trees around the Greywater perimeter— about three quarters of the way through, anyway. Just enough to weaken them, so the turret laser could finish the job quickly when the need arose. It was a desperate idea. But they were desperate men.

The fifth tree was giving him trouble. It was a different species from the others, gnarled and overhung with creepers and rock-hard. He was only halfway through, and already he'd had to change the blade twice. That made him edgy. One slip with the blade, one slash in the skinthins, and the spores could get at him.

"Damn thing," he said, when the teeth began to snap off for the third time. "It cuts like it's half petrified. Damn."

"Look at the bright side," suggested Miterz. "It'll make a mighty big splat when it falls. And even duralloy armor should crumple pretty good."

Delvecchio missed the humor. He changed the blade without comment, and resumed cutting.

"That should do it," he said after a while. "Looks deep enough. But maybe we should use the lasers on this kind, if we hit any more of them."

"That's a lot of power," said Miterz. "Can we afford it?" He raised his laser suddenly, and fired at something behind Delvecchio. The slinker, a four foot long mass of scales and claws, reared briefly from its stomach and then fell again, splattering mud in their direction. Its dying scream was a brief punctuation mark. "Those things are thick today," Miterz commented.

Delvecchio climbed up into the tractor. "You're imagining things," he said.

"No, I'm not." Miterz sounded serious. "I'm the ecologist, remember? I know we don't have a natural ecology around here. The fungus sends us its nasties, and keeps the harmless life forms away. But now there's even more than usual." He gestured with the laser. Off through the underbrush, two big slinkers could be seen chewing at the creepers around a tree, the fungus hanging like a shroud over the back of their skulls. "Look there. What do you think they're doing?"

"Eating," said Delvecchio. "That's normal enough." He started the tractor, and moved it forward jerkily. Mud, turned into a watery slime, spouted out behind the vehicle in great gushes.

"Slinkers are omnivores," Miterz said. "But they prefer meat. Only eat creepers when there's no prey. But there's plenty around here." He stopped, stared at the scene, banged the butt of the laser rifle on the cab floor in a fit of sudden nervous tension.

Then he resumed in a burst of words. "Damn it, damn it. They're clearing a path!" His voice was an accusation. "A path for the soldiers to march on. Starting at our end and working towards them. They'll get here faster if they don't have to cut through the undergrowth."

Delvecchio, at the wheel, snorted. "Don't be absurd."

"What makes you think it's absurd? Who knows what the fungus is up to? A living ecology. It can turn every living thing on this planet against us if it wants to. Eating a path through a swamp is nothing to something like that." Miterz' voice was distant and brooding.

Delvecchio didn't like the way the conversation was going. He kept silent. They went on to the next tree, and then the next. But Miterz, his mind racing, was getting more and more edgy. He kept fidgeting in the tractor, and playing with the rifle, and more than once he absently tried to yank at his mustache, only to be stopped by the filtermask. Finally, Delvecchio decided it was time to head in.

Decontamination took the usual two hours. They waited patiently in the entry chamber and sterilization rooms while the pumps, sprays, heatlamps, and ultraviolet systems did their work on them and the tractor.

They shed their sterilized skinthins as they came through the final airlock.

"Goddamn," said Delvecchio. "I hope we don't have to go out again. Decon takes more time than getting the work done."

Sanderpay met them, smiling. "I think I found something we could use. Nearly forgot about them."

"Yeah? What?" Miterz asked, as he unloaded the laser charge and placed it back in the recharge rack. He punched several buttons absently.

"The sounding rockets."

Delvecchio slapped his head. "Of course. Damn. Didn't even consider them." His mind went back. Blatt, the dead meteorologist, had fired off the six foot sounding rockets regularly for the first few weeks, gaining data on the fungus. They had discovered that spores were frequently found up to 50,000 feet, and a few even reached as high as 80,000. After Blatt discovered that, he still made a twice-daily ritual of firing the sounding rockets, to collect information on the planet's shifting wind patterns. They had weather balloons, but those were next to useless; the swampbats usually vectored in on them soon after they were released. After Blatt's death, however, the readings hadn't meant as much, so the firings were discontinued. But the launching tubes were still functional, as far as he knew.

"You think you can rig them up as small guided missiles?" Delvecchio asked.

"Yep," Sanderpay said with a grin. "I already started. But they won't be very accurate. For one thing, they'll reach about a mile in altitude before we can begin to control them. Then we'll be forcing the trajectory. They'll want to continue in a long arc. We'll want them back down almost to the launching point. It'll be like wrestling a two-headed alligator. I'm thinking of filling half of them with that explosive Andrews is trying to make, and the rest with white phosphorus. But that might be tricky."

"Well, do whatever you can, Otis," said Delvecchio. "This is good news. We needed this kind of punch. Maybe it isn't as hopeless as I thought."

Miterz had been listening carefully, but he still looked glum. "Anything over the commo?" he put in. "From Bill?"

Sanderpay shook his head. "Just the usual solar shit, and some mighty nice whistlers. Must be a helluva thunderstorm somewhere within a thousand miles of here. I'll let you know if anything comes in, though."

Miterz didn't answer. He was looking at the armory and shaking his head.

Delvecchio followed his eyes. Eight lasers were on the racks. Eight lasers and sixteen charges, standard station allotment. Each charge good for maybe 50 fifth-second bursts. Five tranquilizer rifles, an assortment of syringes, darts, and projectiles. All of which would be useless against armored infantry. Maybe if they could adapt some of the heavier projectiles to H.E. . . but such a small amount wouldn't dent duralloy. Hell.

"You know," said Miterz. "If they get inside, we might as well hang it up."

"If," said Delvecchio.

Night at Greywater Station. They had started watch-and-watch. Andrews was topside at the laser turret and sensor board. Delvecchio, Granowicz, and Sanderpay lingered over dinner in the cafeteria below. Miterz and Sheridan had already turned in.

Sanderpay was talking of the day's accomplishments. He figured he had gotten somewhere with the rockets. And Andrews had managed to put together some explosive from the ingredients in Reyn's lab.

"Arnold doesn't like it much, though," Sanderpay was saying. "He wants to get back to his fungus samples. Says he's out of his field, and not too sure he knows what he's doing. He's right, too. Bill was your chemist."

"Bill isn't here," Delvecchio snapped. He was in no mood for criticism. "Someone has to do it. At least Arnold has some background in organic chemistry, no matter how long ago it was. That's more than the rest of us have." He shook his head. "Am *I* supposed to do it? I'm an entomologist. What good is that? I feel useless."

"Yep, I know," said Sanderpay. "Still. It's not easy for me with the rockets, either. I had to take half the propellant from each one. Worked nine hours, finished three. We're gonna be fighting all the known laws of aerodynamics trying to force those things down near their starting point. And everybody else is having problems, too. We tinker and curse and it's all a blind alley. If we do this, we gotta do that. But if we do that, it won't work. This is a research station. So maybe it looks like a fort. That doesn't make it one. And we're scientists, not demolitions experts."

Granowicz gave a thin chuckle. "I'm reminded of that time, back on Earth, in the 20th Century, when that German scientist . . . von Brau? von . . . von Braun and his men were advised that the enemy forces would soon be there. The military began giving them close-order drill and markmanship courses. They wanted them to meet the enemy on the very edge of their missile complex and fight them hand to hand."

"What happened?" said Sanderpay.

"Oh, they ran 300 miles and surrendered," Granowicz replied dryly.

Delvecchio downed his two hundredth cup of coffee, and put his feet up on the table. "Great," he said. "Only we've got no place to run to. So we're going to *have* to meet them on the edge of *our* little missile complex, or whatever. And soon."

Granowicz nodded. "Three days from now, I figure."

"That's if the fungus doesn't help them," said Delvecchio.

The other two looked at him. "What do you mean?" asked Granowicz.

"When Ned and I were out this morning, we saw slinkers. Lots of them. Eating away at the creepers to the west of the station."

Granowicz had a light in his eyes. But Sanderpay, still baffled, said, "So?"

"Miterz thinks they're clearing a path."

"Uh oh," said Granowicz. He stroked his chin with a thin hand. "That's very interesting, and very bad news. Clearing away at both ends, and all along, as I'd think it would do. Hmmmm."

Sanderpay looked from Delvecchio to Granowicz and back, grimaced, uncoiled his legs and then coiled them around his chair again in a different position. He said nothing.

"Ah, yes, yes," Granowicz was saying. "It all fits, all ties in. We should have anticipated this. A total assault, with the life of a planet working for our destruction. It's the fungus . . . a total ecology, as Ned likes to call it. A classic case of the parasitic collective mind. But we can't understand it. We don't know what its basic precepts are, its formative experiences. We don't know. No research has been carried out on anything like it. Except maybe the water jellies of Noborn. But that was a collective organism formed of separate colonies for mutual benefit. A benign form, as it were. As far as I can tell, Greywater, the fungus, is a single, all-encompassing mass, which took over this planet starting from some single central point."

He rubbed his hands together and nodded. "Yes. Based on that, we can make guesses as to what it thinks. And how it will act. And this fits, this total hostility."

"How so?" asked Sanderpay.

"Well, it's never run up against any other intelligence, you see. Only lower forms. That's important. So it judges us by itself, the only mind it has known. *It* is driven to dominate, to take over all life with which it comes in contact. So it thinks we are the same, fears that we are trying to take over this planet as *it* once did.

"Only, like I've been saying all along, it doesn't see us as the intelligence. We're animals, small, mobile. It's known life like that before, and all lower form. But the station itself is something new, something outside its experience. It sees the station as the intelligence, I'll bet. An intelligence like itself. Landing, establishing itself, sending out extensions, poking at it and its hosts. And us, us poor animals, the fungus sees as unimportant tools."

Delvecchio sighed. "Yeah, Ike. We've heard this before. I agree that it's a persuasive theory. But how do you prove it?"

"Proof is all around us," said Granowicz. "The station is under a constant, around-the-clock attack. But we can go outside for samples, and the odds are fifty-fifty whether we'll be attacked or not. Why? Well, we don't kill every slinker we see, do we? Of course not. And the fungus doesn't try to kill us, except if we get annoying. Because we're not important, it thinks. But something like the flyers—mobile but not animal, strange—it tries to eradicate. Because it perceives them as major extensions of Greywater."

"Then why the spores?" Delvecchio said.

Granowicz dismissed that with an airy wave. "Oh, the fungus would like to take us over, sure. To deprive the station of hosts. But it's the station it wants to eradicate. It can't conceive of cooperating with another intelligence—maybe, who knows, it had to destroy rival fungus colonies of its own species before it came to dominate this planet. Once it perceives intelligence, it is threatened. And it perceives intelligence in the station."

He was going to go on. But Delvecchio suddenly took his feet from the table, sat up, and said. "Uh oh."

Granowicz frowned. "What?"

Delvecchio stabbed at him with a finger. "Ike, think about this theory of yours. What if you're right? Then *how* is the fungus going to perceive the spaceship?"

Granowicz thought a moment, nodded to himself, and gave a slow, low whistle.

"So? How?" said Sanderpay. "Whattaya talking about?"

Granowicz turned on him. "The spaceship was mobile, but not animal. Like the station. It came out of the sky, landed, destroyed a large area of the fungus and host forms. And hasn't moved since. Like the station. The fungus probably sees it as another station, another threat. Or an extension of our station."

"Yes," said Delvecchio. "But it gets worse. If you're right, then maybe the fungus is launching an all-out attack right at this moment—on the spaceship hull. While it lets the men march away unharmed."

There was a moment of dead silence. Sanderpay finally broke it, looking at each of the others in turn, and saying, in a low voice, "Oh. Wow. I see."

Granowicz had a thoughtful expression on his face, and he was rubbing his chin again. "No," he said at last. "You'd think that, but I don't think that's what is happening."

"Why not?" asked Delvecchio.

"Well, the fungus may not see the soldiers as the major threat. But it would at least try to take them over, as it does with us. And once it had them, and their weapons, it would have the tools to obliterate the station *and* the spaceship. That's almost sure to happen, too. Those soldiers will be easy prey for the spores. They'll fall to the fungus like ripe fruit."

Delvecchio clearly looked troubled. "Yeah, probably. But this bothers me. If there's even a slight chance that the soldiers might get here without being taken over, we'll have to change our plans."

"But there's no chance of that," Granowicz said, shaking his head. "The fungus already *has* those men. Why else would it be clearing a path?"

Sanderpay nodded in agreement. But Delvecchio wasn't that sure.

"We don't *know* that it's clearing a path," he insisted. "That's just what Miterz *thinks* is happening. Based on very scant evidence. We shouldn't accept it as an accomplished fact."

"It makes sense, though," Granowicz came back. "It would speed up the soldiers getting here, speed up the . . ."

The alarm from the turret began to hoot and clang.

"Slinkers," said Andrews. "I think out by those trees you were working on." He drew on a pair of infrared goggles and depressed a stud on the console. There was a hum.

Delvecchio peered through the binoculars. "Think maybe it's sending them to see what we were up to?"

"Definitely," said Granowicz, standing just behind him and looking out the window from over his shoulder.

"I don't think it'll do anything," said Delvecchio, hopefully. "Mines or anything foreign it would destroy, of course. We've proved that. But all we did is slash a few trees. I doubt that it will be able to figure out why."

"Do you think I should fire a few times?" Andrews asked from the laser console.

"I don't know," said Delvecchio. "Wait a bit. See what they do."

The long, thick lizards were moving around the tree trunks. Some slithered through the fungus and the mud, others scratched and clawed at the notched trees.

"Switch on some of the directional sensors," said Delvecchio. Sanderpay, at the sensor bank, nodded and began flicking on the directional mikes. First to come in was the constant tick of the continual spore bombardment on the receiver head. Then, as the mike rotated, came the hissing screams of the slinkers.

And then the rending sound of a falling tree.

Delvecchio, watching through the binoculars, suddenly felt very cold. The tree came down into the mud with a crashing thud. Slime flew from all sides, and several slinkers hissed out their lives beneath the trunk.

"Shit," said Delvecchio. And then, "Fire, Arnold."

Andrews pushed buttons, sighted in the nightscope, lined the crossnotches up on a slinker near the fallen tree, and fired.

To those not watching through goggles or binoculars, a tiny red-white light appeared in the air between the turret laser and the group of lizards. A gargling sound mixed with the slinker hissing. One of the animals thrashed suddenly, and then lay still. The others began slithering away into the undergrowth. There was stillness for a second.

And on another part of the perimeter, a second tree began to fall.

Andrews hit more buttons, and the big turret laser moved and fired again. Another slinker died. Then, without waiting for another crash, the laser began to swivel to hit the slinkers around the other trees.

Delvecchio lowered the binoculars very slowly. "I think we just wasted a day's work out there," he said. "Somehow the fungus guessed what we were up to. It's smarter than we gave it credit for."

"Reyn," said Granowicz.

"Reyn?" said Delvecchio. With a questioning look.

"He knew we'd try to defend the station. Given that knowledge, it's logical for the fungus to destroy anything we do out there. Maybe Reyn survived the crash of his flyer. Maybe the fungus finally got a human."

"Oh, *shit*," said Delvecchio, with expression. "Yes, sure, you might be right. Or maybe it's all a big coincidence. A bunch of accidents. How do we know? How do we know anything about what the damned thing is thinking or doing or planning?" He shook his head.

"Damn. We're fighting blind. Every time something happens, there are a dozen reasons that might have been behind it. And every plan we make has to have a dozen alternatives."

"It's not that bad," said Granowicz. "We're not entirely in the dark. We've proved that the fungus *can* take over Earth forms. We've proved that it gets at least some knowledge from them; that it absorbs at least part of what they knew. We don't know how big a part, true, however—"

"However, if, but, maybe," Delvecchio swore, looking very disgusted. "Dammit, Ike, how big a part is the crucial question. *If* it has Reyn, and *if* it knows everything he knew, then it knows everything there is to know about Greywater and its defenses. In that case, what kind of a chance will we have?"

"Well," said Granowicz. He paused, frowned, stroked his chin. "I—hmmmmm. Wait, there are other aspects to this that should be thought out. Let me work on this awhile."

"Fine," said Delvecchio. "You do that." He turned to Andrews. "Arnold, keep them off the trees as best you can. I'll be back up to relieve you in four hours."

Andrews nodded. "Okay, I think," he said, his eyes locked firmly on the nightscope.

Delvecchio gave brief instructions to Sanderpay, then turned and left the turret. He went straight to his bunk. It took him the better part of an hour to drift to sleep.

Delvecchio's dream:

He was old, and cool. He saw the station from all sides in a shifting montage of images; some near the ground, some from above, wheeling on silent wings. In one image, he saw, or felt it as a worm must feel the presence of the heavy weight of sunlight.

He saw the station twisted, old, wrecked. He saw the station in a series of images from inside. He saw a skeleton in the corner of an indefinite lab, and saw through the eyes of the skull out into the broken station. Outside, he saw heaped duralloy bodies with greygreen growths sprouting from the cracked faceplates.

And he saw out of the faceplates, out into the swamp. Everywhere was greygreen, and damp and old and cold. Everywhere.

Delvecchio awoke sweating.

His watch was uneventful. The slinkers had vanished as suddenly as they had assembled, and he only fired the laser once, at a careless swampbat that flew near the perimeter. Miterz relieved him. Delvecchio caught several more hours of sleep. Or at least of bunk time. He spent a large chunk of the time lying awake, thinking.

When he walked into the cafeteria the next morning, an argument was raging.

Granowicz turned to him immediately. "Jim, listen," he began, gesturing with his hands. "I've thought about this all night. We've been missing something obvious. If this thing has Reyn, or the soldiers, or *any* human, this is the chance we've been waiting for. The chance to communicate, to begin a mutual understanding. With their knowledge, it will have a common tongue with us. We shouldn't fight it at all. We should try to talk to it, try to make it understand how different we are."

"You're crazy, Granowicz," Sheridan said loudly. "Stark, raving mad. *You* go talk to that stuff. Not me. It's after us. It's been after us all along, and now it's sending those soldiers to kill us all. We have to kill them first."

"But this is our *chance*," Granowicz said. "To begin to understand, to reach that mind, to—"

"That was your job all along," Sheridan snapped. "You're the extee psych. Just because you didn't do your job is no reason to ask us to risk our lives to do it for you."

Granowicz glowered. Sanderpay, sitting next to him, was more vocal. "Sheridan," he said, "sometimes I wish we could throw you out to the fungus. You'd look good with graygreen growths coming out of your ears. Yep."

Delvecchio gave hard glances to all of them. "Shut up, all of you," he said simply. "I've had enough of this nonsense. I've been doing some thinking too."

He pulled up a chair and sat down. Andrews was at another table, quietly finishing his breakfast. Delvecchio motioned him over, and he joined them.

"I've got some things I want to announce," Delvecchio said. "Number one, no more arguments. We waste an incredible amount of time hashing out every detail and yelling at each other. And we don't have time to waste. So no more. I make the decisions, and I don't want any screaming and kicking. If you don't like it, you're free to elect another leader. Understand?" He looked at each of them in turn. Sheridan squirmed a little under the gaze, but none of them objected.

"Okay," Delvecchio said finally. "If that's settled, then we'll move on." He looked at Granowicz. "First thing is this idea of yours, Ike. Now you want us to talk. Sorry, I don't buy it. Just last night you were telling us how the fungus, because of its childhood traumas, was bound to be hostile."

"Yes," began Granowicz, "but with the additional knowledge it will get from—"

"No arguments," Delvecchio said sharply. Granowicz subsided. Delvecchio continued. "What do you think it will be doing while we're talking? Hitting us with everything it's got, if your theory was correct. And it sounded good to me. We're dead men if we're not ready, so we'll be ready. To fight, not talk."

Sheridan was smirking. Delvecchio turned on him next. "But we're not going to hit them with everything we've got as soon as we see them, like you want, Sheridan," he said. "Ike brought up a point last night that's been bothering me ever since. Nagging at me. There's an outside chance the fungus might not even try to take over the soldiers. It might not be smart enough to realize they're important. It might concentrate on the spaceship."

Sheridan sat up straight. "We *have* to hit them," he said. "They'll kill us, Delvecchio. You don't—"

Sanderpay, surprisingly, joined in. "It's eating a path," he said. "And the trees. And this morning, Jim, look out there. Slinkers and swampbats all around. It's got them, I know it. It wouldn't be building up this way otherwise."

Delvecchio waved them both silent. "I know, Otis, I know. You're right. All the signs say that it has them. But we have to be sure. We wait until we see them, until we *know*. Then, if they're taken, hit them with everything, at once. It has to be hard. If it becomes a struggle, we've lost. They outnumber and outgun us, and in a fight, they'd breach the station easy. Only the fungus might just march 'em up. Maybe we can kill them all before they know what hit them."

Granowicz looked doubtful. Sheridan looked more than doubtful. "Delvecchio, that's ridiculous. Every moment we hesitate increases our risk. And for such a ridiculous chance. Of *course* it will take them."

"Sheridan, I've had about enough out of you," Delvecchio said quietly. "Listen for a change. There's two chances. One that the fungus might be too dumb to take them over. And one that it might be too smart."

Granowicz raised his eyebrows. Andrews cleared his throat. Sheridan just looked insulted.

"If it has Reyn," Delvecchio said, "maybe it knows all about us. Maybe it won't take the soldiers over on purpose. It knows from Reyn that we plan to destroy them. Maybe it will just wait."

"But why would it have slinkers clearing a . . ." Sanderpay began, then shut up. "Oh. Oh, no. Jim, it couldn't . . ."

"You're not merely assuming the fungus is very intelligent, Jim," Granowicz said. "You're assuming it's very devious as well."

"No," said Delvecchio. "I'm not assuming *anything*. I'm merely pointing out a possibility. A terrible possibility, but one we should be ready for. For over a year now, we've been constantly underestimating the fungus. At every test, it has proven just a bit more intelligent than we figured. We can't make another mistake like that. No margin for error this time."

Granowicz gave a reluctant nod.

"There's more," said Delvecchio. "I want those missiles finished *today*, Otis. In case they get here sooner than we've anticipated. And the explosive too, Arnold. And I don't want any more griping. You two are relieved of your watches until you finish those projects. The rest of us will double up.

"Also, from now on we all wear skinthins inside the station. In case the attack comes suddenly and the screens are breached."

Everybody was nodding.

"Finally, we throw out all the experiments. I want every bit of fungus and every Greywater life form within this station eradicated." Delvecchio thought of his dream again, and shuddered mentally.

Sheridan slapped the table and smiled. "Now *that's* the kind of thing I like to hear! I've wanted to get rid of those things for weeks."

Granowicz looked unhappy, though. And Andrews looked very unhappy. Delvecchio looked at each in turn.

"All I have is a few small animals, Jim," Granowicz said. "Rootsnuffs and such. They're harmless enough, and safely enclosed. I've been trying to reach the fungus, establish some sort of communications—"

"No," said Delvecchio. "Sorry, Ike, but we can't take the chance. If the walls are breached or the station damaged, we might lose power. Then we'd have contamination inside and out. It's too risky. You can get new animals."

Andrews cleared his throat. "But well, my cultures," he said. "I'm just getting them broken down, isolating the properties of the fungus strains. Six months of research, Jim, and, well, I think—" He shook his head.

"You've got your research. You can duplicate it. If we live through this."

"Yes, well—" Andrews was hesitant. "But the cultures will have to be started over. So much time. And Jim—" He hesitated again, and looked at the others.

Delvecchio smiled grimly. "Go ahead, Arnold. They might die soon. Maybe they should know."

Andrews nodded. "I'm getting somewhere, Jim. With *my* work, the real work, the whole reason for Greywater. I've bred a mutation of the fungus, a non-intelligent variety, very virulent, very destructive of its hosts.

"I'm in the final stages now. It's only a matter of getting the mutant to breed in the Fyndii atmosphere. And I'm near, I'm so near." He looked at each of them in turn, eyes imploring. "If you let me continue, I'll have it soon. And they could dump it on the Fyndii homeworlds, and well, it would end the war. All those lives saved. Think about all the men who will die if I'm delayed."

He stopped suddenly, awkwardly. There was a long silence around the table.

Granowicz broke it. He stroked his chin and gave a funny little chuckle. "And I thought this was such a bold, clean venture," he said, his voice bitter. "To grope towards a new intelligence, unlike any we had known, to try to find and talk to a mind perhaps unique in this universe. And now you tell me all my work was a decoy for biological warfare. Even here I can't get away from that damned war." He shook his head. "Greywater Station. What a lie."

"It had to be this way, Ike," Delvecchio said. "The potential for military application was too great to pass up, but the Fyndii would have easily found out about a big, full-scale biowar research project. But teams like Greywater's—routine planetary investigation teams—are common. The Fyndii can't bother to check on every one. And they don't."

Granowicz was staring at the table. "I don't suppose it matters," he said glumly. "We all may die in a few days anyway. This doesn't change that. But—but —" He stopped.

Delvecchio shrugged. "I'm sorry, Ike." He looked at Andrews. "And I'm sorry about the experiments, too, Arnold. But your cultures have to go. They're a danger to us inside the station."

"But, well, the war—all those people." Andrews looked anguished.

"If we don't make it through this, we lose it all anyway, Arnold," Delvecchio said.

Sanderpay put a hand on Andrews' shoulder. "He's right. It's not worth it."

Andrews nodded.

Delvecchio rose. "All right," he said. "We've got that settled. Now we get to work. Arnold, the explosives. Otis, the rockets. Ike and I will take care of dumping the experiments. But first, I'm going to go brief Miterz. Okay?"

The answer was a weak chorus of agreement.

It took them only a few hours to destroy the work of a year. The rockets, the explosives, and the other defenses took longer, but in time they too were ready. And then they waited, sweaty and nervous and uncomfortable in their skinthins.

Sanderpay monitored the commo system constantly. One day. Two. Three—a day of incredible tension. Four, and the strain began to tell. Five, and they relaxed a bit. The enemy was late.

"You think they'll try to contact us first?" Andrews asked at one point.

"I don't know," said Sanderpay. "Have you thought about it?"

"I have," Granowicz put in. "But it doesn't matter. They'll try either way. If it's them, they'll want to reach us, of course. If it's the fungus, it'll want to throw us off our guard. Assuming that it has absorbed enough knowledge from its hosts to handle a transmission, which isn't established. Still, it will probably try, so we can't trust a transmission."

"Yeah," said Delvecchio. "But that's the problem. We can't trust *anything*. We have to suppose everything we're working on. We don't have *any* concrete information to speak of."

"I know, Jim, I know."

On the sixth day, the storm screamed over the horizon. Spore clouds flowed by in the wind, whipped into rents and gaps. Overhead, the sky darkened. Lightning sheeted in the west.

The radio screeched its agony and crackled. Whistlers

moved up and down the scale. Thunder rolled. In the tower, the men of Greywater Station waited out the last few hours.

The voice had come in early that morning, had faded. Nothing intelligible had come through. Static had crackled most of the day. The soldiers were moving on the edge of the storm, Delvecchio calculated.

Accident? Or planning? He wondered. And deployed his men. Andrews to the turret laser. Sanderpay at the rocket station. Sheridan and himself inside the station, with laser rifles. Granowicz to the flyer port, where the remaining flyers had been stocked with crude bombs. Miterz on the walls.

They waited in their skinthins, filtermasks locked on but not in place. The sky, darkened by the coming storm, was blackening towards twilight anyway. Soon night and the storm would reach Greywater Station hand in hand.

Delvecchio stalked through the halls impatiently. Finally, he returned to the tower to see what was happening. Andrews, at the laser console, was watching the window. A can of beer sat next to him on the nightscope. Delvecchio had never seen the quiet little mycologist drink before.

"They're out there," Andrews said. "Somewhere." He sipped at his beer, put it down again. "I wish that, well, they'd hurry or something." He looked at Delvecchio. "We're all probably going to die, you know. The odds are so against us."

Delvecchio didn't have the stomach to tell him he was wrong. He just nodded, and watched the window. All the lights in the station were out. Everything was down but the generators, the turret controls, and the forcefield. The field, fed with the extra power, was stronger than ever. But strong enough? Delvecchio didn't know.

Near the field perimeter, seven or eight ghosting shapes wheeled against the storm. They were all wings and claw, and a long, razor-barbed tail. Swampbats. Big ones, with six foot wingspans.

They weren't alone. The underbrush was alive with

slinkers. And the big leeches could be seen in the water near the south wall. All sorts of life was being picked up by the sensors.

Driven before the storm? Or massing for the attack? Delvecchio didn't know that, either.

The tower door opened, and Sheridan entered. He threw his laser rifle on the table near the door. "These are useless," he said. "We can't use them unless they get inside. Or unless we go out to meet them, and I'm not going to do *that*. Besides, what good will they do against all the stuff they've got?"

Delvecchio started to answer. But Andrews spoke first. "Look out there," he said softly. "More swampbats. And that other thing. What is it?"

Delvecchio looked. Something else was moving through the sky, on slowly moving leathery wings. It was black, and *big*. Twice the size of a swampbat.

"The first expedition named them hellions," Delvecchio said after a long pause. "They're native to the mountains. A thousand miles from here." Another pause. "That clinches it."

There was general movement on the ground and in the water to the west of Greywater Station. Echoes of thunder rolled. And then, piercing the thunder, came a shrill, whooping shriek.

"What was *that*?" Sheridan asked.

Andrews was white. "That one I know," he said. "It's called a screecher. A sonic rifle, breaks down cell walls with concentrated sound. I saw them used once. I—it almost makes flesh liquify."

"God," said Sheridan.

Delvecchio moved to the intercom. Every box in the station was on, full volume. "Battle stations, gentlemen," he said, flipping down his filtermask. "And good luck."

Delvecchio moved out into the hall and down the stairs. Sheridan picked up his laser and followed. At the base of the stairs, Delvecchio motioned for him to stop. "You stay here, Eldon. I'll take the main entry port."

Rain had begun to spatter the swamps around Greywater, although the field kept it off the station. A great sheet of wind roared from the west. And suddenly the storm was no longer approaching. It was here. The blurred outline of the force bubble could be seen against the churning sky.

Delvecchio strode across the yards, through the halls, and cycled through decon quickly to the main entry port. A large viewplate gave the illusion of a window. Delvecchio watched it, sitting on the hood of a mudtractor. The intercom box was on the wall next to him.

"Burrowing animals are moving against the underfield, Jim," Andrews reported from the turret. "We're getting, oh, five or six shock outputs a minute. Nothing we can't handle, however."

He fell silent again, and the only noise was the thunder. Sanderpay began to talk, gabbing about the rockets. Delvecchio was hardly listening. The perimeter beyond the walls was a morass of rain-whipped mud. Delvecchio could see little. He switched from the monitor he was tuned to, and picked up the turret cameras. He and Andrews watched with the same eyes.

"Underfield contacts are up," Andrews said suddenly. "A couple of dozen a minute now."

The swampbats were wheeling closer to the perimeter, first one, then another, skirting the very edge of the field, riding terribly and silently on the wet winds. The turret laser rotated to follow each, but they were gone before it could fire.

Then there was motion on the ground. A wave of slinkers began to cross the perimeter. The laser wheeled, depressed. A spurt of light appeared, leaving a quick-vanishing roil of steam. One slinker died, then another.

On the south, a leech rose from the grey waters near the basewall of the station. The turret turned. Two quick spurts of red burned. Steam rose once. The leech twisted at the second burst.

Delvecchio nodded silently, clutched his rifle tighter.

And Andrews' voice came over the intercom. "There's a man out there," he said. "Near you, Jim."

Delvecchio slipped on his infrared goggles, and flicked

back to the camera just outside the entry port. There was a dim shape in the undergrowth.

"Just one?" asked Delvecchio.

"All I read," Andrew said.

Delvecchio nodded, and thought. Then: "I'm going out."

Many voices at once on the intercom. "That's not wise, I don't think," said one. Granowicz? Another said, "Watch it, Jim. Careful." Sanderpay, maybe. And Sheridan, unmistakable, *"Don't!* You'll let *them* in."

Delvecchio ignored them all. He hit the switch to open the outer port doors, and slid down into the driver's seat in the mud-tractor. The doors parted. Rain washed into the chamber.

The tractor moved forward, rattling over the entry ramp and sliding smoothly into the slime. Now he was out in the storm, and the rain tingled through his skinthins. He drove with one hand and held the laser with the other.

He stopped the tractor just outside the port, and stood up. "Come out," he screamed, as loud as he could, outshouting the thunder. "Let us see you. If you can understand me—if the fungus doesn't have you—come out now."

He paused, and hoped, and waited a long minute. He was about to shout again when a man came running from the undergrowth.

Delvecchio had a fleeting glimpse of tattered, torn clothes, bare feet stumbling in the mud, rain-drenched dark hair. But he wasn't looking at those. He was looking at the fungus that all but covered the man's face, and trailed across his chest and back.

The man—the thing—raised a fist and released a rock. It missed. He kept running, and screaming. Delvecchio, numb, raised his rifle and fired. The fungus thing fell a few feet beyond the trees.

Delvecchio left the tractor where it was, and walked back to the entry port on foot. The doors were still open. He went to the intercom. "It has them," he said. Then again, "It has them. And it's hostile. So now we kill them."

There were no answers. Just a long silence, and a stifled sob, and then Andrews' slow, detached voice. "A new reading. A body of men—thirty, forty, maybe—moving from the west. In formation. A lot of metal—duralloy, I think."

"The main force," Delvecchio said. "They won't be so easy to kill. Get ready. Remember, everything at once."

He turned back into the rain, cradled his rifle, walked to the ramp. Through his goggles, Delvecchio saw the shapes of men. Only a few, at first. Fanned out.

He went outside the station, to the tractor, knelt behind it. As he watched, the turret turned. A red line reached out, touched the first dim shape. It staggered. New sheets of rain washed in, obliterating the landscape. The laser licked out again. Delvecchio, very slowly, lifted his rifle to his shoulder and joined it, firing at the dim outlines seen through the goggles.

Behind him, he felt the first sounding rocket leave up the launch tube, and he briefly saw the fire of its propellant as it cleared the dome. It disappeared into the rain. Another followed it, then another, then the firings became regular.

The dim shapes were all running together; there was a large mass of men just a few yards deep in the undergrowth. Delvecchio fired into the mass, and noted where they were, and hoped Arnold remembered.

Arnold remembered. The turret laser depressed, sliced at the trunk of a nearby tree. There was the sound of wood tearing. Then the tree began to lean. Then it fell.

From what Delvecchio could see, it missed. Another idea that didn't quite work, he reflected bitterly. But he continued to fire into the forest.

Suddenly, near the edge of the perimeter, water gouted up out of the swamp in a terrific explosion, dwarfing all else. A slinker flew through the air, surprised at itself. It rained leech parts.

The first rocket.

A second later, another explosion, among the trees this time. Then more, one after another. Several very close to the enemy. Two among the enemy. Trees began to fall. And Delvecchio thought he could hear screaming.

He began to hope. And continued to fire.

There was a whine in the sky above. Granowicz and the flyer. Delvecchio took time to glance up briefly, and watch it flit overhead, towards the trees. Other shapes were moving up there too, however, diving on the flyer. But they were slower. Granowicz made a quick pass over the perimeter, dumping bombs. The swamp shook, and the mud and water from the explosions mixed with the rain.

Now, definitely, he *could* hear screaming.

And then the answer began to come.

Red tongues and pencils of light flicked out of the dark, played against the walls, causing steam whirlpools which washed away in the rain. Then projectiles. Explosions. A dull thud rocked the station. A second. And, somewhere in the storm, someone opened up with a screecher.

The wall behind him rang with a humming blow. And there was another explosion, much bigger, overhead, against the forcefield dome. The rain vanished for an instant in a vórtex of exploding gases. Wind whipped the smoke away, and the station rocked. Then the rains touched the dome again, in sheets.

More explosions. Lasers spat and hissed in the rain, back and forth, a grisly light show. Miterz was firing from the walls, Granowicz was making another pass. The rockets had stopped falling. Gone already?

The turret fired, moved, fired, moved, fired. Several explosions rocked the tower. The world was a madness of rain, of noise, of lightning, of night.

Then the rockets began again. The swamp and nearer forest shook to the hits. The eastern corner of the station *moved* as a sounding missile landed uncomfortably close.

The turret began to fire again. Short bursts, lost in rain. Answering fire was thick. At least one screecher was shrieking regularly.

Delvecchio saw the swampbats appear suddenly

around the flyer. They converged from all sides, howling, bent on death. One climbed right up into the engine, folding its wings neatly. There was a terrible explosion that lit the night to ghosts of trailing rain.

More explosions around the force dome. Lasers screamed off the dome and turret. The turret glowed red, steamed. On the south, a section of wall vanished in a tremendous explosion.

Delvecchio was still firing, regularly, automatically. But suddenly the laser went dead. Uncharged. He hesitated, rose. He turned just in time to see the hellion dive on the turret. Nothing stopped it. With a sudden chill, Delvecchio realized that the forcefield was out.

Laser rifles reached out and touched the hellion. But not the turret laser. The turret was still, silent. The hellion hit the windows with a crash, smashing through, shattering glass and plastic and duralloy struts.

Delvecchio began to move back towards the ramp and the entry port. A slinker rose as he darted by, snapped at his leg. There was a red blur of pain, fading quickly. He stumbled, rose again, moved. The leg was numb and bleeding. He used the useless laser as a crutch.

Inside, he hit the switch to shut the outer doors. Nothing happened. He laughed suddenly. It didn't matter. Nothing mattered. The station was breached, the fields were down.

The inner doors still worked. He moved through, limped through the halls, out to the yard. Around him, he could hear the generators dying.

The turret was hit again and again. It exploded and lifted, moaning. Three separate impacts hit the tower at once. The top half rained metal.

Delvecchio stopped in the yard, looking at the tower, suddenly unsure of where he was going. The word Arnold formed on his lips, but stayed there.

The generators quit completely. Lasers and missiles and swampbats steamed overhead. All was night. Lit by lightning, by explosions, by lasers.

Delvecchio retreated to a wall, and propped himself against it. The barrage continued. The ground inside the station was torn, churned, shook. Once there was a scream somewhere, as though someone was calling him in their moment of death.

He lowered himself to the ground and lay still, clutching the rifle, while more shells pounded the station. Then all was silent.

Propped up against a rubble pile, he watched helplessly as a big slinker moved towards him across the yard. It loomed large in the rain. But before it reached him it fell screaming.

There was movement behind him. He turned. A figure in skinthins waved, took up a position near one of the ruined laboratories.

Delvecchio saw shapes moving on what was left of the walls, scrambling over. He wished he had a charge in his laser.

A red pencil of light flashed by him in the rain. One of the shapes crumbled. The man behind him had fired too soon, though, and too obviously. The other figures leveled on him. Stabs of laser fire went searing over Delvecchio's head. Answering fire came briefly, then stopped.

Slowly, slowly, Delvecchio dragged himself through the mud, towards the labs. They didn't seem to see him. After an exhausting effort, he reached the fallen figure in skinthins. Sanderpay, dead.

Delvecchio took the laser. There were five men ahead of him, more in the darkness beyond. Lying on his stomach, Delvecchio fired at one man, then another and another. Steam geysers rose around him as the shapes in duralloy fired back. He fired and fired and fired until all those around him were down. Then he picked himself up, and tried to run.

The heel was shot off his boot, and warmth flooded his foot. He turned and fired, moved on, past the wrecked tower and the labs.

Laser stabs peeled overhead. Four, five, maybe six of them. Delvecchio dropped behind what had been a lab wall. He fired around the wall, saw one shape fall. He fired again. Then the rifle died on him.

Lasers tore into the wall, burning in, almost through. The men fanned. There was no hope.

Then the night exploded into fire and noise. A body, twisted flat, spun by. A stab of laser fire came on the teeth of the explosion, from behind Delvecchio.

Sheridan stood over him, firing into the men caught in the open, burning them down one by one. He quit firing for an instant, lobbed a vial of explosive, then went back to the laser. He was hit by a chunk of flying rubble, went down.

Delvecchio came back up as he did. They stood unsteadily, Sheridan wheeling and looking for targets. But there were no more targets. Sheridan was coughing from exertion inside his skinthins.

The rain lessened. The pain increased.

They picked their way through the rubble. They passed many twisted bodies in duralloy, a few in skinthins. Sheridan paused at one of the armored bodies, turned it over. The faceplate had been burned away with part of the face. He kicked it back over.

Delvecchio tried another. He lifted the helmet off, searched the nostrils, the forehead, the eyes, the ears. Nothing.

Sheridan had moved away, and was standing over a body in skinthins, half covered by rubble. He stood there for a long time. "Delvecchio," he called, finally. *"Delvecchio!"*

Delvecchio walked to him, bent, pulled off the filtermask.

The man was still alive. He opened his eyes. "Oh, God, Jim," he said. "Why? Oh, *why?*"

Delvecchio didn't say anything. He stood stock still, and stared down.

Bill Reyn stared back up.

"I got through, Jim," said Reyn, coughing blood. "Once the flyer was down . . . no trouble . . . close, I walked it. They . . . they were still inside, mostly, with the heat. Only a few had . . . gone out."

Delvecchio coughed once, quietly.

"I got through . . . the vaccine . . . most, anyway. A few had gone out, infected . . . no hope. But . . . but we took away their armor and their weapons. No harm that way . . . we had to fight our way through. Me it left alone . . . but God, those guys in duralloy . . . lost some men . . . leeches, slinkers . . ."

Sheridan turned and dropped his rifle. He began to run towards the labs.

"We tried the suit radios, Jim . . . but the storm . . . should've waited, but the vaccine . . . short-term, wearing off . . . We tried not to . . . hurt you . . . started killing us . . ."

He began to choke on his own blood. Delvecchio, helpless, looked down. "Again," he said in a voice that was dead and broken. "We underestimated it again. We—no, *I*—I—"

Reyn did not die for another three or four hours. Delvecchio never found Sheridan again. He tried to restart the generators alone, but to no avail.

Just before dawn, the skies cleared. The stars came through, bright and white against the night sky. The fungus had not yet released new spores. It was almost like a moonless night on Earth.

Delvecchio sat atop a mound of rubble, a dead soldier's laser rifle in his hands, ten or eleven charges on his belt. He did not look often to where Reyn lay. He was trying to figure out how to get the radio working. There was a supply ship coming.

The sky to the east began to lighten. A swampbat, then another, began to circle the ruins of Greywater Station.

And the spores began to fall.

—*Kansas City, Missouri; Chicago;*
Grand Prairie, Texas;
June–August 1972

THE LONELY SONGS
OF LAREN DORR

There is a girl who goes between the worlds.

She is grey-eyed and pale of skin, or so the story goes, and her hair is a coal-black waterfall with half-seen hints of red. She wears about her brow a circlet of burnished metal, a dark crown that holds her hair in place and sometimes puts shadows in her eyes. Her name is Sharra; she knows the gates.

The beginning of her story is lost to us, with the memory of the world from which she sprang. The end? The end is not yet, and when it comes we shall not know it.

We have only the middle, or rather a piece of that middle, the smallest part of the legend, a mere fragment of the quest. A small tale within the greater, of one world where Sharra paused, and of the lonely singer Laren Dorr and how they briefly touched.

One moment there was only the valley, caught in twilight. The setting sun hung fat and violet on the ridge above, and its rays slanted down silently into a dense forest whose trees had shiny black trunks and colorless ghostly leaves. The only sounds were the cries of the mourning-birds coming out for the night, and the swift rush of water in the rocky stream that cut the woods.

Then, through a gate unseen, Sharra came tired and bloodied to the world of Laren Dorr. She wore a plain white dress, now stained and sweaty, and a heavy fur cloak that had been half-ripped from her back. And her left arm, bare and slender, still bled from three long wounds. She appeared by the side of the stream, shaking, and she threw a quick, wary glance about her before she knelt to dress her wounds. The water, for all its swiftness, was a dark and murky green. No way to tell if it was safe, but Sharra was weak and thirsty. She drank, washed her arm as best she could in the strange and doubtful water, and bound her injuries with bandages ripped from her clothes. Then, as the purple sun dipped lower behind the ridge, she crawled away from the water to a sheltered spot among the trees, and fell into exhausted sleep.

She woke to arms around her, strong arms that lifted her easily to carry her somewhere, and she woke struggling. But the arms just tightened, and held her still. "Easy," a mellow voice said, and she saw a face dimly through gathering mist, a man's face, long and somehow gentle. "You are weak," he said, "and night is coming. We must be inside before darkness."

Sharra did not struggle, not then, though she knew she should. She had been struggling a long time, and she was tired. But she looked at him, confused. "Why?" she asked. Then, not waiting for an answer, "Who are you? Where are we going?"

"To safety," he said.

"Your home?," she asked, drowsy.

"No," he said, so soft she could scarcely hear his voice. "No, not home, not ever home. But it will do." She heard splashing then, as if he were carrying her across the stream, and ahead of them on the ridge she glimpsed a gaunt, twisted silhouette, a triple-towered castle etched black against the sun. Odd, she thought, that wasn't there before.

She slept.

When she woke, he was there, watching her. She lay under a pile of soft, warm blankets in a curtained, canopied bed. But the curtains had been drawn back, and her host sat across the room in a great chair draped by shadows. Candlelight flickered in his eyes, and his hands locked together neatly beneath his chin. "Are you feeling better?" he asked, without moving.

She sat up, and noticed she was nude. Swift as suspicion, quicker than thought, her hand went to her head. But the dark crown was still there, in place, untouched, its metal cool against her brow. Relaxing, she leaned back against the pillows and pulled the blankets up to cover herself. "Much better," she said, and as she said it she realized for the first time that her wounds were gone.

The man smiled at her, a sad wistful sort of smile. He had a strong face, with charcoal-colored hair that curled in lazy ringlets and fell down into dark eyes somehow wider than they should be. Even seated, he was tall. And slender. He wore a suit and cape of some soft grey leather, and over that he wore melancholy like a cloak. "Claw marks," he said speculatively, while he smiled. "Claw marks down your arm, and your clothes almost ripped from your back. Someone doesn't like you."

"Something," Sharra said. "A guardian, a guardian at the gate." She sighed. "There is always a guardian at the gate. The Seven don't like us to move from world to world. Me they like least of all."

His hands unfolded from beneath his chin, and rested on the carved wooden arms of his chair. He nodded, but the wistful smile stayed. "So, then," he said. "You know the Seven, and you know the gates." His eyes strayed to her forehead. "The crown, of course. I should have guessed."

Sharra grinned at him. "You did guess. More than that, you knew. Who are you? What world is this?"

"My world," he said evenly. "I've named it a thousand times, but none of the names ever seem quite right. There was one once, a name I liked, a name that fit. But I've forgotten it. It was a long time ago. *My* name is Laren Dorr, or that was my name, once, when I had use for such a thing. Here and now it seems somewhat silly. But at least I haven't forgotten *it*."

"Your world," Sharra said. "Are you a king, then? A god?"

"Yes," Laren Dorr replied, with an easy laugh. "And more. I'm whatever I choose to be. There is no one around to dispute me."

"What did you do to my wounds?" she asked.

"I healed them." He gave an apologetic shrug. "It's my world. I have certain powers. Not the powers I'd like to have, perhaps, but powers nonetheless."

"Oh." She did not look convinced.

Laren waved an impatient hand. "You think it's impossible. Your crown, of course. Well, that's only half right. I could not harm you with my, ah, powers, not while you wear that. But I can help you." He smiled again, and his eyes grew soft and dreamy. "But it doesn't matter. Even if I could I would never harm you, Sharra. Believe that. It has been a long time."

Sharra looked startled. "You know my name. How?"

He stood up, smiling, and came across the room to sit beside her on the bed. And he took her hand before replying, wrapping it softly in his and stroking her with his thumb. "Yes, I know your name. You are Sharra, who moves between the worlds. Centuries ago, when the hills had a different shape and the violet sun burned scarlet at the very beginning of its cycle, they came to me and told me you would come. I hate them, all Seven, and I will always hate them, but that night I welcomed the vision they gave me. They told me only your name, and that you would come here, to my world. And one thing more, but that was enough. It was a promise. A promise of an ending or a start, of a change. And any change is welcome on this world. I've been alone here through a thousand sun-cycles, Sharra, and each cycle lasts for centuries. There are few events to mark the death of time."

Sharra was frowning. She shook her long black hair, and in the dim light of the candles the soft red highlights glowed. "Are they that far ahead of me, then?" she said. "Do they know what will happen?" Her voice was troubled. She looked up at him. "This other thing they told you?"

He squeezed her hand, very gently. "They told me I would love you," Laren said. His voice still sounded sad. "But that was no great prophecy. I could have told them as much. There was a time long ago—I think the sun was yellow then—when I realized that I would love *any* voice that was not an echo of my own."

Sharra woke at dawn, when shafts of bright purple light spilled into her room through a high arched window that had not been there the night before. Clothing had been laid out for her; a loose yellow robe, a jeweled dress of bright crimson, a suit of forest green. She chose the suit, dressed quickly. As she left, she paused to look out the window.

She was in a tower, looking out over crumbling stone battlements and a dusty triangular courtyard. Two other towers, twisted matchstick things with pointed conical spires, rose from the other corners of the triangle. There was a strong wind that whipped the rows of grey pennants set along the walls, but no other motion to be seen.

And, beyond the castle walls, no sign of the valley, none at all. The castle with its courtyard and its crooked towers was set atop a mountain, and far and away in all directions taller mountains loomed, presenting a panorama of black stone cliffs and jagged rocky walls and shining clean ice steeples that gleamed with a violet sheen. The window was sealed and closed, but the wind *looked* cold.

Her door was open. Sharra moved quickly down a twisting stone staircase, out across the courtyard into the main building, a low wooden structure built against the wall. She passed through countless rooms, some cold and empty save for dust, others richly furnished, before she found Laren Dorr eating breakfast.

There was an empty seat at his side; the table was heavily laden with food and drink. Sharra sat down, and took a hot biscuit, smiling despite herself. Laren smiled back.

"I'm leaving today," she said, in between bites. "I'm sorry, Laren. I must find the gate."

The air of hopeless melancholy had not left him. It never did. "So you said last night," he replied, sighing. "It seems I have waited a long time for nothing."

There was meat, several types of biscuits, fruit, cheese, milk. Sharra filled a plate, face a little downcast, avoiding Laren's eyes. "I'm sorry," she repeated.

"Stay awhile," he said. "Only a short time. You can afford it, I would think. Let me show you what I can of my world. Let me sing to you." His eyes, wide and dark and very tired, asked the question.

She hesitated. "Well . . . it takes time to find the gate. Stay with me for a while, then. But Laren, eventually I must go. I have made promises. You understand?"

He smiled, gave a helpless shrug. "Yes. But look. I know where the gate is. I can show you, save you a search. Stay with me, oh, a month. A month as you measure time. Then I'll take you to the gate." He studied her. "You've been hunting a long, long time, Sharra. Perhaps you need a rest."

Slowly, thoughtfully, she ate a piece of fruit, watching him all the time. "Perhaps I do," she said at last, weighing things. "And there will be a guardian, of course. You could help me then. A month . . . that's not so long. I've been on other worlds far longer than a month." She nodded, and a smile spread slowly across her face. "Yes," she said, still nodding. "That would be all right."

He touched her hand lightly. After breakfast he showed her the world they had given him.

They stood side by side on a small balcony atop the highest of the three towers, Sharra in dark green and

Laren tall and soft in grey. They stood without moving, and Laren moved the world around them. He set the castle flying over restless churning seas, where long black serpent-heads peered up out of the water to watch them pass. He moved them to a vast echoing cavern under the earth, all aglow with a soft green light, where dripping stalactites brushed down against the towers and herds of blind white goats moaned outside the battlements. He clapped his hands and smiled, and steam-thick jungle rose around them; trees that climbed each other in rubber ladders to the sky, giant flowers of a dozen different colors, fanged monkeys that chittered from the walls. He clapped again, and the walls were swept clean, and suddenly the courtyard dirt was sand and they were on an endless beach by the shore of a bleak grey ocean, and above the slow wheeling of a great blue bird with tissue-paper wings was the only movement to be seen. He showed her this, and more, and more, and in the end as dusk seemed to threaten in one place after another, he took the castle back to the ridge above the valley. And Sharra looked down on the forest of black-barked trees where he had found her, and heard the mourning-birds whimper and weep among transparent leaves.

"It is not a bad world," she said, turning to him on the balcony.

"No," Laren replied. His hands rested on the cold stone railing, his eyes on the valley below. "Not entirely. I explored it once, on foot, with a sword and a walking stick. There was a joy there, a real excitement. A new mystery behind every hill." He chuckled. "But that, too, was long ago. Now I know what lies behind every hill. Another empty horizon."

He looked at her, and gave his characteristic shrug. "There are worse hells, I suppose. But this is mine."

"Come with me, then," she said. "Find the gate with me, and leave. There are other worlds. Maybe they are less strange and less beautiful, but you will not be alone."

He shrugged again. "You make it sound so easy," he

said in a careless voice. "I have found the gate, Sharra. I have tried it a thousand times. The guardian does not stop me. I step through, briefly glimpse some other world, and suddenly I'm back in the courtyard. No. I cannot leave."

She took his hand in hers. "How sad. To be alone so long. I think you must be very strong, Laren. I would go mad in only a handful of years."

He laughed, and there was a bitterness in the way he did it. "Oh, Sharra. I have gone mad a thousand times, also. They cure me, love. They always cure me." Another shrug, and he put his arm around her. The wind was cold and rising. "Come," he said. "We must be inside before full dark."

They went up in the tower to her bedroom, and they sat together on her bed and Laren brought them food; meat burned black on the outside and red within, hot bread, wine. They ate and they talked.

"Why are you here?" she asked him, in between mouthfuls, washing her words down with wine. "How did you offend them? Who were you, before?"

"I hardly remember, except in dreams," he told her. "And the dreams—it has been so long, I can't even recall which ones are truth and which are visions born of my madness." He sighed. "Sometimes I dream I was a king, a great king in a world other than this, and my crime was that I made my people happy. In happiness they turned against the Seven, and the temples fell idle. And I woke one day, within my room, within my castle, and found my servants gone. And when I went outside, my people and my world were also gone, and even the woman who slept beside me.

"But there are other dreams. Often I remember vaguely that I was a god. Well, an almost-god. I had powers, and teachings, and they were not the teachings of the Seven. They were afraid of me, each of them, for I was a match for any of them. But I could not meet all Seven together, and that was what they forced me to do. And then they left me only a small bit of my power, and set me here. It was cruel irony. As a god,

I'd taught that people should turn to each other, that they could keep away the darkness by love and laughter and talk. So all these things the Seven took from me.

"And even that is not the worst. For there are other times when I think that I have always been here, that I was born here some endless age ago. And the memories are all false ones, sent to make me hurt the more."

Sharra watched him as he spoke. His eyes were not on her, but far away, full of fog and dreams and half-dead rememberings. And he spoke very slowly, in a voice that was also like fog, that drifted and curled and hid things, and you knew that there were mysteries there and things brooding just out of sight and far-off lights that you would never reach.

Laren stopped, and his eyes woke up again. "Ah, Sharra," he said. "Be careful how you go. Even your crown will not help you should they move on you directly. And the pale child Bakkalon will tear at you, and Naa-Slas feed upon your pain, and Saagael on your soul."

She shivered, and cut another piece of meat. But it was cold and tough when she bit into it, and suddenly she noticed that the candles had burned very low. How long had she listened to him speak?

"Wait," he said then, and he rose and went outside, out the door near where the window had been. There was nothing there now but rough grey stone; the windows all changed to solid rock with the last fading of the sun. Laren returned in a few moments, with a softly shining instrument of dark black wood slung around his neck on a leather cord. Sharra had never quite seen its like. It had sixteen strings, each a different color, and all up and down its length brightly-glowing bars of light were inlaid amid the polished wood. When Laren sat, the bottom of the device rested on the floor and the top came to just above his shoulder. He stroked it lightly, speculatively; the lights glowed, and suddenly the room was full of swift-fading music.

"My companion," he said, smiling. He touched it again, and the music rose and died, lost notes without a tune. And he brushed the light-bars and the very air shimmered and changed color.

He began to sing.

> *I am the lord of loneliness,*
> *Empty my domain . . .*

. . . the first words ran, sung low and sweet in Laren's mellow far-off fog voice. The rest of the song—Sharra clutched at it, heard each word and tried to remember, but lost them all. They brushed her, touched her, then melted away, back into the fog, here and gone again so swift that she could not remember quite what they had been. With the words, the music; wistful and melancholy and full of secrets, pulling at her, crying, whispering promises of a thousand tales untold. All around the room the candles flamed up brighter, and globes of light grew and danced and flowed together until the air was full of color.

Words, music, light; Laren Dorr put them all together, and wove for her a vision.

She saw him then as he saw himself in his dreams; a king, strong and tall and still proud, with hair as black as hers and eyes that snapped. He was dressed all in shimmering white, pants that clung tight and a shirt that ballooned at the sleeves, and a great cloak that moved and curled in the wind like a sheet of solid snow. Around his brow he wore a crown of flashing silver, and a slim, straight sword flashed just as bright at his side. This Laren, this younger Laren, this dream vision, moved without melancholy, moved in a world of sweet ivory minarets and languid blue canals. And the world moved around him, friends and lovers and one special woman whom Laren drew with words and lights of fire, and there was an infinity of easy days and laughter. Then, sudden, abrupt darkness. He was here.

The music moaned; the lights dimmed; the words grew sad and lost. Sharra saw Laren wake, in a familiar castle now deserted. She saw him search from room to room, and walk outside to face a world he'd never seen. She watched him leave the castle, walk off towards the mists of a far horizon in the hope that those mists were smoke. And on and on he walked, and new horizons fell beneath his feet each day, and the great fat sun waxed red and orange and yellow, but still his world was empty. All the places he had shown her he walked to; all those and more; and finally, lost as ever, wanting home, the castle came to him.

By then his white had faded to dim grey. But still the song went on. Days went, and years, and centuries, and Laren grew tired and mad but never old. The sun shone green and violet and a savage hard blue-white, but with each cycle there was less color in his world. So Laren sang, of endless empty days and nights when music and memory were his only sanity, and his songs made Sharra feel it.

And when the vision faded and the music died and his soft voice melted away for the last time and Laren paused and smiled and looked at her, Sharra found herself trembling.

"Thank you," he said softly, with a shrug. And he took his instrument and left her for the night.

The next day dawned cold and overcast, but Laren took her out into the forests, hunting. Their quarry was a lean white thing, half cat, half gazelle, with too much speed for them to chase easily and too many teeth for them to kill. Sharra did not mind. The hunt was better than the kill. There was a singular, striking joy in that run through the darkling forest, holding a bow she never used and wearing a quiver of black wood arrows cut from the same dour trees that surrounded them. Both of them were bundled up tightly in grey fur, and Laren smiled out at her from under a wolf's-head hood. And the leaves beneath their boots, as clear and fragile as glass, cracked and splintered as they ran.

Afterwards, unblooded but exhausted, they returned to the castle and Laren set out a great feast in the main dining room. They smiled at each other from opposite ends of a table fifty feet long, and Sharra watched the clouds roll by the window behind Laren's head, and later watched the window turn to stone.

"Why does it do that?" she asked. "And why don't you ever go outside at night?"

He shrugged. "Ah. I have reasons. The nights are, well, not good here." He sipped hot spice wine from a great jeweled cup. "The world you came from, where you started—tell me, Sharra, did you have stars?"

She nodded. "Yes. It's been so long, though. But I still remember. The nights were very dark and black, and the stars were little pinpoints of light, hard and cold and far away. You could see patterns sometimes. The men of my world, when they were young, gave names to each of those patterns, and told grand tales about them."

Laren nodded. "I would like your world, I think," he said. "Mine was like that, a little. But our stars were a thousand colors, and they moved, like ghostly lanterns in the night. Sometimes they drew veils around them to hide their light. And then our nights would be all shimmer and gossamer. Often I would go sailing at startime, myself and she whom I loved. Just so we could see the stars together. It was a good time to sing." His voice was growing sad again.

Darkness had crept into the room, darkness and silence, and the food was cold and Sharra could scarce see his face fifty long feet away. So she rose and went to him, and sat lightly on the great table near to his chair. And Laren nodded and smiled, and at once there was a whooosh, and all along the walls torches flared to sudden life in the long dining hall. He offered her more wine, and her fingers lingered on his as she took the glass.

"It was like that for us, too," Sharra said. "If the wind was warm enough, and other men were far away, then we liked to lie together in the open. Kaydar and I." She hesitated, looked at him.

His eyes were searching. "Kaydar?"

"You would have liked him, Laren. And he would

have liked you, I think. He was tall and he had red hair and there was a fire in his eyes. Kaydar had powers, as did I, but his were greater. And he had such a will. They took him one night, did not kill him, only took him from me and from our world. I have been hunting for him ever since. I know the gates, I wear the dark crown, and they will not stop me easily."

Laren drank his wine and watched the torchlight on the metal of his goblet. "There are an infinity of worlds, Sharra."

"I have as much time as I require. I do not age, Laren, no more than you do. I will find him."

"Did you love him so much?"

Sharra fought a fond, flickering smile, and lost. "Yes," she said, and now it was her voice that seemed a little lost. "Yes, so much. He made me happy, Laren. We were only together for a short time, but he *did* make me happy. The Seven cannot touch that. It was a joy just to watch him, to feel his arms around me and see the way he smiled."

"Ah," he said, and he did smile, but there was something very beaten in the way he did it. The silence grew very thick.

Finally Sharra turned to him. "But we have wandered a long way from where we started. You still have not told me why your windows seal themselves at night."

"You have come a long way, Sharra. You move between the worlds. Have you seen worlds without stars?"

"Yes. Many, Laren. I have seen a universe where the sun is glowing ember with but a single world, and the skies are vast and vacant by night. I have seen the land of frowning jesters, where there is no sky and the hissing suns burn below the ocean. I have walked the moors of Carradyne, and watched dark sorcerers set fire to a rainbow to light that sunless land."

"This world has no stars," Laren said.

"Does that frighten you so much, that you stay inside?"

"No. But it has something else instead." He looked at her. "Would you see?"

She nodded.

As abruptly as they had lit, the torches all snuffed out. The room swam with blackness. And Sharra shifted on the table to look over Laren's shoulder. Laren did not move. But behind him, the stones of the window fell away like dust and light poured in from outside.

The sky was very dark, but she could see clearly, for against the darkness a shape was moving. Light poured from it, and the dirt in the courtyard and the stones of the battlements and the grey pennants were all bright beneath its glow. Puzzling, Sharra looked up.

Something looked back. It was taller than the mountains and it filled up half the sky, and though it gave off light enough to see the castle by, Sharra knew that it was dark beyond darkness. It had a man-shape, roughly, and it wore a long cape and a cowl, and below that was blackness even fouler than the rest. The only sounds were Laren's soft breathing and the beating of her heart and distant weeping of a mourning-bird, but in her head Sharra could hear demonic laughter.

The shape in the sky looked down at her, in her, and she felt the cold dark in her soul. Frozen, she could not move her eyes. But the shape did move. It turned, and raised a hand, and then there was something else up there with it, a tiny man-shape with eyes of fire that writhed and screamed and called to her.

Sharra shrieked, and turned away. When she glanced back, there was no window. Only a wall of safe, sure stone, and a row of torches burning, and Laren holding her within strong arms. "It was only a vision," he told her. He pressed her tight against him, and stroked her hair. "I used to test myself at night," he said, more to himself than to her. "But there was no need. They take turns up there, watching me, each of the Seven. I have seen them too often, burning with black light against the clean dark of the sky, and holding those I loved. Now I don't look. I stay inside and sing, and my windows are made of night-stone."

"I feel . . . fouled," she said, still trembling a little.

"Come," he said. "There is water upstairs, you can clean away the cold. And then I'll sing for you." He took her hand, and led her up into the tower.

Sharra took a hot bath while Laren set up his instrument and tuned it in the bedroom. He was ready when she returned, wrapped head to foot in a huge fluffy brown towel. She sat on the bed, drying her hair and waiting.

And Laren gave her visions.

He sang his other dream this time, the one where he was a god and the enemy of the Seven. The music was a savage pounding thing, shot through with lightning and tremors of fear, and the lights melted together to form a scarlet battlefield where a blinding-white Laren fought shadows and the shapes of nightmare. There were seven of them, and they formed a ring around him and darted in and out, stabbing him with lances of absolute black, and Laren answered them with fire and storm. But in the end they overwhelmed him, the light faded, and then the song grew soft and sad again and the vision blurred as lonely dreaming centuries flashed by.

Hardly had the last notes fallen from the air and the final shimmers died then Laren started once again. A new song this time, and one he did not know so well. His fingers, slim and graceful, hesitated and retraced themselves more than once, and his voice was shaky too, for he was making up some of the words as he went along. Sharra knew why. For this time he sang of her, a ballad of her quest. Of burning love and endless searching, of worlds beyond worlds, of dark crowns and waiting guardians that fought with claws and tricks and lies. He took every word that she had spoken, and used each, and transformed each. In the bedroom, glittering panoramas formed where hot white suns burned beneath eternal oceans and hissed in clouds of steam, and men ancient beyond time lit rainbows to keep away the dark. And he sang Kaydar, and he sang him true somehow, he caught and drew the fire that had been Sharra's love and made her believe anew.

But the song ended with a question, the halting finale lingering in the air, echoing, echoing. Both of them waited for the rest, and both knew there was no more. Not yet.

Sharra was crying. "My turn, Laren," she said. Then: "Thank you. For giving Kaydar back to me."

"It was only a song," he said, shrugging. "It's been a long time since I had a new song to sing."

Once again he left her, touching her cheek lightly at the door as she stood there with the blanket wrapped around her. Then Sharra locked the door behind him and went from candle to candle, turning light to darkness with a breath. And she threw the towel over a chair and crawled under the blankets and lay a long long time before drifting off to sleep.

It was still dark when she woke, not knowing why. She opened her eyes and lay quietly and looked around the room, and nothing was there, nothing was changed. Or was there?

And then she saw him, sitting in the chair across the room with his hands locked under his chin, just as he had sat that first time. His eyes steady and unmoving, very wide and dark in a room full of night. He sat very still. "Laren?" she called, softly, still not quite sure the dark form was him.

"Yes," he said. He did not move. "I watched you last night, too, while you slept. I have been alone here for longer than you can ever imagine, and very soon now I will be alone again. Even in sleep, your presence is a wonder."

"Oh, Laren," she said. There was a silence, a pause, a weighing and an unspoken conversation. Then she threw back the blanket, and Laren came to her.

Both of them had seen centuries come and go. A month, a moment; much the same.

They slept together every night, and every night Laren sang his songs while Sharra listened. They talked throughout dark hours, and during the day they swam nude in crystalline waters that caught the purple glory of the sky. They made love on beaches of fine white sand, and they spoke a lot of love.

But nothing changed. And finally the time drew near. On the eve of the night before the day that was end, at twilight, they walked together through the shadowed forest where he'd found her.

Laren had learned to laugh during his month with Sharra, but now he was silent again. He walked slowly, clutched her hand hard in his, and his mood was more grey than the soft silk shirt he wore. Finally, by the side of the valley stream, he sat and pulled her down by his side. They took off their boots and let the water cool their feet. It was a warm evening, with a lonely restless wind and already you could hear the first of the mourning-birds.

"You must go," he said, still holding her hand but never looking at her. It was a statement, not a question.

"Yes," she said, and the melancholy had touched her too, and there were leaden echoes in her voice.

"My words have all left me, Sharra," Laren said. "If I could sing for you a vision now, I would. A vision of a world once empty, made full by us and our children. I could offer that. My world has beauty and wonder and mystery enough, if only there were eyes to see it. And if the nights are evil, well, men have faced dark nights before, on other worlds in other times. I would love you, Sharra, as much as I am able. I would try to make you happy."

"Laren . . . ," she started. But he quieted her with a glance.

"No, I could say that, but I will not. I have no right. Kaydar makes you happy. Only a selfish fool would ask you to give up that happiness to share my misery. Kaydar is all fire and laughter, while I am smoke and song and sadness. I have been alone too long, Sharra. The grey is part of my soul now, and I would not have you darkened. But still . . ."

She took his hand in both of hers, lifted it, and kissed it quickly. Then, releasing him, she lay her head on his unmoving shoulder. "Try to come with me, Laren," she said. "Hold my hand when we pass through the gate, and perhaps the dark crown will protect you."

"I will try anything you ask. But don't ask me to believe that it will work." He sighed. "You have countless worlds ahead of you, Sharra, and I cannot see your ending. But it is not here. That I know. And maybe that is best. I don't know anymore, if I ever did. I remember love vaguely, I think I can recall what it was like, and I remember that it never lasts. Here, with both of us unchanging and immortal, how could we help but to grow bored? Would we hate each other then? I'd not want that." He looked at her then, and smiled an aching melancholy smile. "I think that you had known Kaydar for only a short time, to be so in love with him. Perhaps I'm being devious after all. For in finding Kaydar, you may lose him. The fire will go out some day, my love, and the magic will die. And then you may remember Laren Dorr."

Sharra began to weep, softly. Laren gathered her to him, and kissed her, and whispered a gentle "No." She kissed back, and they held each other wordless.

When at last the purple gloom had darkened to near-black, they put back on their boots and stood. Laren hugged her and smiled.

"I *must* go," Sharra said. "I *must*. But leaving is hard, Laren, you must believe that."

"I do," he said. "I love you *because* you will go, I think. Because you cannot forget Kaydar, and you will not forget the promises you made. You are Sharra, who goes between the worlds, and I think the Seven must fear you far more than any god I might have been. If you were not you, I would not think as much of you."

"Oh. Once you said you would love any voice, that was not any echo of your own."

Laren shrugged. "As I have often said, love, *that* was a very long time ago."

They were back inside the castle before darkness, for a final meal, a final night, a final song. They got no sleep that night, and Laren sang to her again just before dawn. It was not a very good song, though; it was an aimless, rambling thing about a wandering minstrel on some nondescript world. Very little of interest ever happened to the minstrel; Sharra couldn't quite get the point of the song, and Laren sang it listlessly. It seemed an odd farewell, but both of them were troubled.

He left her with the sunrise, promising to change clothes and meet her in the courtyard. And sure enough, he was waiting when she got there, smiling at her calm and confident. He wore a suit of pure white; pants that clung, a shirt that puffed up at the sleeves, and a great heavy cape that snapped and billowed in the rising wind. But the purple sun stained him with its shadow rays.

Sharra walked out to him and took his hand. She wore tough leather, and there was a knife in her belt, for dealing with the guardian. Her hair, jet black with lightborn glints of red and purple, blew as freely as his cape, but the dark crown was in place. "Good-bye, Laren," she said. "I wish I had given you more."

"You have given me enough. In all the centuries that come, in all the suncycles that lie ahead, I will remember. I shall measure time by you, Sharra. When the sun rises one day and its color is blue fire, I will look at it and say, 'Yes, this is the first blue sun after Sharra came to me.'"

She nodded. "And I have a new promise. I will find Kaydar, some day. And if I free him, we will come back to you, both of us together, and we will pit my crown and Kaydar's fires against all the darkness of the Seven."

Laren shrugged. "Good. If I'm not here, be sure to leave a message," he said. And then he grinned.

"Now, the gate. You said you would show me the gate."

Laren turned and gestured at the shortest tower, a sooty stone structure Sharra had never been inside. There was a wide wooden door in its base. Laren produced a key.

"Here?" she said, looking puzzled. "In the castle?"

"Here," Laren said. They walked across the courtyard, to the door. Laren inserted the heavy metal key and began to fumble with the lock. While he worked, Sharra took one last look around, and felt the sadness heavy on her soul. The other towers looked bleak and dead, the courtyard was forlorn, and beyond the high icy mountains was only an empty horizon. There was no sound but Laren working at the lock, and no motion but the steady wind that kicked up the courtyard dust and flapped the seven grey pennants that hung along each wall. Sharra shivered with sudden loneliness.

Laren opened the door. No room inside; only a wall of moving fog, a fog without color or sound or light. "Your gate, my lady," the singer said.

Sharra watched it, as she had watched it so many times before. What world was next? she wondered. She never knew. But maybe in the next one, she would find Kaydar.

She felt Laren's hand on her shoulder. "You hesitate," he said, his voice soft.

Sharra's hand went to her knife. "The guardian," she said suddenly. "There is always a guardian." Her eyes darted quickly round the courtyard.

Laren sighed. "Yes. Always. There are some who try to claw you to pieces, and some who try to get you lost, and some who try to trick you into taking the wrong gate. There are some who hold you with weapons, some with chains, some with lies. And there is one, at least, who tried to stop you with love. Yet he was true for all that, and he never sang you false."

And with a hopeless, loving shrug, Laren shoved her through the gate.

Did she find him, in the end, her lover with the eyes of fire? Or is she searching still? What guardian did she face next?

When she walks at night, a stranger in a lonely land, does the sky have stars?

I don't know. He doesn't. Maybe even the Seven do not know. They are powerful, yes, but all power is not theirs, and the number of worlds is greater than even they can count.

There is a girl who goes between the worlds, but her path is lost in legend by now. Maybe she is dead, and maybe not. Knowledge moves slowly from world to world, and not all of it is true.

But this we know; in an empty castle below a purple sun, a lonely minstrel waits, and sings of her.

—*Chicago, May 1974*

NIGHT OF THE VAMPYRES

The announcement came during prime time.

All four major holo networks went off simultaneously, along with most of the independents. There was an instant of crackling grayness. And then a voice, which said, simply, "Ladies and gentlemen, the President of the United States."

John Hartmann was the youngest man ever to hold the office of President, and the commentators were fond of saying that he was the most telegenic as well. His clean-cut good looks, ready wit, and flashing grin had given the Liberty Alliance its narrow plurality in the bitter four-way elections of 1984. His political acumen had engineered the Electoral College coalition with the Old Republicans that had put him in the White House.

Hartmann was not grinning now. His features were hard, somber. He was sitting behind his desk in the Oval Office, looking down at the papers he held in his hands. After a moment of silence, he raised his head slowly, and his dark eyes looked straight out into the living rooms of a nation.

"My fellow countrymen," he said gravely, "tonight our nation faces the most serious crisis in its long and great history. Approximately one hour ago, an American air force base in California was hit by a violent and vicious attack..."

The first casualty was a careless sentry. The attacker was quick, silent, and very efficient. He used a knife.

The sentry died without a whimper, never knowing what was happening.

The other attackers were moving in even before the corpse hit the ground. Circuits were hooked up to bypass the alarm system, and torches went to work on the high electric fence. It fell. From the darkness, more invaders materialized to move through the fresh gap.

But somewhere one alarm system was still alive. Sirens began to howl. The sleepy airbase came to sudden, startled life. Stealth now useless, the attackers began to run. Towards the airfields.

Somebody began to fire. Someone else screamed. Outside the main gate, the guards looked in, baffled, towards the base. A stream of submachine gun fire took them where they stood, hammering them to bloody death against their own fence. A grenade arced through the air, and the gate shattered under the explosion.

"The attack was sudden, well-planned, and utterly ruthless," Hartmann told the nation. "The defense, under the circumstances, was heroic. Nearly one hundred American servicemen died during the course of the action."

The power lines were cut only seconds after the attack got under way. A well-placed grenade took out the emergency generator. Then darkness. It was a moonless night, and the clouds obscured the stars. The only light was the flash of machine gun fire and the brief, shattering brilliance of the explosions around the main gate.

There was little rhyme and less reason to the defense. Startled by the sirens, troops scrambled from the barracks and towards the gate, where the conflict seemed to be centered. On either side of the fence, attackers and defenders hit the ground. A searing crossfire was set up.

The base commandant was as startled and confused as any of his men. Long, valuable minutes passed while he and his staff groped for the facts, and tried to understand what was happening. Their response was almost instinctive. A ring of defenders was thrown around the Command Tower, a second around the base armory. Other men were sent sprinting towards the planes.

But the bulk of the troops were rushed to the main gate, where the battle was at its fiercest.

The defenders brought up heavy weapons from the base armory. The shrubbery outside the base perimeter was blasted by mortars, blown apart by grenades. The attackers' hidden position was systematically pounded. Then, behind a wall of smoke and tear-gas, the defenders poured out of the gate, washed over the enemy positions.

They found them empty, but for corpses. The attackers had melted away as suddenly as they had come.

An order for seach and pursuit was swiftly given. And just as swiftly rescinded. For over the machine gun fire and the explosions, another sound could now be heard.

The sound of a jet taking off.

"The attackers concentrated most of their forces against the main entrance of the air base," Hartmann said. "But for all its fierceness, this assault was simply a diversion. While it was in progress, a smaller force of attackers penetrated another part of the base perimeter, beat off light resistance, and seized a small portion of the airfields."

The President's face was taut with emotion. "The goal of the attack was a squadron of long-range bombers, and their fighter escorts. As part of our first line of defense to deter Communist aggression, the bombers were on stand-by status; fueled and ready to take off in seconds, in the event of an enemy attack."

Hartmann paused dramatically, looked down at his papers, then back up. "Our men reacted swiftly and valiantly. They deserve only our praise. They retook several planes from the attackers, and burned down several others during takeoff.

"Despite this courageous resistance, however, the attackers put seven fighters and two bombers into the air. My fellow countrymen, both of those bombers were equipped with nuclear weaponry."

Again Hartmann paused. Behind him, the Oval Office background dissolved. Suddenly there was only the President, and his desk, outlined against a blank wall of white. On that wall, six familiar sentences suddenly appeared.

"Even while the attack was in progress, an ultimatum was sent to me in Washington," Hartmann said. "Unless certain demands were met within a three-hour deadline, I was told, a hydrogen bomb would be dropped on the city of Washington, D.C. You see those demands before you." He gestured.

"Most of you have seen them before. Some call them the Six Demands," he continued. "I'm sure you know them as well as I. They call for an end to American aid to our struggling allies in Africa and the Mid-East, for the systematic destruction of our defensive capacities, for an end to the Special Urban Units that have restored law and order to our cities, for the release of thousands of dangerous criminals, for the repeal of federal restrictions on obscene and subversive literature, and, of course,"—he flashed his famous grin—"for my resignation as President of the United States."

The grin faded. "These demands are a formula for national suicide, a recipe for surrender and disgrace. They would return us to the lawlessness and anarchy of a permissive society that we have left behind. Moreover, they are opposed by the great majority of the American people.

"However, as you know, these demands are vocally advocated by a small and dangerous minority. They represent the political program of the so-called American Liberation Front."

The background behind Hartmann changed again. The blowup of the Six Demands vanished. Now the President sat before a huge photograph of a bearded, long-haired young man in a black beret and baggy black uniform. The man was quite dead; most of his chest had been blown away.

"Behind me you see a photograph of one of the

casualties of tonight's attack," Hartmann said. "Like all the other attackers we found, he wears the uniform of the paramilitary wing of the A. L. F."

The photo vanished. Hartmann looked grim. "The facts are clear. But this time the A. L. F. has gone too far. I will not submit to nuclear blackmail. Nor, my fellow countrymen, is there cause for alarm. To my fellow citizens of Washington I say especially, fear not. I promise that the A.L.F. pirate planes will be tracked down and destroyed long before they reach their target.

"Meanwhile, the leaders of the A.L.F. are about to learn that they erred in attempting to intimidate this administration. For too long they have divided and weakened us, and given aid and comfort to those who would like to see this nation enslaved. They shall do so no longer.

"There can be only one word for tonight's attack. That word is treason.

"Accordingly, I will deal with the attackers like traitors."

"I've got them," McKinnis said, his voice crackling with static. "Or something."

Reynolds didn't really need the information. He had them too. He glanced briefly down at the radarmap. They were on the edge of the scope, several miles ahead, heading due east at about 90,000 feet. High, and moving fast.

Another crackle, then Bonetto, the flight leader. "Looks like them, alright. I've got nine. Let's go get 'em."

His plane nosed up and began to climb. The others followed, behind and abreast of him in a wide V formation. Nine LF-7 Vampyre fighter/interceptors. Red, white, and blue flags on burnished black metal, silvery teeth slung underneath.

A hunting pack closing for the kill.

Yet another voice came over the open channel. "Hey,

whattaya figure the odds? All over they're looking. Betcha it gets us promotions. Lucky us."

That had to be Dutton, Reynolds thought. A brash kid, hungry. Maybe *he* felt lucky. Reynolds didn't. Inside the acceleration suit he was sweating suddenly, coldly.

The odds had been all against it. The kid was right about that. The Alfie bombers were LB-4s, laser-armed monsters with speed to spare. They could've taken any route of a dozen, and still make it to Washington on time. And every damn plane and radar installation in the country was looking for them.

So what were the odds against them running into Reynolds and his flight out over northern Nebraska on a wild goose chase?

Too damn good, as it turned out.

"They see us," Bonetto said. "They're climbing. And accelerating. Move it."

Reynolds moved it. His Vampyre was the last in one arm of the V, and it held its formation. Behind the oxygen mask, his eyes roamed restlessly, and watched the instruments. Mach 1.3. Then 1.4. Then higher.

They were gaining. Climbing and gaining.

The radarmap showed the Alfie positions. And there was a blur up ahead on the infrared scope. But through the narrow eyeslit, nothing. Just cold black sky and stars. They were above the clouds.

The dumb bastards, Reynolds thought. They steal the most sophisticated hunk of metal ever built, and they don't know how to use it. They weren't even using their radar scramblers. It was almost like they were asking to be shot down.

Cracklings. "They're leveling off." Bonetto again. "Hold your missiles till my order. And remember, those big babies can give you a nasty hotfoot."

Reynolds looked at the radarmap again. The Alfies were now flat out at about 100,000 feet. Figured. The LB-4s could go higher, but ten was about the upper limit for the fighter escorts. Rapiers. Reynolds remembered his briefing.

They wanted to stick together. That made sense. The

Alfies would need their Rapiers. Ten *wasn't* the upper limit for Vampyres.

Reynolds squinted. He thought he saw something ahead, through the eyeslit. A flash of silver. Them? Or his imagination? Hard to tell. But he'd see them soon enough. The pursuit planes were gaining. Fast as they were, the big LB-4s were no match for the Vampyres. The Rapiers were; but they had to stay with the bombers.

So it was only a matter of time. They'd catch them long before Washington. And then?

Reynolds shifted uneasily. He didn't want to think about that. He'd never flown in combat before. He didn't like the idea.

His mouth was dry. He swallowed. Just this morning he and Anne had talked about how lucky he was, made plans for a vacation. And beyond. His term was almost up, and he was still safe in the States. So many friends dead in the South African War. But he'd been lucky.

And now this. And suddenly the possibility that tomorrow might not be bright. The possibility that tomorrow might not be. It scared him.

There was more, too. Even if he lived, he was still queasy. About the killing.

That shouldn't have bothered him. He knew it might happen when he enlisted. But it was different then. He thought he'd be flying against Russians, Chinese—enemies. The outbreak of the South African War and the U.S. intervention had disturbed him. But he could have fought there, for all that. The Pan-African Alliance was Communist-inspired, or so they said.

But Alfies weren't distant foreigners. Alfies were people, neighbors. His radical college roommate. The black kids he had grown up with back in New York. The teacher who lived down the block. He got along with Alfies well enough, when they weren't talking politics.

And sometimes even when they were. The Six Demands weren't all that bad. He'd heard a lot of nasty rumors about the Special Urban Units. And God knows what the U.S. was doing in South Africa and the Mid-East.

He grimaced behind the oxygen mask. Face it, Reynolds, he told himself. The skeleton in his closet. He had actually thought about voting A.L.F. in '84, although in the end he'd chickened out and pulled the lever for Bishop, the Old Democrat. No one on the base knew but Anne. They hadn't argued politics for a long time, with anyone. Most of his friends were Old Republicans, but a few had turned to the Liberty Alliance. And that scared him.

Bonetto's crackling command smashed his train of thought. "Look at that, men. The Alfies are going to fight. At 'em!"

Reynolds didn't need to look at his radarmap. He could see them now, above. Lights against the sky. Growing lights.

The Rapiers were diving on them.

Of all the commentators who followed President Hartmann over the holo networks, Continental's Ted Warren seemed the least shell-shocked. Warren was a gritty old veteran with an incisive mind and razor tongue. He had tangled with Hartmann more than once, and was regularly denounced by the Liberty Alliance for his "Alfie bias."

"The President's speech leaves many questions still unanswered," Warren said in his post-mortem newscast. "He has promised to deal with the A.L.F. as traitors, but as yet, we are unsure exactly what steps will be taken. There is also some question, in my mind at any rate, as to the A.L.F.'s motivation for this alleged attack. Bob, any thoughts on that?"

A new face on camera; the reporter who covered A.L.F. activities for Continental had been hustled out of bed and rushed to the studio. He still looked a little rumpled.

"No, Ted," he replied. "As far as I know, the A.L.F. was not planning any action of this kind. Were it not for the fact that this attack was so well-planned, I might question whether the A.L.F. national leadership was involved at all. It might have been an unauthorized action by a group of local extremists. You'll recall that the assault on the Chicago Police Headquarters during the 1985 riots was of this nature. However, I think the planning that went into this attack, and the armament that was used, precludes this being a similar case."

Warren, at the Continental anchordesk, nodded sagely. "Bob, do you think there is any possibility that the paramilitary arm of the A.L.F. might have acted unilaterally, without the knowledge of the party's political leaders?"

The reporter paused and looked thoughtful. "Well, it's possible, Ted. But not likely. The kind of assault that the President described would require too much planning. I'd think that the whole party would have to be involved in an effort on that scale."

"What reasons would the A.L.F. have for an action like this?" Warren asked.

"From what the President said, a hope that a nuclear threat would bring immediate agreement to the A.L.F.'s Six Demands would seem to be the reason."

Warren was insistent. "Yes. But why should the A.L.F. resort to such an extreme tactic? The latest Gallup poll gave them the support of nearly 29% of the electorate, behind only the 38% of President Hartmann's Liberty Alliance. This is a sharp increase from the 13% of the vote the A.L.F. got in the presidential elections of 1984. With only a year to go before the new elections, it seems strange that the A.L.F. would risk everything on such a desperate ploy."

Now the reporter was nodding. "You have a point, Ted. However, we've been surprised by the A.L.F. before. They've never been the easiest party to predict, and I think—"

Warren cut him off. "Excuse me, Bob. Back to you later. Correspondent Mike Petersen is at the A.L.F.'s national headquarters in Washington, and he has Douglass Brown with him. Mike, can you hear me?"

The picture changed. Two men standing before a desk, one half slouched against it. Behind them, on the wall, the A.L.F. symbol; a clenched black fist superimposed over the peace sign. The reporter held a microphone. The man he was with was tall, black, youthful. And angry.

"Yes, Ted, we've got you," the reporter said. He turned to the black man. "Doug, you were the A.L.F. presidential candidate in 1984. How do you react to President Hartmann's charges?"

Brown laughed lightly. "Nothing that man does surprises me any more. The charges are vicious lies. The American Liberation Front had nothing to do with this so-called attack. In fact, I doubt that this attack ever took place. Hartmann is a dangerous demagogue, and he's tried this sort of smear before."

"Then the A.L.F. claims that no attack took place?" Petersen asked.

Brown frowned. "Well, that's just a quick guess on my part, not an official A.L.F. position," he said quickly. "This has all been very sudden, and I don't really have the facts. But I'd say that was a possibility. As you know, Mike, the Liberty Alliance has made wild charges against us before."

"In his statement tonight, President Hartmann said he would deal with the A.L.F. as traitors. Would you care to comment on that?"

"Yeah," said Brown. "It's more cheap rhetoric. I say that Hartmann's the traitor. He's the one that has betrayed everything this country is supposed to stand for. *His* creation of the Special Suuies to keep the ghettoes in line, *his* intervention in the South African War, *his* censorship legislation; there's your treason for you."

The reporter smiled. "Thank you, Doug. And now back to Ted Warren."

Warren reappeared. "For those of you who have flicked on late, a brief recap. Earlier this evening, an American air base in California was attacked, and two bombers and seven fighter planes were seized. The bombers were equipped with nuclear weaponry, and the attackers have threatened to destroy Washington, D.C., unless certain demands are met within three hours. Only an hour-and-a-half now remain. Continental News will stay on the air until the conclusion of the crisis..."

Somewhere over western Illinois, Reynolds climbed towards ten, and sweated, and tried to tell himself that the advantages were all his.

The Rapiers were good planes. Nothing with wings was any faster, or more maneuverable. But the Vampyres had all the other plusses. Their missiles were more sophisticated, their defensive scramblers better. And they had their Vampyre fangs: twin gas-dynamic lasers mounted on either wing that could slice through steel like it was jello. The Rapiers had nothing to match that. The Vampyres were the first operational Laser/Fighters.

Besides, there were nine Vampyres and only seven Rapiers. And the Alfies weren't as familiar with their planes. They couldn't be.

So the odds were all with Reynolds. But he still sweated.

The arms of the V formation slowly straightened, as Reynolds and the other wingmen accelerated to come even with Bonetto's lead jet. In the radarmap, the Rapiers were already on top of them. And even through the eyeslit he could see them now, diving out of the black, their silver-white sides bright against the sky. The computer tracking system was locked in, the warheads armed. But still no signal from Bonetto.

And then, "Now." Sharp and clear.

Reynolds hit the firing stud, and missiles one and eight shot from beneath the wings, and etched a trail of flame up into the night. Parallel to his, others. Dutton, on his wing, had fired four. Eager for the kill.

Red/orange against black through the eyeslit. Black on red in the infrared scope. But all the same, really. The climbing streaks of flame that were the Vampyre missiles intersecting with a descending set. Crisscrossing briefly.

Then explosion. The Alfies had rigged one of theirs for timed detonation. A small orange fireball bloomed briefly. When it vanished, both sets of missiles were gone, save for one battered survivor from the Vampyre barrage that wobbled upward without hitting anything.

Reynolds glanced down. The radarmap was having an epileptic fit. The Alfies were using their scramblers.

"Split," said Bonetto, voice crackling. "Scatter and hit them."

The Vampyres broke formation. Reynolds and Dutton pulled up and to the left, McKinnis dove. Bonetto and most of his wing swung away to the right. And Trainor climbed straight on, at the diving Rapiers.

Reynolds watched him from the corner of his eye. Two more missiles jumped from Trainor's wings, then two more, then the final two. And briefly, the laser seared a path up from his wingtips. A futile gesture; he was still out of range.

The Rapiers were sleek silver birds of prey, spitting missiles. And suddenly, another fireball, and one of them stopped spitting.

But no time for cheering. Even as the Rapier went up, Trainor's Vampyre tried to swerve from the hail of Alfie missiles. His radar scrambler and heat decoys had confused them. But not enough. Reynolds was facing away from the explosion, but he felt the impact of the shock, and he could see the nightblack plane twisting and shattering in his mind.

Reynolds felt a vague pang, and tried to remember what Trainor had looked like. But there was no time. He twisted the Vampyre around in a sharp loop. Dutton flew parallel. They dove back towards the fight.

Far below a new cloud of flame blossomed. McKinnis, Reynolds thought, fleetingly, bitterly. He dove. The Alfies got on his tail. The goddamn Alfies.

But there was no way to be sure, no leisure to consider the question. Even a brief glance out the eyeslit was a luxury; a dangerous luxury. The infrared scope, the radarmap, the computer tracking systems all screamed for his attention.

Below him, two Alfies were swinging around. The computer locked on. His fingers moved as if by instinct. Missiles two and seven leapt from their launchers, towards the Rapiers.

A scream sounded briefly from his radio, mingled with the static and the sudden shrill cry of the proximity alarms. Something had locked on him. He activated the lasers. The computer found the incoming missile, tracked it, burned it from the sky when it got within range. Reynolds had never even seen it. He wondered how close it had come.

A flood of bright orange light washed through the eye slit as a Rapier went up in flame in front of him. His missile? Dutton's? He never knew. It was all he could do to pull the Vampyre up sharply, and avoid the expanding ball of fire.

There were a few seconds of peace. He was above the fight, and he took time for a quick glance at the infrared. A tangle of confused black dots on a red field. But two were higher than the rest. Dutton; with an Alfie on his tail.

Reynolds swung his Vampyre down again, came in above and behind the Rapier just as it was discharging its missiles. He was close. No need to waste the four missiles he had left. His hand went to the lasers, fired.

Converging beams of light lanced from the black wingtips, to bite into the Rapier's silver fuselage on either side of the cockpit. The Alfie pilot dove for escape. But the Vampyre minicomputer held the lasers steady.

The Rapier exploded.

Almost simultaneously there was another explosion; the Alfie missiles, touched off by Dutton's lasers. Reynolds' radio came alive with Dutton's laughter, and breathless thanks.

But Reynolds was paying more attention to the infrared and the radarmap. The radar was clear again.

Only three blips showed below him.

It was over.

Bonetto's voice split the cabin again. "Got him," he was yelling. "Got them all. Who's left up there?"

Dutton replied quickly. Then Reynolds. The fourth surviving Vampyre was Ranczyk, Bonetto's wingman. The others were gone.

There was a new pang, sharper than during the battle. It had been McKinnis after all, Reynolds thought. He'd known McKinnis. Tall, with red hair, a lousy poker player who surrendered his money gracefully when he lost. He always did. His wife made good chili. They'd voted Old Democrat, like Reynolds. Damn, damn, damn.

"We're only halfway there," Bonetto was saying. "The LB-4s are still ahead. Picked up some distance. So let's go."

Four Vampyres weren't nearly as impressive in formation as nine. But they climbed. And gave chase.

Ted Warren looked tired. He had taken off his jacket and loosened the formal black scarf knotted around his neck, and his hair was mussed. But still he went on.

"Reports have been coming in from all over the nation on the sighting of the pirate planes," he said. "Most of them are clearly misidentifications, but no word has yet come from the administration on the hunt for the stolen jets, so the rumors continue to flow unabated. Meanwhile, barely an hour remains before the threatened nuclear demolition of Washington."

Behind him a screen woke to sudden churning life. Pennsylvania Avenue, with the Capitol outlined in the distance, was choked with cars and people. "Washington itself is in a state of panic," Warren commented. "The populace of the city has taken to the streets en masse in an effort to escape, but the resulting traffic jams have effectively strangled all major arteries. Many have abandoned their cars and are trying to leave the city on foot. Helicopters of the Special Urban Units have been attempting to qwell the disturbances, ordering the citizens to return to their homes. And President Hartmann himself has announced that he intends to set an example for the people of the city, and remain in the White House for the duration of the crisis."

The Washington scenes faded. Warren looked off-camera briefly. "I've just been told that Chicago correspondent Ward Emery is standing by with Mitchell

Grinstein, the chairman of the A.L.F.'s Community Defense Militia. So now to Chicago."

Grinstein was standing outdoors, on the steps of a gray, fortress-like building. He was tall and broad, with long black hair worn in a pony tail and a drooping Fu Manchu mustache. His clothes were a baggy black uniform, a black beret, and an A.L.F. medallion on a length of rawhide. Two other men, similarly garbed, lounged behind him on the steps. Both carried rifles.

"I'm here with Mitchell Grinstein, whose organization has been accused of participating in this evening's attack on a California air base, and the hijacking of two nuclear bombers," Emery said. "Mitch, your reactions?"

Grinstein flashed a vaguely sinister smile. "Well, I only know what I see on the holo. I didn't order any attack. But I applaud whoever did. If this speeds up the implementation of the Six Demands, I'm all for it."

"Douglass Brown has called the charges of A.L.F. participation in this attack 'vicious lies,'" Emery continued. "He questions whether any attack ever took place. How does this square with what you just said?"

Grinstein shrugged. "Maybe Brown knows more than I do. We didn't order this attack, like I said. But it could be that some of our men finally got fed up with Hartmann's fourth-rate fascism, and decided to take things into their own hands. If so, we're behind them."

"Then you think there *was* an attack?"

"I guess so. Hartmann had pictures. Even he wouldn't have the gall to fake *that*."

"And you support the attack?"

"Yeah. The Community Defenders have been saying for a long time that black people and poor people aren't going to get justice anywhere but in the streets. This is a vindication of what we've been calling for all along."

"And what about the position of the A.L.F.'s political arm?"

Another shrug. "Doug Brown and I agree on where we're going. We don't see eye to eye on how to get there."

"But isn't the Community Defense Militia subordinate to the A.L.F. political apparatus, and thus to Brown?"

"On paper. It's different in the streets. Are the Liberty Troopers subordinate to President Hartmann when they go out on freak-hunts and black busting expeditions? They don't act like it. The Community Defenders are committed to the protection of the community. From thugs, Liberty Troopers, and Hartmann's Special Suuies. And anyone else who comes along. We're also committed to getting the Six Demands. And maybe we'd go a bit further to realize those demands than Doug and his men."

"One last question," said Emery. "President Hartmann, in his speech tonight, said that he intended to treat the A.L.F. like traitors."

"Let him try," Grinstein said, smiling. "Just let him try."

The Alfie bombers had edged onto the radarmap again. They were still at 100,000 feet, doing about Mach 1.7. The Vampyre pack would be on them in minutes.

Reynolds watched for LB-4s, almost numbly, through his eyeslit. He was cold and drenched with his own sweat. And very scared.

The lull between battles was worse than the battles themselves, he had decided. It gave you too much time to think. And thinking was bad.

He was sad and a little sick about McKinnis. But grateful. Grateful that it hadn't been him. Then he realized that it still might be. The night wasn't over. The LB-4s were no pushovers.

And all so needless. The Alfies were vicious fools. There were other ways, better ways. They didn't have to do this. Whatever sympathy he had ever felt for the A.L.F. had gone down in flames with McKinnis and Trainor and the others.

They deserved whatever they had coming to them. And Hartmann, he was sure, had something in mind.

So many innocent people dead. And for nothing. For a grandstand, desperado stunt without a prayer of success.

That was the worst part. The plan was so ill-conceived, so hopeless. The A.L.F. couldn't possibly win. They could shoot him down, sure. Like McKinnis. But there were other planes. They'd be found and taken out by someone. And if they got as far as Washington, there was still the city's ring of defensive missiles to deal with. Hartmann had had trouble forcing that through Congress. But it would come in handy now.

And even if the A.L.F. got there, so what? Did they really think Hartmann would give in? No way. Not him. He'd call their bluff, and either way they lost. If they backed down, they were finished. And if they dropped the bomb, they'd get Hartmann—but at the expense of millions of their own supporters. Washington was nearly all black. Hell, it gave the A.L.F. a big plurality in '84. What was the figure? Something like 65%, he thought. Around there, anyway.

It didn't make sense. It couldn't be. But it was.

There was a knot in his stomach. Churning and twisting. Through the eyeslit, he saw flickers of motion against the star field. The Alfies. The goddamn Alfies. His mind turned briefly to Anne. And suddenly he hated the planes ahead of him, and the men who flew them.

"Hold your missiles till my order," Bonetto said. "And watch it."

The Vampyres accelerated. But the Alfies acted before the attack.

"Hey, look!" That was Dutton.

"They're splitting." A bass growl distorted by static; Ranczyk.

Reynolds looked at his radarmap. One of the LB-4s was diving sharply, picking up speed, heading for the sea of clouds that rolled below in the starlight. The other was going into a shallow climb.

"Stay together!" Bonetto again. "They want us to break up. But we're faster. We'll take out one and catch the other."

They climbed. Together at first, side by side. But then one of the sleek planes began to edge ahead.

"Dutton!" Bonetto's voice was a warning.

"I want him." Dutton's Vampyre screamed upward, into range of the bandit ahead. From his wings, twin missiles roared, closed.

And suddenly were not. The bomber's lasers burned them clean from the sky.

Bonetto tried to shout another order. But it was too late. Dutton was paying no attention. He was already shrieking to his kill.

This time Reynolds saw it all.

Dutton was way out ahead of the others, still accelerating, trying to close within laser range. He was out of missiles.

But the Alfie laser had a longer range. It locked on him first.

The Vampyre seemed to writhe. Dutton went into a sharp dive, pulled up equally sharply, threw his plane from side to side. Trying to shake free of the laser. Before it killed. But the tracking computers in the LB-4s were faster than he could ever hope to be. The laser held steady.

And then Dutton stopped fighting. Briefly, his Vampyre closed again, climbing right up into the spear of light, its own lasers flashing out and converging. Uselessly; he was still too far away. And only for an instant.

Before the scream.

Dutton's Vampyre never even exploded. It just seemed to go limp. Its laser died suddenly. And then it was in a spin. Flames licking at the black fuselage, burning a hole in the black velvet of night.

Reynolds didn't watch the fall. Bonetto's voice had snapped him from his nightmare trance. "Fire!"

He let go on three and six, and they shrieked away from him towards the Alfie. Bonetto and Ranczyk had also fired. Six missiles rose together. Two more slightly behind them. Ranczyk had let loose with a second volley.

"At him!" Bonetto shouted. "Lasers!"

Then his plane was moving away quickly, Ranczyk

with him. Black shadows against a black sky, following their missiles and obscuring the stars. Reynolds hung back briefly, still scared, still hearing Dutton's scream and seeing the fireball that was McKinnis. Then, shamed, he followed.

The bomber had unleashed its own missiles, and its lasers were locked onto the oncoming threats. There was an explosion; several missiles wiped from the air. Others burned down.

But there were two Vampyres moving in behind the missiles. And then a third behind them. Bonetto and Ranczyk had their lasers locked on the Alfie, burning at him, growing hotter and more vicious as they climbed. Briefly, the bomber's big laser flicked down in reply. One of the Vampyres went up in a cloud of flame, a cloud that still screamed upwards at the Alfie.

Almost simultaneously, another roar. A fireball under the wing of the bomber, rocked it. Its laser winked off. Power trouble? Then on again, burning at the hail of missiles. Reynolds flicked on his laser, and watched it lance out towards the chaos above. The other Vampyre —Reynolds wasn't sure which—was firing its remaining missiles.

They were almost on top of each other. In the radar-map and the infrared they were. Only in the eyeslit was there still space between the two.

And then they were together. Joining. One big ball, orange and red and yellow, swallowing both Vampyre and prey, growing, growing, growing.

Reynolds sat almost frozen, climbing towards the swelling inferno, his laser firing ineffectively into the flames. Then he came out of it. And swerved. And dove. His laser fired once more, to wipe out a chunk of flaming debris that came spinning towards him.

He was alone. The fire fell and faded, and there was only one Vampyre, and the stars, and the blanket of cloud far below him. He had survived.

But how? He had hung back. When he should have attacked. He didn't deserve survival. The others had earned it, with their courage. But he had hung back. He felt sick.

But he could still redeem himself. Yes. Down below, there was still one Alfie in the air. Headed towards Washington with its bombs. And only he was left to stop it.

Reynolds nosed the Vampyre into a dive, and began his grim descent.

After a brief station identification, Warren was back. With two guests and a new wrinkle. The wrinkle was the image of a large clock that silently counted down the time remaining while the newsmen talked. The guests were a retired Air Force general and a well-known political columnist.

Warren introduced them, then turned to the general. "Tonight's attack, understandably, has frightened a lot of people," he began. "Especially those in Washington. How likely is it that the threatened bombing will take place?"

The general snorted. "Impossible, Ted. I know what kind of air defense systems we've got in this country. They were designed to handle a full-fledged attack, from another nuclear power. They can certainly handle a cheap-shot move like this."

"Then you'd say that Washington is in no danger?"

"Correct. Absolutely none. This plan was militarily hopeless from its conception. I'm shocked that even the A.L.F. would resort to such a foredoomed venture."

Warren nodded, and swiveled to face the columnist. "How about from a political point of view? You've been a regular observer of President Hartmann and the Washington scene for many years, Sid. In your opinion, did this maneuver have any chances of practical political success?"

"It's still very early," the columnist cautioned. "But from where I sit, I'd say the A.L.F. has committed a major blunder. This attack is a political disaster—or at least it looks like one, in these early hours. Because of Washington's large black population, I'd guess that this threat to the city will seriously undermine the the A.L.F.'s support among the black community. If so, it would be a catastrophe for the party. In 1984,

Douglass Brown drew more black votes than the other three candidates combined. Without these votes, the A.L.F. presidential campaign would have been a farce."

"How will this affect other A.L.F. supporters?" Warren asked.

"That's a key question. I'd say it would tend to drive them away from the party. Since its inception, the A.L.F. has always had a large pacifist element, which frequently clashed with the more militant Alfies who made up the Community Defense Militia. I think that tonight's events might be the final blow for these people."

"Who do you think would benefit from these desertions?"

The columnist shrugged. "Hard to say. There's the possibility of a new splinter party being formed. And President Hartmann, I'm sure, will enjoy a large swing of support his way. The most likely possibility would be a revival of the Old Democratic Party, if it can regain the black voters and white radicals it has lost to the A.L.F. in recent years."

"Thank you," said Warren. He turned back to the camera, then glanced down briefly at the desk in front of him, checking the latest bulletins. "We'll have more analysis later," he said. "Right now, Continental's man in California is at Collins Air Base, where tonight's attack took place."

Warren faded. The new reporter was tall and thin and young. He was standing before the main gate of the air base. Behind him was a bustling tangle of activity, several jeeps, and large numbers of police and soldiers. The spotlights were on again, and the destruction was clearly evident in the battered gatehouse and the twisted, shattered wire of the fence itself.

"Deke Hamilton here," the man began. "Ted, Continental came out here to check whether any attack did take place, since the A.L.F. has charged that the President was lying. Well, from what I've seen out here, it's the A.L.F. that's been lying. There *was* an attack, and it was a vicious one. You can see some of the damage behind you. This is where the attackers struck hardest."

Warren's voice cut in. "Have you seen any bodies?"

The reporter nodded. "Yes. Many of them. Some have been horribly mangled by the fighting. More than one hundred men from the base, I'd estimate. And about fifty Alfies."

"Have any of the attackers been identified?" Warren asked.

"Well, they're clearly Alfies," the reporter said. "Beards, long hair, A.L.F. uniforms. And many had literature in their pockets. Pamphlets advocating the Six Demands, that sort of thing. However, as of yet, no specific identifications have been announced. Except for the air men, of course. The base has released its own casualty lists. But not for the Alfies. As I said, many bodies are badly damaged, so identification may be difficult. I think some sort of mass burial is being planned."

"Deke," said Warren, "has there been any racial breakdown on the casualties?"

"Uh—none has been released. The bodies I saw were all white. But then, the black population in this area is relatively small."

Warren started to ask another question. He never finished his sentence. Without warning, the picture from California suddenly vanished, and was replaced by chaos.

"This is Mike Petersen in Washington," the reporter said. He was awash in a sea of struggling humanity, being pushed this way and that. All around him fights were in progress, as a squad of Special Urban Police, in blue and silver, waded through a crowd of resisting Alfies. The A.L.F. symbol was on the wall behind Petersen.

"I'm at A.L.F. national headquarters," he said, trying valiantly to stay before the cameras. "I—" he was shoved to one side, fought back. "We've got quite a scene here. Just a few minutes ago, a detachment of Special Urban Police broke into the building, and arrested several of the A.L.F.'s national leaders, including Douglass Brown. Some of the other people here tried to stop them, and the police are now trying to make more arrests. There's been—damn!" Someone had spun into him. The cops were using clubs.

Petersen was trying to untangle himself from the battle. He looked up briefly and started to say something. Then something hit the camera, and suddenly he was gone.

Reynolds was very much conscious of being alone. He was at 60,000 feet and dropping rapidly, ripping through layer on layer of wispy cloud. In an empty sky. The Alfie was somewhere below him, but he couldn't see it yet.

He knew it was there, though. His radarmap was acting up. That meant a scrambler nearby.

His eyes roamed, his thoughts wandered. It was one on one now. There might be help. Bonetto had radioed down when they first sighted the bandits. Maybe someone had tracked them. Maybe another flight was on its way to intercept the bomber.

And then again, maybe not.

Their course had been erratic. They were over Kentucky now. And they'd been up high, with scramblers going to confuse radar. Maybe their position wasn't known.

He could radio down. Yes. He should do that. But no, come to think of it. That would alert the Alfie. Maybe they didn't know he was behind them. Maybe he could take them by surprise.

He hoped so. Otherwise he was worried. There were only two missiles left. And Reynolds wasn't all that sure that a Vampyre could take an LB-4 one on one.

Loose facts rolled back and forth in his mind. The lasers. The bomber had a big power source. Its laser had a range nearly twice that of the smaller model on the Vampyre. With a bigger computer to keep it on target.

What did he have? Speed. Yes. And maneuverability. And maybe he was a better pilot, too.

Or was he? Reynolds frowned. Come to think of it, the Alfies had pretty much held their own up to now. Strange. You wouldn't think they'd be so good. Especially when they made elementary mistakes like forgetting to throw in their scramblers.

But they had been. They flew almost like veterans. Maybe they were veterans. Hartmann had discharged a lot of A.L.F. sympathizers from the armed forces right after his election. Maybe some of them had gone all the way and actually joined the Alfies. And were coming back for revenge.

But that was three years ago. And the LB-4s were new. It shouldn't have been all that easy for the Alfies to master them.

Reynolds shook his head and shoved the whole train of thought to one side. It wasn't worth pursuing. However it had happened, the fact was the Alfies were damn good pilots. And any advantage he had there was negligible.

He looked at his instruments. Still diving at 40,000 feet. The LB-4 still below him somewhere, but closer. The radarmap was a useless dancing fuzz now. But there was an image on the infrared scope.

Through the eyeslit, he could see lightning flashes far below. A thunderstorm. And the bomber was diving through it. And slowing, according to his instruments. Probably going to treetop level.

He'd catch it soon.

And what then?

There were two missiles left. He could close and fire them. But the Alfie had its own missiles, and its laser net. What if his missiles didn't get through?

Then he'd have to go in with his own lasers.

And die. Like Dutton.

He tried to swallow, but the saliva caught in his throat. The damn Alfie had such a big power source. They'd be slicing him into ribbons long before he got close enough for his smaller weapon to be effective.

Oh, sure, he might take them, too. It took even a

big gas dynamic laser a few seconds to burn through steel. And in those few seconds he'd be close enough to return the attentions.

But that didn't help. He'd die, with them.

And he didn't want to die.

He thought of Anne again. Then of McKinnis.

The Alfies would never reach Washington, he thought. Another flight of hunters would sight the LB-4, and catch it. Or the city's ABMS would knock it out. But they'd never get through.

There was no reason for him to die to stop the bomber. No reason at all. He should pull up, radio ahead, land and sound the alarm.

Thick, dark clouds rolled around the plane, swallowed it. Lightning hammered at the nightblack wings, and shook the silver missiles in their slots.

And Reynolds sweated. And the Vampyre continued to dive.

"The question of what President Hartmann meant when he promised to treat the A.L.F. like traitors has been resolved," Ted Warren said, looking straight out of millions of holocubes, his face drawn and unreadable. "Within the last few minutes, we've had dozens of reports. All over the nation, the Special Urban Units are raiding A.L.F. headquarters and the homes of party leaders. In a few cities, including Detroit, Boston, and Washington itself, mass arrests of A.L.F. members are reported to be in progress. But for the most part, the S.U.U. seems to be concentrating on those in positions of authority with the Community Defense Militia or the party itself.

"Meanwhile, the Pentagon reports that the bandit planes that the A.L.F. is accused of taking have been tracked over Kentucky, heading towards Washington. According to informed Air Force sources, only one of the hijacked bombers is still in the air, and it is being pursued by a interceptor. Other flights are now being rushed to the scene."

Warren looked outcube briefly, scowled at someone unseen, and turned back. "We have just been informed that the White House is standing by with a statement. I give you now the President of the United States."

The image changed. Again the Oval Office. This time Hartmann was standing, and he was not alone. Vice-President Joseph Delaney, balding and middle-aged, stood next to him, before a row of American flags.

"My fellow patriots," Hartmann began, "I come before you again to announce that the government is taking steps against the traitors who have threatened the very capital of this great nation. After consulting with Vice-President Delaney and my Cabinet, I have ordered the arrest of the leaders of the so-called American Liberation Front."

Hartmann's dark eyes were burning, and his voice had a marvelous, fatherly firmness. Delaney, beside him, looked pale and frightened and uncertain.

"To those of you who have supported these men in the past, let me say now that they will receive every safeguard of a fair trial, in the American tradition," Hartmann continued. "As for yourselves, your support of the so-called A.L.F. was well-intentioned, no matter how misguided. No harm will come to you. However, your leaders have tonight betrayed your trust, and your nation. They have forfeited your support. To aid them now would be to join in their treason.

"I say this especially to our black citizens, who have been so cruelly misled by A.L.F. sloganeering. Now is the time to demonstrate your patriotism, to make up for past mistakes. And to those who would persist in their error, I issue this warning; those who aid the traitors in resisting lawful authority will be treated as traitors themselves."

Hartmann paused briefly, then continued. "Some will question this move. With a legitimate concern for the American system of checks and balances, they will argue that I had no authority for deploying the Special Urban Units as I have done. They are right. But special situations call for special remedies, and in this night of crisis, there was no time to secure Congressional approval. However, I did not act unilaterally." He looked towards Delaney.

The Vice-President cleared his throat. "President Hartmann consulted me on this matter earlier tonight," he began, in a halting voice. "I expressed some reluctance, at first, to approve his proposed course of action. But, after the President had presented me with all the facts, I could see that there was no realistic alternative. Speaking for myself, and for those Cabinet members who like me represent the Republican Party, I concur with the President's actions."

Hartmann began to speak again, but the voice suddenly faded on the holocast, and a short second later, the image also vanished. Ted Warren returned to the air.

"We will bring you the rest of the President's statement later," the anchorman said, "after several special bulletins. We have just been informed that all 32 A.L.F. members of the House of Representatives have been placed under arrest, as well as two of the three A.L.F. Senators. S.U.U. national headquarters reports that Senator Jackson Edwards is still at large, and is currently being sought after."

Warren shuffled some papers. "We also have reports of scattered street-fighting in several cities between the S.U.U. and the Community Defenders. The fighting appears to be most intense in Chicago, where Special Urban forces have surrounded the national center of the A.L.F.'s paramilitary wing. We take you now to Ward Emery, on the scene."

The image shifted. Emery was standing on the steps of the new Chicago Police Headquarters on South State Street. Every light in the building behind him burned brightly, and a steady stream of riot-equipped police was hurrying up and down the stairs.

"Not quite on the scene, Ted," he began. "Our crew was forcibly excluded from the area where the fighting is now in progress. We're here at Chicago Police Headquarters now, which you will recall was the focus of the battle during the 1985 riots. The local police and the Special Urban Units are doing their planning and coordinating from here."

Warren cut in with a voice-over. "What precisely has taken place?"

"Well," said Emery, "it started when a detachment of Special Urban Police arrived at Community Defender Central, as it's called, to arrest Mitchell Grinstein and several other organization leaders. I'm not sure who opened fire. But someone did, and there were several casualties. The Community Defenders have their headquarters heavily guarded, and they drove back the S.U.U. in the early skirmish that I witnessed. But things have changed since then. Although the local police have cordoned off a large portion of Chicago's South Side and excluded me and other reporters, I now understand that Grinstein and his Militiamen are holed up inside their building, which is under S.U.U. siege."

He looked around briefly. "As you can see, there's a lot of activity around here," he continued. "The local police are on overtime, and the Special Urban Units have mobilized their entire Chicago battalion. They're using their regular armored cars, plus some heavier weapons. And I've also heard reports that something new has been deployed by the S.U.U.—a light tank with street tires instead of treads, designed for city use."

"Are all the A.L.F. forces concentrated around Grinstein's headquarters?" Warren asked.

Emery shook his head. "No, not at all. The ghettos on the South and West sides are alive with activity. The local police have suffered several casualties, and there's been one case of a squad car being Molotov-cocktailed. Also, there are rumors of an impending A.L.F. counterattack on Police Headquarters. The building is symbolic to both sides, of course, since the renegade local Militiamen seized and razed the earlier building on this site during the 1985 fighting."

"I see," said Warren. "The A.L.F. is known to have active chapters on several college campuses in your area. Have you gotten any reports from them?"

"Some," Emery replied. "The police have been ignoring the campus chapters up to now, but we understand that a strong force of Liberty Troopers moved in on the University of Illinois' Chicago campus in an attempt to make citizens' arrests. Some fighting was reported, but resistance was only light. The students were mostly without arms while the Liberty Troopers, of course, are a paramilitary force."

"Thank you, Ward," Warren said, as the image suddenly shifted. "We'll be back to you later for an update. Now, we will continue with the rest of President Hartmann's most recent statement.

"For those who just flicked on, the President has just ordered the arrest of the A.L.F. leaders. This move was made with the support of the Vice-President, and thus presumably with the support of the Old Republicans, the President's partners in his coalition government. It's an important shift on the part of the Old Republicans. Last year, you will recall, Hartmann's efforts to pass his Subversive Registration Bill were thwarted when Vice-President Delaney and his followers refused to back the measure.

"Since the Liberty Alliance and the Old Republicans, between them, command a majority in both houses of Congress, Delaney's support of Hartmann guarantees Congressional approval of the President's actions tonight.

"And now, the rest of the Presidential message . . ."

There were hills below, and dark forests in a shroud of night. And the only light was the sudden jagged brilliance of the lightning. But there were two thunders.

One was the thunder of the storm that churned above the forest. The other was the thunder of the jet, screaming between the stormclouds and the trees and laying down a trail of sonic booms across the landscape.

That was the Alfie. Reynolds watched it in his infrared scope, watched it play at Mach 1, slip back and forth over the barrier. And while he watched he gained on it.

He had stopped sweating, stopped thinking, stopped fearing. Now he only acted. Now he was part of the Vampyre.

He descended through the stormclouds, blind but for his instruments, lashed by the lightning. Everything that was human in him told him to pull up and let something else take the Alfie. But something else, some drive, some compulsion, told him that he must not hang back again.

So he descended.

The Alfie knew he was there. That was inevitable. It was simply holding its fire. As he was holding his missiles. He would save them until the last second, until the Alfie lasers were locked on him.

The Vampyre moved at half again the bomber's speed. Ripped through the last bank of clouds. Framed by the lightning. Fired its lasers.

The beams cut the night, touched the bomber, converged. Too far away. Hardly hot. But warming, warming. Every microsecond brought the sleek black interceptor closer, and the wand of light grew deadlier.

And then the other beam jumped upward from the bomber's tail. Swords of light crossed in the night. And the shrieking Vampyre impaled itself upon the glowing stake.

Reynolds was watching his infrared when it died. The mere touch of the enemy laser had been too much for the system's delicate optics. But he didn't need it, now. He could see the bomber, ahead and below, outlined in the flashes.

There were alarms ringing, clamoring, slamming at his ears. He ignored them. It was too late now. Too late to pull away and up. Too late to shake the lasers.

Now there was only time to find a victim.

Reynolds' eyes were fixed on the bomber, and it grew larger by the microsecond. His hand was on the missile stud, waiting, waiting. The warheads were armed. The computers were locked, tracking.

The Alfie loomed large and larger in the eyeslit. And he saw its laser slicing through the dark. And around him, he could feel the Vampyre shake and shudder.

And he fired.

Four and five were flaming arrows in the night, climbing down at the Alfie. It seemed, almost, like they were sliding down the laser path that the Vampyre had burned.

Reynolds, briefly, saw his plane as the others must have seen it. Black and ominous, howling from the stormclouds down at them, lasers afire, draped in lightning, spitting missiles. Exhilaration! Glorydeath! He held the vision tightly.

The Alfie laser was off him, suddenly. Too late. The alarms still rang. His control was gone.

The Vampyre was burning, crippled. But from the flames the laser still licked out.

The bomber burned one missile from the sky. But the other was climbing up a jet. And the Vampyre's fangs now had a bite to them.

And then the night itself took flame.

Reynolds saw the fireball spread over the forest, and something like relief washed over him, and he shuddered. And then the sweat came back, in a rushing flood.

He watched the woods come up at him, and he thought briefly of ejecting. But he was too low and too fast and it was hopeless. He tried to capture his vision again. And he wondered if he'd get a medal.

But the vision was elusive, and the medal didn't seem to matter now.

Suddenly all he could think about was Anne. And his cheeks were wet. And it wasn't sweat.

He screamed.

And the Vampyre hit the trees at Mach 1.4.

There were circles under Warren's eyes, and an ache in his voice. But he continued to read.

" . . . in Newark, New Jersey, local police are engaged in pitched street battles with the Special Urban Units. City officials in Newark, elected by the A.L.F., mobilized the police when the S.U.U. attempted to arrest them . . .

" . . . latest announcement from S.U.U. headquarters

says that Douglass Brown and six other leading A.L.F. figures died while attempting to escape from confinement. The attempted escape came during a surprise attack by Community Defense Militiamen on the jail where Brown and the others were imprisoned, the release says ...

" ... both the Community Defense Militia and the Liberty Troopers have been mobilized from coast-to-coast by their leaders, and have taken to the streets. The Liberty Troopers are assisting the Special Urban Units in their campaign against the Community Defenders ...

" ... President Hartmann has called out the National Guard ...

" ... riots and looting reported in New York, Washington, and Detroit, and numerous smaller cities ...

"... in Chicago is a smoldering ruin. Mitchell Grinstein is reported dead, as well as other top A.L.F. leaders. A firebombing has destroyed a wing of the new Police Headquarters ... Loop reported in flames ... bands of armed men moving from the ghetto sections into the Near North ...

"... Community Defenders in California charge that they had nothing to do with original attack ... have demanded that the bodies be produced and identified ... mass burial, already ordered ...

" ... bombing of Governor's mansion in Sacramento ...

" ... Liberty Alliance has called all citizens to take up arms, and wipe out the A.L.F. ... that an attempted revolution is in progress ... this was the plan all along, Alliance charges ... California attack a signal ...

" ... A.L.F. charges that California attack was Hartmann ploy ... cites Reichstag fire ...

" .... Governor Horne of Michigan has been assassinated ...

" ... national curfew imposed by S.U.U. ... has called on all citizens to return to their homes ... still out in one hour will be shot on sight ...

" ... A.L.F. reports that Senator Jackson Edwards

of New Jersey was dragged from his police sanctuary in Newark and shot by Liberty Troopers...

"... martial law declared...

"... reports that last bandit plane has been shot down...

"... Army has been mobilized...

"... Hartmann has declared death penalty for any who aid so-called revolutionaries...

"... alleges...

"... charges...

"... reports..."

In Kentucky, a forest was burning. But no one came to put it out.

There were bigger fires elsewhere.

—Chicago,
June 1972

THE RUNNERS

There were times, between cases, when Colmer grew strangely restless. He could never quite put his finger on the reason. Most of the time he chalked it up to boredom, but somewhere in the back of his head he knew it was more than that.

Colmer was a man of resources, though. He had his remedies when the moods came upon him. The best thing, he'd found, was just to get back into action. There was always a demand for his services. He was a Master Probe, one of less than a hundred in all of known space. Sometimes, if they couldn't meet his standard fee, he'd take a smaller one. If the case was interesting enough, and he was bored.

Colmer had other pursuits for the times when he couldn't find a case. He would often occupy himself with games and friends and sports and sex. And food, frequently with food. He was a small, quiet chipmunk of a man, and he loved to eat, especially when the moods came upon him and there was nothing else to do. It was all part of the full life, Colmer felt.

He was sitting in the Old Lady, waiting for his dinner in a lull between cases, when Bryl found him.

The Old Lady had been a schooner once. Now it floated off Sullivan's Wharf, in the heart of the fisherman's district of Old Poseidon. Nearby, the sleek silver boats came and went daily, harvesting the wealth of Poseidon's Big Sea. They dragged great nets full of bluespawn and tiny silver winkles. Others packed their holds with salt-rich hunter crabs. And the smaller ships, oddly, brought back the giant spikefins and the vampire eels, whose meat was black and buttery.

The whole district smelled of fish and salt and sea, and Colmer loved it. Whenever time lay heavy on his hands, he'd take a day off to walk the twisting woodplank streets. He'd watch the fisherships set out at dawn, then drink till noon in the wharfside bars, then hunt for curios in the mustiest shops he could find. By late afternoon, he'd usually have worked up an appetite. Then he'd head for the Old Lady. There were dozens of seafood places in the district, but the Old Lady was the best.

He'd just finished his appetizer that day when Bryl pulled up a chair and sat down at his table. "I need your help," he said, quickly and simply.

Colmer wanted dinner, not company. He frowned a little. "I have an office," he said.

"You keep records of every client?"

"Of course," said Colmer.

"I don't want any records kept. That's why I hung out around this place. They told me Adrian Colmer always eats at the Old Lady, that I'd find you here if I waited long enough. I didn't know if I could wait long enough. But I got lucky. Please help me."

Colmer was suddenly interested, his curiosity aroused. He studied the stranger across from him. He saw a tall, thin man, a dark face framed by shoulder-length black hair and dominated by a hawk nose, nondescript dress that a thousand men might have worn. But the face was oddly ageless, the man fidgeted a lot, and his eyes moved constantly. That was all Colmer could tell from a glance.

He could have probed, of course. Some Talents would have done that, professional ethics notwithstanding. But Colmer only opened for a fee.

He poured Bryl a glass of wine from the bottle on the table. "All right," he said. "Eat, if you like. And tell me why you want help."

Bryl took the wine, sipped at it. His eyes never stopped moving. "My name is Ted Bryl. I want you to probe me. There are some people after me, you see. They've been hunting me for years. I'm sure they want to kill me, but I don't know why. As far back as I can remember, they've been following me, and I've been running."

Colmer wove his hands together and set his chin upon them. "You sound paranoid," he said. He didn't believe in wasting words.

Bryl laughed. "It sounds like that. But I'm not. I've gone to the police, you know. They've probed me, they know it's real. Sometimes they've even arrested some of the people after me. But then they always let them go. They won't do anything to help me."

"Very paranoid."

"The police have probed me, I tell you."

Colmer smiled tolerantly. "Police probes," he said. Like a doctor saying 'chiropractor.'

"All right," Bryl said. "Probe me. See for yourself."

"Don't get upset. If you're paranoid, I can probably help you. A Master Probe is a qualified psipsych, among other things. However, you haven't mentioned a fee."

"I can't afford your fee. I don't have much money. I get jobs, but I don't keep them long. I have to run. *They* are never far behind me."

"I see." Colmer studied him a minute. "Well, I've got nothing else going at the moment. I might as well see what your problem is. But if you tell anyone I worked without a fee, I'll deny it. Of course."

"Of course," Bryl agreed.

Colmer probed him.

It was over in less than a minute; a quick opening of Colmer's mind, a drinking, a draining. To an outsider, just a long vacant stare.

Then Colmer sat back and stroked his chin and reached for the wine. "It's real," he said. "How very strange."

Bryl smiled. "That's what the police probes said. But *why? Why* are they after me?"

"You don't know. So I can't know, unless I probe one of them. You have a barrier, by the way."

"A barrier?"

"A mind block. Your memory goes back five years and a few months, then skips to your adolescence. Which was quite a long time ago, by the way. Undoubtedly you've had rejuves. There's a big hole in your head. Someone's shielded you good up there, for some reason."

Bryl suddenly looked afraid. "I know," he said. "I think *they* did it. I must know something, something important. So they took away my memory. But they're afraid I'll get it back. So they want to kill me. That's it, isn't it?"

"No," said Colmer. "It can't be that simple. If they were just criminals, the police wouldn't keep letting them go. That happens over and over again, remember. On Newholme, on Baldur, on Silversky. You've really been around. I envy you your travels." He smiled.

Bryl did not smile. "My running, you mean. I don't think you'd envy it if you had to live it. Look, Colmer, I live in constant fear. Every time I look over a shoulder, I wonder if they'll be behind me. Sometimes they are."

"Agreed, I saw those moments. The time the fat girl was sitting in your apartment when you entered. The man waiting at the spaceport, when you returned from that stint on the orbital docks. The blonde following you through the carnival. Very vivid memories. Very chilling."

Bryl was staring at him, shock written on his face. "God! How can you talk like that? You're a cold fish, Colmer."

"I have to be. I'm a Probe."

"What else can you tell me?"

"The three of them are working together. But you know that, don't you? The blonde is a telepath. That's how she follows you. The man is her protection. The fat girl—I don't know. She's very strange. She smiles like an idiot. I don't understand her function. But she seems to terrify you."

Bryl shivered. "Yes. You'd understand if you'd seen her. She's gross. Huge and white, like a fat maggot. And always smiling, dammit, always smiling at me. I never know where she's going to turn up. That time on Newholme, when I opened the door and she was sitting there, smiling at me—it was like—like finding a cockroach in a bowl of cereal you've half eaten. God!"

"You're convinced that she's going to kill you," Colmer said. "I don't know why. If any killing was to be done, the man is the logical one to do it. He's bigger, looks very strong. You've seen the gun he carries."

Bryl nodded. "I know. But it won't be him. She'll do it. I *know* it. That's why she's always smiling."

"You could buy a gun and kill them, you know," Colmer said.

Bryl looked at him. "I—I never thought of that."

"True. Yet it's odd that you haven't. Don't you think?"

"Yes. But, somehow, I couldn't do that. I'm not a violent man."

"You're a very violent man," Colmer said. "But I agree. You will not use force against them, for some reason even you don't know."

Bryl fidgeted. "Can you help me? Before they find me?"

"Perhaps I can help you. However, they've already found you. The blonde just entered the restaurant. They're giving her a table."

Bryl gasped and whirled about in his seat. Across the width of the bare plank floor, the maitre d' was escorting a shapely fair-haired young women to a seat. Bryl looked at her, his mouth hanging open. "God," he said. "They won't leave me alone." Then suddenly he was on his feet, running, literally *running,* from the Old Lady. The blonde never even looked at him.

Colmer watched him go, then glanced out the porthole. Bryl would be even more terrified when he reached the wharf. Down aways, an immense fat girl with an idiot grin was sitting on the edge of the pier, watching the fisherships spill their catch.

"Very dramatic," Colmer said. His meal arrived just then, a plate of fat bluespawn cooked in cheese. But he stood up. "I'll be joining that young lady," he told the waiter, pointing. "Bring it over there."

He walked across the restaurant and sat down. The waiter followed and put the fish in front of him.

The blonde looked up. "Adrian Colmer," she said. "I've heard of you."

Colmer *tsk*-ed. "Probing without permission. Very unprofessional, young lady. But I'll forgive you. I'm sure you didn't get much. My defenses are very good."

She smiled. "True. I suppose it was inevitable that he'd go to a private Probe eventually. How much do you know?"

"Everything he knows. Enough to have you arrested, unless you explain things to me."

"He's had us arrested from time to time. The police always let us go. But go ahead, probe. It's all right."

"You won't resist?"

"No. I'm honored."

Colmer probed.

He didn't go very deep. After all, she was a Talent. Just a quick skim, but it was enough. Afterward, he sat back, blinking rapidly in confusion. "Curiouser and curiouser. He *hired* you?"

"He doesn't remember it, of course. Part of the deal. But we have all the papers. Enough documentation to convince the police whenever they haul us in. They can't tell him. That's in the papers too. It would break the barrier, and there'd be a lawsuit you wouldn't believe."

"Edward Bryllanti," Colmer mused. "Yes, the name rings a bell. Very wealthy. He could do it. But why would he *want* to? A life of constant fear, constant running...."

"It's his idea," the woman said. "He even picked Freda. She's a moron, of course. A brain-wipe. We have to lead her around by the hand, put her where he can see her. But something about her terrifies him. So he wanted her in on it. To keep him running."

Colmer began eating his dinner. He chewed it slowly, thoughtfully. "I don't understand," he finally admitted, between bites.

The woman smiled. "You didn't go deep enough. I understand. Didn't you find it? Tell me, haven't you ever had moments when you wondered whether it was all worthwhile? When it suddenly hit you that it was all meaningless, all empty?"

Colmer stared, chewing.

"Bryllanti had more of those than most. He had psi-psychs in, saw Probes. Got him nowhere. Finally he did this. Now he doesn't wonder any more. He lives every day to the fullest, because he thinks it might be his last. He's got constant excitement, constant fear, and he never has time to think whether life is worth living. He's too busy just staying alive. You see?"

Colmer stared on, suddenly feeling very cold. The fish in his mouth tasted like damp sawdust. "But he *runs*," he said finally. "His life *is* empty. Just running, meaningless running, on a treadmill of his own creation."

The woman sighed. "You disappoint me. I expected more insight from a Master Probe. Don't you see? We *all* run."

After that, Colmer lowered his fees, to get himself more cases. But still the moods come often.

—*Chicago, June 1973*

NIGHT SHIFT

Dennison fed his card into the office time clock, listened for the heavy thunk, and snatched the card back when the machine spat it out. He slid it into its slot among the other night crew cards, and walked through the office door out onto the loading dock.

It was like walking into a furnace. The office, a plastoid pimple on the face of the elevated circular dock, was air-conditioned. But the loading area itself was not. The concrete underfoot had taken plenty of punishment during hours under an August sun, and now it was getting its own with a vengeance.

Dennison had just begun a prayer for the souls of the poor bastards who had to work out here during the day when poor bastard foreman McAllister walked up and handed him a clipboard.

"Busy?" Dennison asked.

McAllister nodded. "Yeah," he said. "And you're gonna be busier. That damn Y-324 is over an hour late. I'm not complaining, though. That puts it on your shift."

Dennison riffled through the papers on the clipboard, then glanced around the loading dock. Six of the ten berths along the rim of the great concrete circle were occupied. The squat, discolored spaceships formed an uneven, broken ring around the dock, their yawning freight ports almost obscured by the huge containers and stacked crates that clustered around each berth.

"How come P-22 isn't loaded yet?" Dennison said, flipping through the papers to find the right one. "It says here it's due out at six. That's an hour, Mac. And it can't be half loaded, by the looks of it."

McAllister shrugged. "One of the big Ivans is out," he said. "Left us only two to work with. And those are fucking *big* containers going into P-22. The little Ivans can't handle 'em."

"Shit," said Dennison. "And, of course, the big Ivan hasn't been fixed yet. So that makes it my problem." He looked over at P-22 with disgust. "Shit," he repeated.

"Don't complain to me," McAllister said. "I didn't break the fucking Ivan. You night boys got it easy, anyhow. Start at five, just when it's getting cool. No boss to bitch at you from the office. Lighter traffic most of the time. You deserve a few problems once in a while."

"Yeah. Right. Look, Mac, I was on days for years. Nights are no easier. And when I was on days I didn't leave any headaches for the night crew to take care of. I solved my own problems."

"So solve this one," McAllister said, turning towards the office. "Me, I'm going home for a beer."

Dennison followed him through the door, clipboard in hand. As usual, his crew was loitering around the small office, taking advantage of the air-conditioning until the last possible minute. That was in violation of company policy; dock workers were supposed to stay out of the office except on business. That was also routine; the station chief quit at five, and skeleton night office staff didn't give a damn.

McAllister frowned at the night shift, wove a path through them, and stepped into the elevator that would take him down into the underground garage. Dennison halted just inside the door.

"Alright," he announced. "We've got a broken big Ivan and a ship leaving in an hour, so we'll have to sweat tonight. Tony, Dirk, get the other two big Ivans going and shove those containers into P-22. Hi-Lo, I'll talk to you in a second."

He paused, flipped a page on the clipboard. "Get the

little Ivans to work unloading K-918," he continued. "Sweat crew get started loading K-490."

The men began to shuffle past him, out onto the loading dock. Dennison looked up from the clipboard. "And for Christ sake, check the ship numbers. I know they all look alike, but that's no excuse for unloading the wrong one."

A short, wizened black in a spotlessly clean coverall was the last in line. He paused before the door and looked expectantly at Dennison. "Well?" he said.

"I've only got two big Ivans, Hi-Lo, but I've got three operators," Dennison said. "So I'm going to have to find something else for you to do."

The little man smiled. "I'm a little old for the sweat crew, don't you think? I'm pushing retirement age. Besides, I'm the best Ivan man you've got. Why don't you rest Tony?"

"I wasn't thinking of the sweat crew," the foreman replied. "I had something else in mind. We'll never get those containers aboard P-22 in time with only two Ivans. But I think the company's still got some old fork lifts downstairs in the storage garage. Still know how to run one?"

"Shit, sure. That's why they call me Hi-Lo. Drove one for years before they even thought of the Ivan. Easy as hell."

"Alright," Dennison said. "Go down there and see if you can find one still in working order. A big one. Big enough to handle those containers for P-22. Then use one of the dock elevators to get it up here."

Hi-Lo nodded, and started towards the elevator. Halfway there he paused. "Gas," he said.

"What?"

"Gas. The old fork lifts worked on gas. No power cells like the Ivans. Where do I gas it up?"

Dennison looked puzzled. He looked over at Marshall, the night dispatcher who was lounging in front of his computer console and listening to the whole conversation. "Marsh?" he asked.

The thin, antiseptic-looking dispatcher clucked thoughtfully. "Well," he said. "None of the port trucks use gas. But I think a couple client companies still have some old models in operation. Maybe he could borrow some." He waved vaguely. "Siphon it, or something."

"Our best chance," Dennison agreed. "We'll never make it with two big Ivans alone. There should be some trucks down there now, picking up the stuff from K-918. Check with them for gas if you can find a decent fork lift."

Hi-Lo nodded again, and vanished into the elevator, leaving Dennison alone with the two office workers. The office looked empty, even with the supervisor's room darkened and locked up. The day staff was a lot bigger, so the desks and chairs far outnumbered the night personnel.

Marshall, the dispatcher, had turned his attention back to the master console of the office computer, and his fingers flew over the control studs with practiced ease. The night shift was really a headless operation, but Marshall was the boss if anyone was. Dennison merely took charge of loading and unloading. It was Marshall who kept track of incoming and outgoing ships, who knew which cargo was to be transferred to another ship and which unloaded onto the elevators for the trucks waiting below, and who assigned incoming freight to the proper ship.

"What do we have coming in tonight?" Dennison asked Marshall as he watched the console over his shoulder.

The dispatcher never looked up. "Two ships. Y-324 is late, could come in any minute. And there's another one scheduled to come in at nine. P-22 is the only one leaving tonight, though, so it shouldn't be too tight. A couple others go out first thing in the morning."

"We'll have to finish those two tonight, then," Dennison said. He checked his clipboard to make sure he had the numbers right. "Alright."

He turned, and nodded absently in recognition towards the other office worker, a fat college kid with a soft, pink face who had been hired for the summer to prepare sky manifests and other papers. The kid had only been around for about a week, and Dennison kept forgetting his name. Getting a nod in return, the foreman went back out onto the loading dock.

The air still swam with the late afternoon heat, and the sun still burned down on the broad expanse of white concrete. The only shade in sight was in the shadow cast by the piled freight around each of the occupied ship berths.

Three of the berths were alive with activity. Alive, but hardly humming. Nobody worked very hard until the sun went down in weather like this. Including Dennison.

The foreman drifted over to berth four, where a dozen little Ivans were rapidly emptying K-918. The squat gray machines lumbered in and out of the open hold on tank-like treads, lifting and carrying the cargo containers with tractor beams. They were stacking it on a dock elevator, a concrete slab that would later descend to surface level and the waiting trucks with the unloaded freight.

Dennison watched for a few minutes, barked orders to keep things moving quickly, and bitched at one Ivan operator who collided with the stack of containers. But the job was almost finished. The day crew had already sent down several loads. Dennison checked his clipboard.

"This tub leaves tomorrow morning," he said. "When you've got it empty, send the load downstairs. Then break open K-06 and move the stuff over here for transhipment."

He headed over towards berth six, detouring around the large black chasm left by a descending dock elevator. Things were going less well over here. The two big Ivans were massive creatures, tank-like in size as well as appearance. But the pre-sealed metal containers that were awaiting loading were equally imposing. Even drawing on their reserve power cells to push the tractor beams to max power, the Ivans could handle only one at a time.

Dennison studied the situation for only a second before giving up on the half-formed idea of setting the little Ivans to work on P-22 in teams. It would never work, he decided. Several light tractor beams *did not* have the power of one heavy-duty one, simply because it was difficult to coordinate them. To be at all effective, paired tractors had to lift at the same time and yank in the same direction. With two, maybe that could be worked out. With six, chaos. And containers of this size and weight would require at least six little Ivans.

Tony and Dirk were pushing their machines as hard as possible, but there was no way they were going to make it. The load was just too big. Dennison shrugged mentally, and moved on.

Berth one was directly opposite six on the circular loading dock, so Dennison had to walk across half of the loading area to get there. The sweat crew, as usual, was goofing off.

The cargo stacked up in front of K-490 was a potpourri. There was a mountain of small wooden crates, a couple of mail bags, a lot of heavy trunks, and a chaotic pile of packages of widely differing sizes and shapes. The contents of the crates and packages varied just as widely, Dennison knew, and included everything from personal effects to single shipments of a household appliance.

It was cargoes like this that kept the sweat crews in business—freight too small, too light, and too varied for the Ivans to handle economically. Containerization had vastly decreased the need for unskilled labor, but it had not eliminated it. Sweaters were still cheaper and more efficient than Ivans for this sort of thing.

"Cirelli," Dennison shouted as he walked up to the hold. The man jumped, and nearly knocked over the crate he'd been sitting on.

"Get off your ass," the foreman continued. "This ship has to be loaded by morning."

"Uh—yeah, sorry," Cirelli said. He picked up a crate and started towards the ship. Several of his fellow workers popped out of crannies in the mazelike stack of crates, each loaded down with several boxes. Dennison pondered briefly how many boxes they'd been carrying before he shouted.

As Cirelli entered the ship cargo hold, another man exited. He walked towards Dennison, lifted one of the crates near where the foreman was standing, and turned back towards the ship. Then he paused, looked back, and grinned.

"Say—uh, what's in these things?" he asked.

Dennison checked the shipment number stenciled on the crate, and looked down at his clipboard. "Something called Corn Crunchers," he said. "Sounds like a snack or something."

The other man grinned again. "Sure does," he said. He walked off and vanished into the hold.

Seconds later, there was the sound of wood protesting and breaking. A head popped out of the hold. "Say, boss, I dropped that crate. Stupid. It's broken open all over the place." He grinned.

Dennison returned the grin. "Careless, aren't you?" he said. "Well, we can't ship it loose. Give each of the men a couple boxes, and open the rest and eat 'em here. And put aside a box or two for me."

The man nodded, and Dennison turned and headed back towards berth six and problem ship P-22. Even less progress was being made than he had hoped. He shook his head grimly, told Tony to speed it up, and moved on.

Work on K-918 was all but finished, so Dennison sent half of the little Ivans over to berth two to open up K-06 and start lugging its cargo over to the empty ship. While he was watching the others unload the last few containers, the Ivan operator who had been involved in the earlier collision managed to do it again. This time a whole stack of small containers collapsed on top of the Ivan.

Dennison got there just in time to nearly get run over by the Ivan when it emerged from beneath the pile. The plastoid control bubble had kept the driver from injury, but he was shaken.

Dennison lifted the bubble and shook him some more. "Who the hell told you you could drive an Ivan?" he finally said, when his string of obscenities had sputtered to a halt. "He was a damn liar, whoever he was."

The driver, a sullen youth of about twenty, climbed out of the cab. "I only got promoted from the sweat gang two weeks ago," he protested.

"You just got de-promoted," Dennison said. "Get over to berth one. I'll give you another crack at it when I've got some time to watch you, but tonight I'm too busy."

The youth glared at him, shrugged, and stalked off. Dennison climbed into the Ivan, stashed his clipboard alongside the seat, yanked down the bubble, and swung the machine back into action.

On his third trip back from the hold, he nearly had a collision himself. He was lifting a container atop a crooked stack with his tractors when an ear-splitting, coughing roar sounded somewhere behind him. The sudden noise startled him. The container jiggled a little in mid-air, and the pile began to lean.

But Dennison recovered quickly. He shoved the pile back in place with his beam, and placed his container neatly on top. Then he guided the little Ivan down the narrow canyon between two large stacks of containers, out into the open. He stopped and climbed out.

Hi-Lo had found his fork lift.

The old machine was roaring and belching and running in circles in front of P-22, with Hi-Lo perched on top grinning like an idiot. It was huge. It didn't have the width or weight of the squat big Ivans, but it was higher. The big tires, nearly treadless, were an imposing sight themselves. The fork on front of the battered yellow monster looked almost large enough to pick up a big Ivan *and* its load.

Nearly all work had ground to a halt on the loading dock, and a crowd of enthusiastic spectators was forming around P-22. The old fork lift was a fascinatingly ramshackle piece of machinery, and the men took turns shouting caustic comments and advice to Hi-Lo.

Dennison, smiling in spite of himself, drifted over and elbowed his way through the crowd. "Alright, back to work," he shouted. Hi-Lo braked the machine to a sudden halt, and the men began to wander off.

Dennison kicked one of the tires, and shook his head. "Christ," he said. "I never knew they made these things so fucking *big*."

Hi-Lo was fingering the steering wheel lovingly. "Sure," he replied. "They didn't have tractor beams, so they had to have size instead. This was a heavy-duty model. Used for outdoor work, mostly. Not nearly as common as the little jobs they used inside warehouses. But it should do the job for us."

Dennison ran his hand along the body of the machine, and dry flakes of dirty yellow paint peeled off and fluttered to the ground. "I hope so," he said. "Does the fork work? The muffler sure as hell doesn't."

Hi-Lo grinned and pulled at a lever mounted on the floor of the cab. There was a squeal of protest, but the lift tilted and the fork began to move up. "It works okay. Only one thing."

"What's that?"

"These things were built to work with pallets. The fork has to slide underneath a container before it can lift it."

Dennison nodded, and turned to look around. He gestured, and a little Ivan came rumbling over from berth four. Dennison told the driver what he wanted, and the man nodded and moved the small machine forward slowly.

Its tractor beam reached out, took hold, and yanked. One of the big P-22 containers rose awkwardly on one side. It rose less than a foot, and hung there tilted, but that was enough.

Hi-Lo grinned again and slammed the fork lift into reverse. It backed up a few feet, and halted, then tilted its forks forward like a bull lowering its horns and moved slowly towards the container. The forks slid neatly in underneath the container, and the lift tilted back. The little Ivan released its tractor. Hi-Lo hit his lever again, and the forks began to rise, lifting the heavy container into the air.

"Good enough," said Dennison with a smile. "Charlie,

you stay here and work with Hi-Lo," he told the Ivan operator. The man nodded. Hi-Lo gunned his machine forward with a roar and careened towards the freight hold, the container wobbling in its forks.

Dennison walked back to the little Ivan he had been running, got his clipboard, then headed over to K-490 and assigned a sweater to take over the machine for the rest of the night. He watched the man for a while until he was certain that this guy really did know how to drive. Finally satisfied, he went back to the office.

The air-conditioning was nice, since it was still hot outside and he was starting to work up a sweat. The sun was sinking, but not yet sunk.

There was a third man in the office, sitting on top of a desk and drinking a mug of coffee. His coverall was sky blue instead of loading crew gray. A driver. Dennison knew him from previous stops. He nodded politely, and headed for the water cooler.

"I'm due out in fifteen minutes," the man said, looking at his watch. "Gonna be on time?"

Dennison shook his head. "No way," he said. He paused, drained a cup of water, refilled it, and drained it again. "We've got three loaders on it now, so that will speed things up a little. But you'll still be late. Forty-five minutes. Maybe an hour."

"Damn," the man said. But he didn't appear too concerned. He sipped at his coffee slowly.

The college kid in the corner looked up from his manifests with interest. "Where are you headed?" he asked.

"The Belt," the driver said. "Ceres, then a couple of other stops."

"What's the cargo?" the kid asked.

"Uh—mining machinery, I think. Something like that. Isn't that right, Denny?"

Dennison checked his clipboard. "Yeah," he said.

The driver nodded. "With the Belt, it's always mining machinery. What the hell else would they send out there?"

"Well, a lot of things," the kid said. "I've been watching the manifests, sort of, since I started on Monday.

It's interesting. You'd be surprised at some of the stuff they ship out. On Tuesday, there was a lot of portable heaters for the Mercury Research Station. Can you imagine that? *Heaters!* For *Mercury!*" He laughed.

The driver didn't seem to think it was funny, and looked at the kid strangely. Then he turned back to Dennison.

"Well, tell your boys to hustle," he said. "I've got a four-day haul ahead of me, and I don't take any longer than I have to."

The kid was shuffling through his manifests again. "Four days," he said, without looking up. "Must be fascinating work," he continued. "Alone out there, you and your ship and the stars and millions of miles of space."

The driver climbed off the desk and finished his coffee. "It's a living," he said. He walked past Dennison out onto the loading dock.

Marshall, who had been tending his computer oblivious of the conversation, finally looked up from his console. "Close out the manifest on P-22, Greg," he said to the kid.

The kid looked up, and nodded assent. "Easy," he said, picking up a couple of the cards on the desk before him and stuffing them into a manifest folder. "There's nothing to these big unit-shipments. It's the assorted freight loads that foul me up."

He gestured towards a chaotic pile of cards before him, and Dennison smiled in sympathy. A small package of chocolates demanded just as much paperwork as twelve tons of mining machinery, so the same mixed cargoes that provided work for the sweat crews were the office man's nightmare.

"Those for K-490?" Dennison asked, nodding towards the cards.

"They're for the Mars freighter," the kid replied. "I forget the number. It stops at Bradbury and Burroughs City. Carrying all sorts of junk."

Dennison looked at his clipboard. "Yeah," he said. "K-490 is headed out to Mars. Same ship."

Marshall was staring across the room at the kid,

looking annoyed. "How could you forget the *number?*" he said. "The number's what's *important*. No wonder you're so slow, if you're going through the manifests looking to see where the ships are *going*."

He got up from his console, and minced across the room, frowning. Standing over the kid, he jabbed at the top of one of the cards with his finger. "Look, I showed you how to do it on Monday. Each card represents a shipment. Just look up *here*—" his finger jabbed "—for a number. That'll tell you what ship it goes on. If there's no number, look here"—jab again—"or here" —again. "In that order. You fouled up enough on Tuesday because you looked in the wrong places. Separated two manifests from their cargoes. God knows the foulups that will cause. After you separate them by ship, use the console to check for weight and times and payment."

He went on and on. The kid stared down at the cards morosely, his face screwed up with a martyr's expression. Dennison wandered back outside.

It was starting to get a little cooler. The mountain of containers waiting to be loaded on P-22 was shrinking visibly with the rumbling big Ivans and roaring fork lift at work on it, but it would still be a while before the ship could be sealed up and moved out across the port for takeoff. The little Ivans, meanwhile, were moving the cargo from K-06 over to K-918.

Dennison picked up the visiphone mounted outside the office and punched port control. Marshall, of course, had already arranged for a takeoff slot for P-22, but Dennison had to order the spaceport's monstrous super Ivans that would haul the ship out to the loading field with their giant tractor beams.

He made the necessary arrangements, then chatted briefly with the freight port's night supervisor. It was a little after six when he rang off and walked over to K-490 to wake up the sweat crew again. Small cellophane bags of Corn Crunchers were everywhere, full, half-full, and empty, and the concrete was littered with the remains of stray Crunchers that had been crushed underfoot.

Dennison caught Cirelli loafing again and bawled him out, then set aside his clipboard and lugged crates with the sweaters for a while. A makeshift bowl, full of Corn Crunchers, had been rigged just inside the hold, and the men snatched handfuls as they went back and forth. Dennison decided the snacks were a bit too salty, but otherwise pretty good.

He quit about a quarter to seven and resumed his rounds. Work on P-22 was near completion. Only a few more containers awaited loading. The driver was standing by impatiently, his manifests in hand, while the big Ivans and Hi-Lo's fork lift shoved the last freight aboard. Down below, on surface level, Dennison could hear the growl of the port superIvans, standing by to lug the freighter out for takeoff.

The foreman studied his clipboard, flipping back and forth between papers. There was nothing urgent until Y-324 came in, so he could use the big Ivans for whatever he pleased. Probably be best to use one to help the little Ivans load K-918, just to make sure that was wrapped up and sealed away by morning. The other big Ivan and the fork lift he could set to work unloading D-3 over at berth ten, and lugging the freight over to the vacant berth five. That was no rush job; the ship the freight was to be transferred to wasn't due in until after the weekend. But it would keep them busy until Y-324 arrived.

Satisfied, he shouted orders to Dirk, Tony, and Hi-Lo, and watched while P-22 was sealed up and towed off. Then he drifted on to K-918, commandeered a little Ivan, and began shuttling containers back and forth between berth two and berth four. He hardly noticed P-22 when it finally took off, its flame mingling with the sunset, an hour and ten minutes late.

It was a little after eight, dark and growing darker, when he pulled himself from the cab of the Ivan and bellowed orders to his crew to break for lunch. There was a buzzer that was supposed to sound to announce lunch and quitting time. But it had been acting peculiar for several weeks now.

"I'm making the run down to Talbott's tonight," Hi-

Lo said after he climbed down from his fork lift. His once-immaculate coverall was stained with grease and covered with sweat. "You want something? Burger? Beer?"

Dennison shook his head. "Nah," he said. "Brought my lunch with me." He smiled. "And I'm not supposed to know about the beers, remember? It's against company policy."

"Oh, yeah," Hi-Lo said. He put on a shocked look, vastly exaggerated. "What beers are you talking about, boss?" Then he grinned and stalked off to the elevators.

On the way back to the office, Dennison stopped to turn on the dock night lamps. Marshall was already eating when he got inside, but the kid was nowhere to be seen. Dennison dug his hotbox out of the desk drawer where he had stashed it. "Where's the kid?" he asked Marshall idly. "Whatisname. Greg, or whatever."

"Greg Masetti," Marshall supplied helpfully. He waved towards the door vaguely. "He's eating out there somewhere. God knows why. The kid doesn't know it, but this is his last night."

Dennison had unsealed his hotbox and was chewing thoughtfully on a roast beef sandwich, dripping hot barbeque sauce. He paused between bites. "His last night? He just started Monday. That's only a week, hell. Give him a chance."

Marshall shook his head. "Look, we've got a new station chief, and he's determined to make this place more efficient. So I can't fool around. The job's not tough, but God, this kid. All he does is daydream. He's too slow. And when I try to speed him up he makes mistakes. No, he's got to go. There's plenty of people looking for summer jobs. We'll get someone new on Monday. Someone better."

Dennison finished the sandwich, started another, and nibbled from a bag of hot fried onion rings. "Have you told him?" he asked.

"No," said Marshall. "Not going to, either. He might get mad and walk out or something. I'll phone him Monday morning, before he comes in. Tell him business has slowed down and we can't afford him."

Dennison scowled, but said nothing. He polished off the sandwich and onion rings, then drained two plastic cartons of chocolate milk, before he crumpled up the disposable hotbox and wandered back outside.

Hi-Lo had just returned, so most of the crew was only starting lunch. A few of them, however, had brought their food with them, and were finished already. Some of them were gathered around the office, pitching coins against the wall. Others were sprawled out on crates and containers, half-asleep.

Dennison found the kid sitting on the edge of the dock at berth six, alone, his legs hanging over into emptiness. The half-eaten remains of an unappetizing gray synwich lay alongside him.

The foreman stooped and picked up the plastic wrapper. "It's SYNfully delicious," he read, laughing. "Christ, kid, how can you eat this stuff?"

The fat kid gestured at the synwich remains, and smiled faintly. "I can't," he said. "That's the problem." His eyes wandered back out across the spaceport.

"This is sort of an interesting job," he said after a long silence. "The manifests are tedious, but I kind of enjoy working around the ships. There's a romance there, a mystery sort of. You know what I mean?"

Dennison frowned. "No," he said. "Can't say that I do. I never really thought of this place as particularly exciting. It's a job. A drudge. Sweat and oil and crates and paper. That's all."

The kid looked at him curiously, then turned back to the spaceport. "I think you underrate the place. You're at the crossroads of the solar system here. Ships coming and going every day, from all the far, distant places most people never get to see. Long, cold hauls between the planets. Cargoes both exotic and humdrum, going out to men all over the system for dozens of different purposes. There are a lot of stories here, I think."

Dennison shook his head, smiling. "You've been reading too many books at college, kid. This is a dull, dead-end job for guys like me who couldn't cut it. There's nothing exciting or adventurous or romantic about it. That's all in your head. Space itself is just tedium. Ask the drivers."

"Tedium? Hardly. The ultimate adventure, I'd say. Lonely, maybe. But there's a romance in loneliness too, if it's the right kind of loneliness. Your ships are the galleons of the 21st century, and the freight runs are the equivalent of a modern Spanish Main."

"Galleons—" Dennison mused. He grinned. It was an odd, incongruous thought. "No, I'll tell you what the ships are. They're the—"

Across the spaceport there was a booming roar, and a thin pillar of fire lit the night sky in the distance. Atop the flames, slowly descending, was a squat black cigar shape.

Dennison and the kid spoke almost simultaneously.

"Titan," the kid said. "The Titan freighter."

"Y-324," Dennison said. "Almost four goddamn hours late."

Then the mischievous buzzer buzzed, and Dennison checked his watch, and it was time to go back to work. He strode off towards the office to find his clipboard. The kid lingered on the dock for a few minutes, watching as the Titan freighter settled to earth and the superIvans moved in around it.

The three hours to quitting time were hectic ones. Y-324 was badly behind schedule on its run from Titan to Venus Station, and there was a fleet of trucks down below waiting impatiently for its cargo, as well as a consignment for Venus that had to be loaded. So Dennison set everything—big Ivans, little Ivans, and fork lift—at work on it as soon as the superIvans moved it into berth seven. The sweat crew he kept on K-490, however; they'd only be in the way with a containerized cargo.

As soon as the ship was berthed and unsealed, the driver came stalking out, swearing a blue streak with a thick Martian accent.

"Shit! Shit!" he told Dennison when he had calmed down a little. "That ship's a flying shit pile. A wreck. A death-trap. It's been acting up all the way from Titan. I'll be damned if I'm going to move it another foot until some repairs are made. I'm not *about* to push that shit pile on to Venus the way it is."

Dennison shrugged, and continued with his loading. The driver strode into the office and repeated his declarations to Marshall. Marshall didn't raise his voice. The dispatcher simply pointed out that Y-324 was already behind schedule, and that the driver would be fired if he didn't finish the run. The ship could be examined on Venus.

It was a heroic feat to get Y-324 emptied and reloaded before the quitting buzzer sounded at midnight. Especially since another ship came in less than a half-hour later. But Dennison managed it somehow. The ship and its penitent driver took off at a quarter to twelve.

The sweat crew, meanwhile, had finished and sealed K-490, and were set to work unloading the newcomer in berth nine. After Y-324 left, Dennison moved the Ivans back over to finish loading K-918. They had to run about a half-hour overtime to do it, but they managed that one too, and sealed it up for a morning takeoff before leaving.

Dennison hit the office water cooler while they were sealing it up. Marshall, finished for the night, lounged against his console and looked bored, waiting to lock up. The kid was still working feverishly. The rush to prepare a manifest for Y-324 had put him way behind, and he still didn't have complete papers ready for the two morning departures.

When K-918 was wrapped up, the night crew began to drift into the office, one by one, to punch out and head for the elevator. Hi-Lo was the last of them.

"Uh, what should I do with the fork lift?" he asked Dennison when he entered the office. "Take it back below? Or leave it there?"

"Leave it," Dennison replied. "We'll use it until the big Ivan gets fixed. Besides, McAllister won't have anybody who can run it, and it'll bug the hell out of him."

Hi-Lo laughed. "Right," he called back, as he vanished into the elevator.

Dennison went back outside, doused the lights, and punched out himself. The kid had just finished the manifest for K-490. Marshall was rattling his keys impatiently.

"Got a ride?" Dennison asked the kid.

"Uh—no. I take the tubes."

"Don't run too often this time of night. C'mon, I'll take you home," Dennison said, turning to wave goodbye to Marshall. "See you, Marsh. Take it easy."

The kid muttered thanks, and they entered the elevator together, shooting down to the underground garage and the expressway buried beneath the spaceport. On the way to the kid's house, Dennison asked polite, stupid questions about the kid's college and courses. He thought of telling him that tonight was his last, but the idea was distasteful. That was Marshall's job, not his. So he avoided the subject, and the drive was a patchwork of meaningless noises and awkward silences.

It was not until they were almost there that the kid started in about the job again. Dennison listened politely. But inside he was muttering. Galleons. Romance. Far-off places and exotic cultures. Bah, he thought. Maybe Marshall was right. The kid was nice enough, but he was a little weird.

Finally, when they had pulled up to a stop in front of the kid's apartment complex, Dennison turned towards him. "No," he said. "You've got it all wrong."

The kid stopped in the middle of some hazily romantic generality. "How so?"

"Space isn't precisely like anything else," Dennison said carefully. "But it's certainly not the sea. Everybody thinks it is. But it's not. Spaceships aren't clipper ships, or whalers, or even tramp steamers. Nothing like that."

The kid got out of the car, and hesitated a moment, with the door open. "I think you're wrong," he said. "Maybe when I've worked around the port all summer I'll feel the same way. Maybe. But I hope not. Good night." He closed the door.

Dennison sat there for a second, debating whether he should call the kid back and tell him that he wouldn't even be working there next week, let alone all summer.

No, he decided. Let him enjoy the weekend. Summer jobs are hard to find this year, so no sense upsetting him.

The kid vanished inside the building. Dennison restarted the car. He realized suddenly the kid had never bothered to ask him what *he* thought spaceships were.

"Trucks," he muttered, half to himself, half to the vanished kid. "Big fucking ugly trucks."

He pulled away from the curb, and decided to have a beer or two before heading home.

—Bayonne, New Jersey; June 1971

". . . FOR A SINGLE YESTERDAY"

Keith was our culture, what little we had left. He was our poet and our troubadour, and his voice and his guitar were our bridges to the past. He was a time-tripper too, but no one minded that much until Winters came along.

Keith was our memory. But he was also my friend.

He played for us every evening after supper. Just beyond sight of the common house, there was a small clearing and a rock he liked to sit on. He'd wander there at dusk, with his guitar, and sit down facing west. Always west; the cities had been east of us. Far east, true, but Keith didn't like to look that way. Neither did the rest of us, to tell the truth.

Not everybody came to the evening concerts, but there was always a good crowd, say three-fourths of the people in the commune. We'd gather around in a rough circle, sitting on the ground or lying in the grass by ones and twos. And Keith, our living hi-fi in denim and leather, would stroke his beard in vague amusement and begin to play.

He was good, too. Back in the old days, before the Blast, he'd been well on his way to making a name for himself. He'd come to the commune four years ago for a rest, to check up on old friends and get away from the musical rat race for a summer. But he'd figured on returning.

Then came the Blast. And Keith had stayed. There was nothing left to go back to. His cities were graveyards full of dead and dying, their towers melted tombstones that glowed at night. And the rats—human and animal—were everywhere else.

In Keith, those cities still lived. His songs were all of the old days, bittersweet things full of lost dreams and loneliness. And he sang them with love and longing. Keith would play requests, but mostly he stuck to his kind of music. A lot of folk, a lot of folk-rock, and a few straight rock things and show tunes. Lightfoot and Kristofferson and Woody Guthrie were particular favorites. And once in a while he'd play his own compositions, written in the days before the Blast. But not often.

Two songs, though, he played every night. He always started with "They Call the Wind Maria" and ended with "Me and Bobby McGee." A few of us got tired of the ritual, but no one ever objected. Keith seemed to think the songs fit us, somehow, and nobody wanted to argue with him.

Until Winters came along, that is. Which was in a late-fall evening in the fourth year after the Blast.

His first name was Robert, but no one ever used it, although the rest of us were all on a first name basis. He'd introduced himself as Lieutenant Robert Winters the evening he arrived, driving up in a jeep with two other men. But his Army didn't exist anymore, and he was looking for refuge and help.

That first meeting was tense. I remember feeling very scared when I heard the jeep coming, and wiping my palms on my jeans as I waited. We'd had visitors before. None of them very nice.

I waited for them alone. I was as much a leader as we had in those days. And that wasn't much. We voted on everything important, and nobody gave orders. So I wasn't really a boss, but I was a greeting committee. The rest scattered, which was good sense. Our last visitors had gone in big for slugging people and raping the girls. They'd worn black-and-gold uniforms and called themselves the Sons of the Blast. A fancy name for a rat pack. We called them SOB's too, but for other reasons.

Winters was different, though. His uniform was the good ol' U.S. of A. Which didn't prove a thing, since some Army detachments are as bad as the rat packs. It was our own friendly Army that went through the area in the first year after the Blast, scorching the towns and killing everyone they could lay their hands on.

I don't think Winters was part of that, although I never had the courage to flat-out ask him. He was too decent. He was big and blond and straight, and about the same age as the rest of us. And his two "men" were scared kids, younger than most of us in the commune. They'd been through a lot, and they wanted to join us. Winters kept saying that he wanted to help us rebuild.

We voted them in, of course. We haven't turned anyone away yet, except for a few rats. In the first year, we even took in a half-dozen citymen and nursed them while they died of radiation burns.

Winters changed us, though, in ways we never anticipated. Maybe for the better. Who knows? He brought books and supplies. And guns, too, and two men who knew how to use them. A lot of the guys on the commune had come there to get away from guns and uniforms, in the days before the Blast. So Pete and Crazy Harry took over the hunting, and defended us against the rats that drifted by from time to time. They became our police force and our army.

And Winters became our leader.

I'm still not sure how that happened. But it did. He started out making suggestions, moved on to leading discussions, and wound up giving orders. Nobody objected much. We'd been drifting ever since the Blast, and Winters gave us a direction. He had big ideas, too. When I was spokesman, all I worried about was getting us through until tomorrow. But Winters wanted to rebuild. He wanted to build a generator, and hunt for more survivors, and gather them together into a sort of village. Planning was his bag. He had big dreams for the day after tomorrow, and his hope was catching.

I shouldn't give the wrong impression, though. He

wasn't any sort of a tin tyrant. He led us, yeah, but he was one of us, too. He was a little different from us, but not *that* different, and he became a friend in time. And he did his part to fit in. He even let his hair get long and grew a beard.

Only Keith never liked him much.

Winters didn't come out to concert rock until he'd been with us over a week. And when he did come, he stood outside the circle at first, his hands shoved into his pockets. The rest of us were lying around as usual, some singing, some just listening. It was a bit chilly that night, and we had a small fire going.

Winters stood in the shadows for about three songs. Then, during a pause, he walked closer to the fire. "Do you take requests?" he asked, smiling uncertainly.

I didn't know Winters very well back then. But I knew Keith. And I tensed a little as I waited for his answer.

But he just strummed the guitar idly and stared at Winters' uniform and his short hair. "That depends," he said at last. "I'm not going to play 'Ballad of the Green Berets,' if that's what you want."

An unreadable expression flickered over Winters' face. "I've killed people, yes," he said. "But that doesn't mean I'm proud of it. I wasn't going to ask for that."

Keith considered that, and looked down at his guitar. Then, seemingly satisfied, he nodded and raised his head and smiled. "Okay," he said. "What do you want to hear?"

"You know 'Leavin' on a Jet Plane'?" Winters asked.

The smile grew. "Yeah. John Denver. I'll play it for you. Sad song, though. There aren't any jet planes anymore, Lieutenant. Know that? 'S true. You should stop and think why."

He smiled again, and began to play. Keith always had the last word when he wanted it. Nobody could argue with his guitar.

A little over a mile from the common house, beyond the fields to the west, a little creek ran through the hills and the trees. It was usually dry in the summer and the fall, but it was still a nice spot. Dark and quiet at night, away from the noise and the people. When the weather was right, Keith would drag his sleeping bag out there and bunk down under a tree. Alone.

That's also where he did his timetripping.

I found him there that night, after the singing was over and everyone else had gone to bed. He was leaning against his favorite tree, swatting mosquitoes and studying the creekbed.

I sat down next to him. "Hi, Gary," he said, without looking at me.

"Bad times, Keith?" I asked.

"Bad times, Gary," he said, staring at the ground and idly twirling a fallen leaf. I watched his face. His mouth was taut and expressionless, his eyes hooded.

I'd known Keith for a long time. I knew enough not to say anything. I just sat next to him in silence, making myself comfortable in a pile of fresh-fallen leaves. And after a while he began to talk, as he always did.

"There ought to be water," he said suddenly, nodding at the creek. "When I was a kid, I lived by a river. Right across the street. Oh, it was a dirty little river in a dirty little town, and the water was as polluted as all hell. But it was still water. Sometimes, at night, I'd go over to the park across the street, and sit on a bench, and watch it. For hours, sometimes. My mother used to get mad at me."

He laughed softly. "It was pretty, you know. Even the oil slicks were pretty. And it helped me think. I miss that, you know. The water. I always think better when I'm watching water. Strange, right?"

"Not so strange," I said.

He still hadn't looked at me. He was still staring at the dry creek, where only darkness flowed now. And his hands were tearing the leaf into pieces. Slow and methodical, they were.

"Gone now," he said after a silence. "The place was too close to New York. The water probably glows now, if there is any water. Prettier than ever, but I can't go back. So much is like that. Every time I remember something, I have to remember that it's gone now. And

I can't go back, ever. To anything. Except . . . except with that . . . ." He nodded toward the ground between us. Then he finished with the leaf, and started another.

I reached down by his leg. The cigar box was where I expected it. I held it in both hands, and flipped the lid with my thumbs. Inside, there was the needle, and maybe a dozen small bags of powder. The powder looked white in the starlight. Bt seen by day, it was pale, sparkling blue.

I looked at it and sighed. "Not much left," I said.

Keith nodded, never looking. "I'll be out in a month, I figure." His voice sounded very tired. "Then I'll just have my songs, and my memories."

"That's all you've got now," I said. I closed the box with a snap and handed it to him. "Chronine isn't a time machine, Keith. Just a hallucinogen that happens to work on memory."

He laughed. "They used to debate that, way back when. The experts all said chronine was a memory drug. But they never *took* chronine. Neither have you, Gary. But I know. I've timetripped. It's not memory. It's more. You go back, Gary, you really do. You live it again, whatever it was. You can't change anything, but you know it's real, all the same."

He threw away what was left of his leaf, and gathered his knees together with his arms. Then he put his head atop them and looked at me. "You ought to timetrip someday, Gary. You really ought to. Get the dosage right, and you can pick your yesterday. It's not a bad deal at all."

I shook my head. "If I wanted to timetrip, would you let me?"

"No," he said, smiling but not moving his head. "I found the chronine. It's mine. And there's too little left to share. Sorry, Gary. Nothing personal, though. You know how it is."

"Yeah," I said. "I know how it is. I didn't want it anyway."

"I knew that," he said.

Ten minutes of thick silence. I broke it with a question. "Winters bother you?"

"Not really," he said. "He seems okay. It was just the uniforms, Gary. If it wasn't for those damn bastards in uniform and what they did, I *could* go back. To my river, and my singing."

"And Sandi," I said.

His mouth twisted into a reluctant smile. "And Sandi," he admitted. "And I wouldn't even need chronine to keep my dates."

I didn't know what to say to that. So I didn't say anything. Finally, wearying, Keith slid forward a little, and lay back under the tree. It was a clear night. You could see the stars through the branches.

"Sometimes, out here at night, I forget," he said softly, more to himself than to me. "The sky still looks the same as it did before the Blast. And the stars don't know the difference. If I don't look east, I can almost pretend it never happened."

I shook my head. "Keith, that's a game. It *did* happen. You can't forget that. You know you can't. And you can't go back. You know that, too."

"You don't listen, do you, Gary? I *do* go back. I really do."

"You go back to a dream world, Keith. And it's dead, that world. You can't keep it up. Sooner or later you're going to have to start living in reality."

Keith was still looking up at the sky, but he smiled gently as I argued. "No, Gary. You don't see. The past is as real as the present, you know. And when the present is bleak and empty, and the future more so, then the only sanity is living in the past."

I started to say something, but he pretended not to hear. "Back in the city, when I was a kid, I never saw this many stars," he said, his voice distant. "The first time I got into the country, I remember how shocked I was at all the extra stars they'd gone and stuck in my sky." He laughed softly. "Know when that was? Six years ago, when I was just out of school. Also last night. Take your pick. Sandi was with me, both times."

He fell silent. I watched him for a few moments, then stood up and brushed myself off. It was never any use. I couldn't convince him. And the saddest part of it was, I couldn't even convince myself. Maybe he was right. Maybe, for him, that was the answer.

"You ever been in the mountains?" he asked suddenly. He looked up at me quickly, but didn't wait for an answer. "There was this night, Gary—in Pennsylvania, in the mountains. I had this old beat-up camper, and we were driving through, bumming it around the country.

"Then, all of a sudden, this fog hit us. Thick stuff, gray and rolling, all kind of mysterious and spooky. Sandi loved stuff like that, and I did too, kind of. But it was hell to drive through. So I pulled off the road, and we took out a couple of blankets and went off a few feet.

"It was still early, though. So we just lay on the blankets together, and held each other, and talked. About us, and my songs, and that great fog, and our trip, and her acting, and all sorts of things. We kept laughing and kissing, too, although I don't remember what we said that was so funny. Finally, after an hour or so, we undressed each other and made love on the blankets, slow and easy, in the middle of that dumb fog."

Keith propped himself up on an elbow and looked at me. His voice was bruised, lost, hurt, eager. And lonely. "She was beautiful, Gary. She really was. She never liked me to say that, though. I don't think she believed it. She liked me to tell her she was pretty. But she was more than pretty. She *was* beautiful. All warm and soft and golden, with red-blond hair and these dumb eyes that were either green or gray, depending on her mood. That night they were gray, I think. To match the fog." He smiled, and sank back, and looked up at the stars again.

"The funniest thing was the fog," he said. Very slowly. "When we'd finished making love, and we lay back together, the fog was gone. And the stars were out, as bright as tonight. The stars came out for us. The silly goddamn voyeuristic stars came out to watch us make it. And I told her that, and we laughed, and I held her warm against me. And she went to sleep in my arms, while I lay there and looked at stars and tried to write a song for her."

"Keith . . ." I started.

"Gary," he said. "I'm going back there tonight. To the fog and the stars and my Sandi."

"Damnit, Keith," I said. "Stop it. You're getting yourself hooked."

Keith sat up again and began unbuttoning his sleeve. "Did you ever think," he said, "that maybe it's not the drug that I'm addicted to?" And he smiled very broadly, like a cocky, eager kid.

Then he reached for his box, and his timetrip. "Leave me alone," he said.

That must have been a good trip. Keith was all smiles and affability the next day, and his glow infected the rest of us. The mood lasted all week. Work seemed to go faster and easier than usual, and the nightly song sessions were as boisterous as I can remember them. There was a lot of laughter, and maybe more honest hope than we'd had for quite a while.

I shouldn't give Keith all the credit, though. Winters was already well into his suggestion-making period, and things were happening around the commune. To begin with, he and Pete were already hard at work building another house—a cabin off to the side of the common house. Pete had hooked up with one of the girls, and I guess he wanted a little more privacy. But Winters saw it as the first step toward the village he envisioned.

That wasn't his only project, either. He had a whole sheaf of maps in his jeep, and every night he'd drag someone off to the side and pore over them by candlelight, asking all sorts of questions. He wanted to know which areas we'd searched for survivors, and which towns might be worth looting for supplies, and where the rat packs liked to run, and that sort of thing. Why? Well, he had some "search expeditions" in mind, he said.

There was a handful of kids on the commune, and Winters thought we ought to organize a school for them, to replace the informal tutoring they'd been getting. Then he thought we ought to build a generator and get the electricity going again. Our medical resources were limited to a good supply of drugs and medicines; Winters thought that one of us should quit the fields permanently and train himself as a village doctor. Yeah, Winters had a lot of ideas, all right. And a good portion of 'em were pretty good, although it was clear that the details were going to require some working out.

Meanwhile, Winters had also become a regular at the evening singing. With Keith in a good mood, that didn't pose any real problems. In fact, it livened things up a little.

The second night that Winters came, Keith looked at him very pointedly and swung into "Vietnam Rag," with the rest of us joining in. Then he followed it up with "Universal Solider." In between lyrics, he kept flashing Winters this taunting grin.

Winters took it pretty well, however. He squirmed and looked uncomfortable at first, but finally entered into the spirit of the thing and began to smile. Then, when Keith finished, he stood up. "If you're so determined to cast me as the commune's very own friendly reactionary, well I guess I'll have to oblige," he said. He reached out a hand. "Give me that guitar."

Keith looked curious but willing. He obliged. Winters grabbed the instrument, strummed it a few times uncertainly, and launched into a robust version of "Okie from Muskogee." He played like his fingers were made of stone, and sang worse. But that wasn't the point.

Keith began laughing before Winters was three bars into the song. The rest of us followed suit. Winters, looking very grim and determined, plowed on through to the bitter end, even though he didn't know all the words and had to fake it in spots. Then he did the Marine hymn for an encore, ignoring all the hissing and moaning.

When he was finished, Pete clapped loudly. Winters bowed, smiled, and handed the guitar back to Keith with an exaggerated flourish.

Keith, of course, was not one to be topped easily.

He nodded at Winters, took the guitar, and promptly did "Eve of Destruction."

Winters retaliated with "Welfare Cadillac." Or tried to. Turned out he knew hardly any of the words, so he finally gave that up and settled for "Anchors Aweigh."

That sort of thing went on all night, as they jousted back and forth, and everybody else sat around laughing. Well, actually we did more than laugh. Generally we had to help Winters with his songs, since he didn't really know any of them all the way through. Keith held his own without us, of course.

It was one of the more memorable sessions. The only thing it really had in common with Keith's usual concerts was that it began with "They Call the Wind Maria," and ended with "Me and Bobby McGee."

But the next day, Keith was more subdued. Still some kidding around between him and Winters, but mostly the singing slipped back into the older pattern. And the day after, the songs were nearly all Keith's kind of stuff, except for a few requests from Winters, which Keith did weakly and halfheartedly.

I doubt that Winters realized what was happening. But I did, and so did most of the others. We'd seen it before. Keith was getting down again. The afterglow from his latest timetrip was fading. He was getting lonely and hungry and restless. He was itching, yet again, for his Sandi.

Sometimes, when he got that way, you could almost see the hurt. And if you couldn't see it, you could hear it when he sang. Loud and throbbing in every note.

Winters heard it too. He'd have had to be deaf to miss it. Only I don't think he understood what he heard, and I know he didn't understand Keith. All he knew was the anguish he heard. And it troubled him.

So, being Winters, he decided to do something about it. He came to Keith.

I was there at the time. It was midmorning, and Keith and I had come in from the field for a break. I was sitting on the well with a cup of water in my hand, and Keith was standing next to me talking. You could tell that he was getting ready to timetrip again, soon.

He was very down, very distant, and I was having trouble reaching him.

In the middle of all this, Winters comes striding up, smiling, in his Army jacket. His house was rising quickly, and he was cheerful about it, and he and Crazy Harry had already mapped out the first of their "search expeditions."

"Hello, men," he said when he joined us at the well. He reached for the water, and I passed my cup.

He took a deep drink and passed it back. Then he looked at Keith. "I enjoy your singing," he said. "I think everybody else does, too. You're very good, really." He grinned. "Even if you are an anarchistic bastard."

Keith nodded. "Yeah, thanks," he said. He was in no mood for fooling around.

"One thing, though, has been bothering me," Winters said. "I figured maybe I could discuss it with you, maybe make a few suggestions. Okay?"

Keith stroked his beard and paid a little more attention. "Okay. Shoot, Colonel."

"It's your songs. I've noticed that most of them are pretty . . . down, let's say. Good songs, sure. But sort of depressing, if you know what I mean. Especially in view of the Blast. You sing too much about the old days, and things we've lost. I don't think that's good for morale. We've got to stop dwelling so much on the past if we're ever going to rebuild."

Keith stared at him, and slumped against the well. "You gotta be kidding," he said.

"No," said Winters. "No, I mean it. A few cheerful songs would do a lot for us. Life can still be good and worthwhile if we work at it. You should tell us that in your music. Concentrate on the things we still have. We need hope and courage. Give them to us."

But Keith wasn't buying it. He stroked his beard, and smiled, and finally shook his head. "No, Lieutenant, no way. It doesn't work like that. I don't sing propaganda, even if it's well-meant. I sing what I feel."

His voice was baffled. "Cheerful songs, well . . . no. I can't. They don't work, not for me. I'd like to believe it, but I can't, you see. And I can't make other people believe if I don't. Life is pretty empty around here, the way I see it. And not too likely to improve. And . . . well, as long as I see it that way, I've got to sing it that way. You see?"

Winters frowned. "Things aren't *that* hopeless," he said. "And even if they were, we can't admit it, or we're finished."

Keith looked at Winters, at me, then down into the well. He shook his head again, and straightened. "No," he said simply, gently, sadly. And he left us at the well to stalk silently in the fields.

Winters watched him go, then turned to me. I offered him more water, but he shook his head. "What do you think, Gary?" he said. "Did I have a point? Or did I?"

I considered the question, and the asker. Winters sounded very troubled and very sincere. And the blond stubble on his chin made it clear that he was trying his best to fit in. I decided to trust him, a little.

"Yes," I said. "I know what you were driving at. But it's not that easy. Keith's songs aren't just songs. They mean things to him."

I hesitated, then continued. "Look, the Blast was hell for everybody, I don't have to tell you that. But most of us out here, we chose this kind of life, 'cause we wanted to get away from the cities and what they stood for. We miss the old days, sure. We've lost people, and things we valued, and a lot that made life joyful. And we don't much care for the constant struggle, or for having to live in fear of the rat packs. Still, a lot of what we valued is right here on the commune, and it hasn't changed that much. We've got the land, and the trees, and each other. And freedom of a sort. No pollution, no competition, no hatred. We like to remember the old days, and the *good* things in the cities—that's why we like Keith's singing—but now has its satisfactions too.

"Only, Keith is different. He didn't choose this way, he was only visiting. His dreams were all tied up with the cities, with poetry and music and people and noise.

And he's lost his world; everything he did and wanted to do is gone. And . . . and well, there was this girl. Sandra, but he called her Sandi. She and Keith lived together for two years, traveled together, did everything together. They only split for a summer, so she could go back to college. Then they were going to join up again. You understand?"

Winters understood. "And then the Blast?"

"And then the Blast. Keith was here, in the middle of nowhere. Sandi was in New York City. So he lost her, too. I think sometimes that if Sandi had been with him, he'd have gotten over the rest. She was the most important part of the world he lost, the world they shared together. With her here, they could have shared a new world and found new beauties and new songs to sing. But she wasn't here, and . . ."

I shrugged.

"Yeah," said Winters solemnly. "But it's been four years, Gary. I lost a lot too, including my wife. But I got over it. Sooner or later, mourning has to stop."

"Yes," I said. "For you, and for me. I haven't lost that much, and you . . . you think that things will be good again. Keith doesn't. Maybe things were *too* good for him in the old days. Or maybe he's just too romantic for his own good. Or maybe he loved harder than we did. All I know is that *his* dream tomorrow is like his yesterday, and mine isn't. I've never found anything I could be that happy with. Keith did, or thinks he did. Same difference. He wants it back."

I drank some more water, and rose. "I've got to get back to work," I said quickly, before Winters could continue the conversation. But I was thoughtful as I walked back to the fields.

There was, of course, one thing I hadn't told Winters, one important thing. The timetripping. Maybe if Keith was forced to settle for the life he had, he'd come out of it. Like the rest of us had done.

But Keith had an option; Keith could go back. Keith still had his Sandi, so he didn't *have* to start over again.

That, I thought, explained a lot. Maybe I should have mentioned it to Winters. Maybe.

Winters skipped the singing that night. He and Crazy Harry were set to leave the next morning, to go searching to the west. They were off somewhere stocking their jeep and making plans.

Keith didn't miss them any. He sat on his rock, warmed by a pile of burning autumn leaves, and outsung the bitter wind that had started to blow. He played hard and loud, and sang sad. And after the fire went out, and the audience drifted off, he took his guitar and his cigar box and went off toward the creek.

I followed him. This time the night was black and cloudy, with the smell of rain in the air. And the wind was strong and cold. No, it didn't sound like people dying. But it moved through the trees and shook the branches and whipped away the leaves. And it sounded ... restless.

When I reached the creek, Keith was already rolling up his sleeve.

I stopped him before he took his needle out. "Hey, Keith," I said, laying a hand on his arm. "Easy. Talk first, okay?"

He looked at my hand and his needle, and returned a reluctant nod. "Okay, Gary," he said. "But short. I'm in a rush. I haven't seen Sandi for a week."

I let go his arm and sat down. "I know."

"I was trying to make it last, Gar. I only had a month's worth, but I figured I could make it last longer if I only timetripped once a week." He smiled. "But that's hard."

"I know," I repeated. "But it would be easier if you didn't think about her so much."

He nodded, put down the box, and pulled his denim jacket a little tighter to shut out the wind. "I think too much," he agreed. Then, smiling, he added, "Such men are dangerous."

"Ummm, yeah. To themselves, mostly." I looked at him, cold and huddled in the darkness. "Keith, what will you do when you run out?"

"I wish I knew."

"I know," I said. "Then you'll forget. Your time machine will be broken, and you'll have to live today. Find somebody else and start again. Only it might be easier if you'd start now. Put away the chronine for a while. Fight it."

"Sing cheerful songs?" he asked sarcastically.

"Maybe not. I don't ask you to wipe out the past, or pretend it didn't happen. But try to find something in the present. You know it can't be as empty as you pretend. Things aren't black and white like that. Winters was part right, you know—there *are* still good things. You forget that."

"Do I? What do I forget?"

I hesitated. He was making it hard for me. "Well ... you still enjoy your singing. You know that. And there could be other things. You used to enjoy writing your own stuff. Why don't you work on some new songs? You haven't written anything to speak of since the Blast."

Keith had picked up a handful of leaves and was offering them to the wind, one by one. "I've thought of that. You don't know how much I've thought of that, Gary. And I've *tried*. But nothing comes." His voice went soft right then. "In the old days, it was different. And you know why. Sandi would sit out in the audience every time I sang. And when I did something new, something of mine, I could see her brighten. If it was good, I'd know it, just from the way she smiled. She was proud of me, and my songs."

He shook his head. "Doesn't work now, Gary. I write a song now, and sing it, and ... so what? Who cares? You? Yeah, maybe you and a few of the others come up after and say, 'Hey, Keith, I liked that.' But that's not the same. My songs were *important* to Sandi, the same way her acting was important to me. And now my songs aren't important to anyone. I tell myself that shouldn't matter. I should get my own satisfaction from composing, even if no one else does. I tell myself that a lot. But saying it doesn't make it so."

Sometimes I think, right then, I should have told

Keith that his songs were the most important thing in the world to me. But hell, they weren't. And Keith was a friend, and I couldn't feed him lies, even if he needed them.

Besides, he wouldn't have believed me. Keith had a way of recognizing truth.

Instead, I floundered. "Keith, you could find someone like that again, if you tried. There are girls in the commune, girls as good as Sandi, if you'd open yourself up to them. You could find someone else."

Keith gave me a calm stare, more chilling than the wind. "I don't need someone else, Gary," he said. He picked up the cigar box, opened it, and showed me the needle. "I've got Sandi."

Twice more that week Keith timetripped. And both times he rushed off with a feverish urgency. Usually he'd wait an hour or so after the singing, and discreetly drift off to his creek. But now he brought the cigar box with him, and left even before the last notes of "Me and Bobby McGee" had faded from the air.

Nobody mentioned anything, of course. We all knew Keith was timetripping, and we all knew he was running out. So we forgave him, and understood. Everybody understood, that is, except Pete, Winters' former corporal. He, like Winters and Crazy Harry, hadn't been filled in yet. But one evening at the singing, I noticed him looking curiously at the cigar box that lay by Keith's feet. He said something to Jan, the girl he'd been sleeping with. And she said something back. So I figured he'd been briefed.

I was too right.

Winters and Crazy Harry returned a week, to the day, after their departure. They were not alone. They brought three young teen-agers, a guy and two girls, whom they'd found down west, in company with a group of rats. "In company," is a euphemism, of course. The kids had been slaves. Winters and Crazy had freed them.

I didn't ask what had happened to the rats. I could guess.

There was a lot of excitement that night and the night after. The kids were a little frightened of us, and it took a lot of attention to convince them that things would be different here. Winters decided that they should have their own place, and he and Pete began planning a second new cabin. The first one was nearing its crude completion.

As it turned out, Winters and Pete were talking about more than a cabin. I should have realized that, since I caught Winters looking at Keith very curiously and thoughtfully on at least two occasions.

But I didn't realize it. Like everyone else, I was busy getting to know the newcomers and trying to make them feel at ease. It wasn't simple, that.

So I didn't know what was going on until the fourth evening after Winters' return. I was outside, listening to Keith sing. He'd just barely finished "They Call the Wind Maria," and was about to swing into a second song, when a group of people suddenly walked into the circle. Winters led them, and Crazy Harry was just behind him with the three kids. And Pete was there, with his arm around Jan. Plus a few others who hadn't been at the concert when it started but had followed Winters from the common house.

Keith figured they wanted to listen, I guess. He began to play. But Winters stopped him.

"No, Keith," he said. "Not right now. We've got business to take care of now, while everybody's together. We're going to talk tonight."

Keith's fingers stopped, and the music faded. The only sounds were the wind and the crackle of the nearby burning leaves. Everyone was looking at Winters.

"I want to talk about timetripping," Winters said.

Keith put down his guitar and glanced at the cigar box at the base of concert rock. "Talk," he said.

Winters looked around the circle, studying the impassive faces, as if he was weighing them before speaking. I looked too.

"I've been told that the commune has a supply of chronine," Winters began. "And that you use it for timetripping. Is that true, Keith?"

Keith stroked his beard, as he did when he was nervous or thoughtful. "Yeah," he said.

"And that's the *only* use that's ever been made of this chronine?" Winters said. His supporters had gathered behind him in what seemed like a phalanx.

I stood up. I didn't feel comfortable arguing from the ground. "Keith was the first one to find the chronine," I said. "We were going through the town hospital after the Army had gotten through with it. A few drugs were all that were left. Most of them are in the commune stores, in case we need them. But Keith wanted the chronine. So we gave it to him, all of us. Nobody else cared much."

Winters nodded. "I understand that," he said very reasonably. "I'm not criticizing that decision. Perhaps you didn't realize, however, that there are other uses for chronine besides timetripping."

He paused. "Listen, and try to judge me fairly, that's all I ask," he said, looking at each of us in turn. "Chronine is a powerful drug; it's an important resource, and we need all our resources right now. And timetripping—anyone's timetripping—is an *abuse* of the drug. Not what it was intended for."

That was a mistake on Winters' part. Lectures on drug abuse weren't likely to go over big in the commune. I could feel the people around me getting uptight.

Rick, a tall, thin guy with a goatee who came to the concerts every night, took a poke at Winters from the ground. "Bullshit," he said. "Chronine's time travel, Colonel. Meant to be used for tripping."

"Right," someone else said. "And we gave it to Keith. I don't want to timetrip, but he does. So what's wrong with it?"

Winters defused the hostility quickly. "Nothing," he said. "*If* we had an unlimited supply of chronine. But we don't. Do we, Keith?"

"No," Keith said quietly. "Just a little left."

The fire was reflected in Winters' eyes when he looked at Keith. It made it difficult to read his expression. But his voice sounded heavy. "Keith, I know what those time trips mean to you. And I don't want to hurt you, really I don't. But we need that chronine, all of us."

"How?" That was me. I wanted Keith to give up chronine, but I'd be damned before I'd let it be taken from him. "How do we *need* the chronine?"

"Chronine is not a time machine," Winters said. "It is a memory drug. And there are things we *must* remember." He glanced around the circle. "Is there anyone here who ever worked in a hospital? An orderly? A candy-striper? Never mind. There might be, in a group this size. And they'd have seen things. Somewhere in the back of their skulls they'd *know* things we need to know. I'll bet some of you took shop in high school. I'll bet you learned all sorts of useful things. But how much do you remember? With chronine, you could remember it all. We might have someone here who once learned to make arrows. We might have a tanner. We might have someone who knows how to build a generator. We might have a *doctor!*"

Winters paused and let that sink in. Around the circle, people shifted uneasily and began to mutter.

Finally Winters continued. "If we found a library, we wouldn't burn the books for heat, no matter how cold it got. But we're doing the same thing when we let Keith timetrip. *We're* a library—all of us here, we have books in our heads. And the only way to read those books is with chronine. We should use it to help us remember the things we must know. We should hoard it like a treasure, calculate every recall session carefully, and make sure—make *absolutely* sure—that we don't waste a grain of it."

Then he stopped. A long, long silence followed; for Keith, an endless one. Finally Rick spoke again. "I never thought of that," he said reluctantly. "Maybe you have something. My father was a doctor, if that means anything."

Then another voice, and another; then a chorus of people speaking at once, throwing up half-remembered experiences that might be valuable, might be useful. Winters had struck paydirt.

He wasn't smiling, though. He was looking at me.

I wouldn't meet his eyes. I couldn't. He had a point—an awful, awful point. But I couldn't admit that, I couldn't look at him and nod my surrender. Keith was my friend, and I had to stand by him.

And of all of us in the circle, I was the only one standing. But I couldn't think of anything to say.

Finally Winters' eyes moved. He looked at concert rock. Keith sat there, looking at the cigar box.

The hubbub went on for at least five minutes, but at last it died of its own weight. One by one the speakers glanced at Keith, and remembered, and dropped off into awkward silence. When the hush was complete, Keith rose and looked around, like a man coming out of a bad dream.

"No," he said. His voice was hurt and disbelieving; his eyes moved from person to person. "You can't. I don't . . . don't *waste* chronine. You know that, all of you. I visit Sandi, and that's not wasting. I need Sandi, and she's gone. I have to go back. It's my only way, my time machine." He shook his head.

My turn. "Yes," I said, as forcefully as I could manage. "Keith's right. Waste is a matter of definition. If you ask me, the biggest waste would be sending people back to sleep through college lectures a second time."

Laughter. Then other voices backed me. "I'm with Gary," somebody said. "Keith needs Sandi, and we need Keith. It's simple. I say he keeps the chronine."

"No way," someone else objected. "I'm as compassionate as anyone, but *hell*—how many of our people have died over the last few years 'cause we've bungled it when they needed doctoring? You remember Doug, two years ago? You shouldn't need chronine for that. A bad appendix, and he dies. We butchered him when we tried to cut it out. If there's a chance to prevent that from happening again—even a long shot—I say we gotta take it."

"No guarantee it won't happen anyway," the earlier voice came back. "You have to hit the right memories to accomplish anything, and even *they* may not be as useful as you'd like."

"Shit. We have to *try*...."

"I think we have an obligation to Keith...."

"I think Keith's got an obligation to *us*...."

And suddenly everybody was arguing again, hassling back and forth, while Winters and Keith and I stood and listened. It went on and on, back and forth over the same points. Until Pete spoke.

He stepped around Winters, holding Jan. "I've heard enough of this," he said. "I don't even think we got no argument. Jan here is gonna have my kid, she tells me. Well, damnit, I'm not going to take any chances on her or the kid dying. If there's a way we can learn something that'll make it safer, we take it. Especially I'm not gonna take no chances for a goddamn weakling who can't face up to life. Hell, Keithie here wasn't the only one hurt, so how does *he* rate? I lost a chick in the Blast too, but I'm not begging for chronine to dream her up again. I got a new chick instead. And that's what you better do, Keith."

Keith stood very still, but his fists were balled at his sides. "There are differences, Pete," he said slowly. "Big ones. My Sandi was no chick, for one thing. And I loved her, maybe more than you can ever understand. I know you don't understand pain, Pete. You've hardened yourself to it, like a lot of people, by pretending that it doesn't exist. So you convinced everybody you're a tough guy, a strong man, real independent. And you gave up some of your humanity, too." He smiled, very much in control of himself now, his voice sure and steady. "Well, I won't play that game. I'll cling to my humanity, and fight for it if I must. I loved once, really loved. And now I hurt. And I won't deny either of those things, or pretend that they mean any less to me than they do."

He looked to Winters. "Lieutenant, I want my Sandi, and I won't let you take her away from me. Let's have a vote."

Winters nodded.

It was close, very close. The margin was only three votes. Keith had a lot of friends.

But Winters won.

Keith took it calmly. He picked up the cigar box, walked over, and handed it to Winters. Pete was grinning happily, but Winters didn't even crack a smile.

"I'm sorry, Keith," he said.

"Yeah," said Keith. "So am I." There were tears on his face. Keith was never ashamed to cry.

There was no singing that night.

Winters didn't timetrip. He sent men on "search expeditions" into the past, all very carefully planned for minimum risk and maximum reward.

We didn't get any doctor out of it. Rick made three trips back without coming up with any useful memories. But one of the guys remembered some valuable stuff about medicinal herbs after a trip back to a bio lab, and another jaunt recalled some marginally good memories about electricity.

Winters was still optimistic, though. He'd turned to interviewing by then, to decide who should get to use the chronine next. He was very careful, very thorough, and he always asked the right questions. No one went back without his okay. Pending that approval, the chronine was stored in the new cabin, where Pete kept an eye on it.

And Keith? Keith sang. I was afraid, the night of the argument, that he might give up singing, but I was wrong. He couldn't give up song, any more than he could give up Sandi. He returned to concert rock the very next evening, and sang longer and harder than ever before. The night after that he was even better.

During the day, meanwhile, he went about his work with a strained cheerfulness. He smiled a lot, and talked a lot, but he never *said* anything much. And he never mentioned chronine, or timetripping, or the argument.

Or Sandi.

He still spent his nights out by the creek, though. The weather was getting progressively colder, but Keith didn't seem to mind. He just brought out a few blankets and his sleeping bag, and ignored the wind, and the chill, and the increasingly frequent rains.

I went out with him once or twice to sit and talk.

Keith was cordial enough. But he never brought up the subjects that really mattered, and I couldn't bring myself to force the conversations to places he obviously didn't want to go. We wound up discussing the weather and like subjects.

These days, instead of his cigar box, Keith brought his guitar out to the creek. He never played it when I was there, but I heard him once or twice from a distance, when I was halfway back to the common house after one of our fruitless talks. No singing, just music. Two songs, over and over again. You know which two.

And after a while, just one. "Me and Bobby McGee." Night after night, alone and obsessed, Keith played that song, sitting by a dry creek in a barren forest. I'd always liked the song, but now I began to fear it, and a shiver would go through me whenever I heard those notes on the frosty autumn wind.

Finally, one night, I spoke to him about it. It was a short conversation, but I think it was the only time, after the argument, that Keith and I ever really reached each other.

I'd come with him to the creek, and wrapped myself in a heavy woolen blanket to ward off the cold, wet drizzle that was dripping from the skies. Keith lay against his tree, half into his sleeeping bag, with his guitar on his lap. He didn't even bother to shield it against the damp, which bothered me.

We talked about nothing, until at last I mentioned his lonely creek concerts. He smiled. "You know why I play that song," he said.

"Yeah," I said. "But I wish you'd stop."

He looked away. "I will. After tonight. But tonight I play it, Gary. Don't argue, please. Just listen. The song is all I have left now, to help me think. And I've needed it, 'cause I been thinking a lot."

"I warned you about thinking," I said jokingly.

But he didn't laugh. "Yeah. You were right, too. Or I was, or Shakespeare . . . whoever you want to credit the warning to. Still, sometimes you can't help thinking. It's part of being human. Right?"

"I guess."

"I know. So I think with my music. No water left to think by, and the stars are all covered. And Sandi's gone. Really gone now. You know, Gary . . . if I kept on, day to day, and didn't think so much, I might forget her. I might even forget what she looked like. Do you think Pete remembers his chick?"

"Yes," I said. "And you'll remember Sandi. I'm sure of that. But maybe not quite so much . . . and maybe that's for the best. Sometimes it's good to forget."

Then he looked at me. Into my eyes. "But I *don't want* to forget, Gary. And I won't. I won't."

And then he began to play. The same song. Once. Twice. Three times. I tried to talk, but he wasn't listening. His fingers moved on, fiercely, relentlessly. And the music and the wind washed away my words.

Finally I gave up and left. It was a long walk back to the common house, and Keith's guitar stalked me through the drizzle.

Winters woke me in the common house, shaking me from my bunk to face a grim, gray dawn. His face was even grayer. He said nothing; he didn't want to wake the others, I guess. He just beckoned me outside.

I yawned and stretched and followed him. Just outside the door, Winters bent and handed me a broken guitar.

I looked at it blankly, then up at him. My face must have asked the question.

"He used it on Pete's head," Winters said. "And took the chronine. I think Pete has a mild concussion, but he'll probably be all right. Lucky. He could be dead, real easy."

I held the guitar in my hands. It was shattered, the wood cracked and splintered, several strings snapped. It must have been a hell of a blow. I couldn't believe it. "No," I said. "Keith . . . no, he couldn't . . ."

"It's his guitar," Winters pointed out. "And who else would take the chronine?" Then his face softened. "I'm sorry, Gary. I really am. I think I understand why he did it. Still, I want him. Any idea where he could be?"

I knew, of course. But I was scared. "What . . . what will you do?"

"No punishment," he said. "Don't worry. I just want the chronine back. We'll be more careful next time."

I nodded. "Okay," I said. "But nothing happens to Keith. I'll fight you if you go back on your word, and the others will too."

He just looked at me, very sadly, like he was disappointed that I'd mistrust him. He didn't say a thing. We walked the mile to the creek in silence, me still holding the guitar.

Keith was there, of course. Wrapped in his sleeping bag, the cigar box next to him. There were a few bags left. He'd used only one.

I bent to wake him. But when I touched him and rolled him over, two things hit me. He'd shaved off his beard. And he was very, very cold.

Then I noticed the empty bottle.

We'd found other drugs with the chronine, way back when. They weren't even guarded. Keith had used sleeping pills.

I stood up, not saying a word. I didn't need to explain. Winters had taken it all in very quickly. He studied the body and shook his head.

"I wonder why he shaved?" he said finally.

"I know," I said. "He never wore a beard in the old days, when he was with Sandi."

"Yes," said Winters. "Well, it figures."

"What?"

"The suicide. He always seemed unstable."

"No, Lieutenant," I said. "You've got it all wrong. Keith didn't commit suicide."

Winters frowned. I smiled.

"Look," I said. "If you did it, it would be suicide. You think chronine is only a drug for dreaming. But Keith figured it for a time machine. He didn't kill himself. That wasn't his style. He just went back to his Sandi. And this time, he made sure he stayed there."

Winters looked back at the body. "Yes," he said.

"Maybe so." He paused. "For his sake, I hope that he was right."

The years since then have been good ones, I guess. Winters is a better leader than I was. The timetrips never turned up any knowledge worth a damn, but the search expeditions proved fruitful. There are more than two hundred people in town now, most of them people that Winters brought in.

It's a real town, too. We have electricity and a library, and plenty of food. And a doctor—a real doctor that Winters found a hundred miles from here. We got so prosperous that the Sons of the Blast heard about us and came back for a little fun. Winters had his militia beat them off and hunt down the ones who tried to escape.

Nobody but the old commune people remember Keith. But we still have singing and music. Winters found a kid named Ronnie on one of his trips, and Ronnie has a guitar of his own. He's not in Keith's league, of course, but he tries hard, and everybody has fun. And he's taught some of the youngsters how to play.

Only thing is, Ronnie likes to write his own stuff, so we don't hear many of the old songs. Instead we get postwar music. The most popular tune, right now, is a long ballad about how our army wiped out the Sons of the Blast.

Winters says that's a healthy thing; he talks about new music for a new civilization. And maybe he has something. In time, I'm sure, there will be a new culture to replace the one that died. Ronnie, like Winters, is giving us tomorrow.

But there's a price.

The other night, when Ronnie sang, I asked him to do "Me and Bobby McGee." But nobody knew the words.

—*Chicago, October 1972*

AND SEVEN TIMES
NEVER KILL MAN

—⊰ ⊱—

*Ye may kill for yourselves, and your mates,
  and your cubs as they need, and ye can;*

*But kill not for pleasure of killing,
  and seven times never kill Man!*
                              —RUDYARD KIPLING

Outside the walls the Jaenshi children hung, a row of small grayfurred bodies still and motionless at the ends of long ropes. The oldest among them, obviously, had been slaughtered before hanging; here a headless male swung upside down, the noose around the feet, while there dangled the blast-burned carcass of a female. But most of them, the dark hairy infants with the wide golden eyes, most of them had simply been hung. Toward dusk, when the wind came swirling down out of the ragged hills, the bodies of the lighter children would twist at the ends of their ropes and bang against the city walls, as if they were alive and pounding for admission.

But the guards on the walls paid the thumping no mind as they walked their relentless rounds, and the rust-streaked metal gates did not open.

"Do you believe in evil?" Arik neKrol asked Jannis Ryther as they looked down on the City of the Steel

Angels from the crest of a nearby hill. Anger was written across every line of his flat yellow-brown face, as he squatted among the broken shards of what once had been a Jaenshi worship pyramid.

"Evil?" Ryther murmured in a distracted way. Her eyes never left the redstone walls below, where the dark bodies of the children were outlined starkly. The sun was going down, the fat red globe that the Steel Angels called the Heart of Bakkalon, and the valley beneath them seemed to swim in bloody mists.

"Evil," neKrol repeated. The trader was a short, pudgy man, his features decidedly mongoloid except for the flame-red hair that fell nearly to his waist. "It is a religious concept, and I am not a religious man. Long ago, when I was a very child growing up on ai-Emerel, I decided that there was no good or evil, only different ways of thinking." His small, soft hands felt around in the dust until he had a large, jagged shard that filled his fist. He stood and offered it to Ryther. "The Steel Angels have made me believe in evil again," he said.

She took the fragment from him wordlessly and turned it over in her hands. Ryther was much taller than neKrol, and much thinner; a hard bony woman with a long face, short black hair, and eyes without expression. The sweat-stained coveralls she wore hung loosely on her spare frame.

"Interesting," she said finally, after studying the shard for several minutes. It was as hard and smooth as glass, but stronger; colored a translucent red, yet so very dark it was almost black. "A plastic?" she asked, throwing it back to the ground.

NeKrol shrugged. "That was my very guess, but of course it is impossible. The Jaenshi work in bone and wood and sometimes metal, but plastic is centuries beyond them."

"Or behind them," Ryther said. "You say these worship pyramids are scattered all through the forest?"

"Yes, as far as I have ranged. But the Angels have smashed all those close to their valley, to drive the

Jaenshi away. As they expand, and they *will* expand, they will smash others."

Ryther nodded. She looked down into the valley again, and as she did the last sliver of the Heart of Bakkalon slid below the western mountains and the city lights began to come on. The Jaenshi children swung in pools of soft blue illumination, and just above the city gates two stick figures could be seen working. Shortly they heaved something outward, a rope uncoiled, and then another small dark shadow jerked and twitched against the wall. "Why?" Ryther said, in a cool voice, watching.

NeKrol was anything but cool. "The Jaenshi tried to defend one of their pyramids. Spears and knives and rocks against the Steel Angels with lasers and blasters and screechguns. But they caught them unaware, killed a man. The Proctor announced it would not happen again." He spat. "Evil. The children trust them, you see."

"Interesting," Ryther said.

"Can you do anything?" neKrol asked, his voice agitated. "You have your ship, your crew. The Jaenshi need a protector, Jannis. They are helpless before the Angels."

"I have four men in my crew," Ryther said evenly. "Perhaps four hunting lasers as well." That was all the answer she gave.

NeKrol looked at her helplessly. *"Nothing?"*

"Tomorrow, perhaps, the Proctor will call on us. He has surely seen the *Lights* descend. Perhaps the Angels wish to trade." She glanced again into the valley. "Come, Arik, we must go back to your base. The trade goods must be loaded."

Wyatt, Proctor of the Children of Bakkalon on the World of Corlos, was tall and red and skeletal, and the muscles stood out clearly on his bare arms. His blue-black hair was cropped very short, his carriage was stiff and erect. Like all the Steel Angels, he wore a uniform of chameleon cloth (a pale brown now, as he stood in the full light of day on the edge of the small, crude spacefield), a mesh-steel belt with hand-laser and communicator and screechgun, and a stiff red Roman collar. The tiny figurine that hung on a chain about his neck—the pale child Bakkalon, nude and innocent and bright-eyed, but holding a great black sword in one small fist—was the only sign of Wyatt's rank.

Four other Angels stood behind him: two men, two women, all dressed identically. There was a sameness about their faces, too; the hair always cropped tightly, whether it was blond or red or brown, the eyes alert and cold and a little fanatic, the upright posture that seemed to characterize members of the military-religious sect, the bodies hard and fit. NeKrol, who was soft and slouching and sloppy, disliked everything about the Angels.

Proctor Wyatt had arrived shortly after dawn, sending one of his squad to pound on the door of the small gray prefab bubble that was neKrol's trading base and home. Sleepy and angry, but with a guarded politeness, the trader had risen to greet the Angels, and had escorted them out to the center of the spacefield, where the scarred metal teardrop of the *Lights of Jolostar* squatted on three retractable legs.

The cargo ports were all sealed now: Ryther's crew had spent most of the evening unloading neKrol's trade goods and replacing them in the ship's hold with crates of Jaenshi artifacts that might bring good prices from collectors of extraterrestrial art. No way of knowing until a dealer looked over the goods: Ryther had dropped neKrol only a year ago, and this was the first pickup.

"I am an independent trader, and Arik is my agent on this world," Ryther told the Proctor when she met him on the edge of the field. "You must deal through him."

"I see," Proctor Wyatt said. He still held the list he had offered Ryther, of goods the Angels wanted from the industrialized colonies on Avalon and Jamison's World. "But neKrol will not deal with us."

Ryther looked at him blankly.

"With good reason," neKrol said. "I trade with the Jaenshi, you slaughter them."

The Proctor had spoken to neKrol often in the months since the Steel Angels had established their city-colony, and the talks had all ended in arguments; now he ignored him. "The steps we took were needed," Wyatt said to Ryther. "When an animal kills a man, the animal must be punished, and other animals must see and learn, so that beasts may know that man, the seed of Earth and child of Bakkalon, is the lord and master of them all."

NeKrol snorted. "The Jaenshi are not beasts, Proctor, they are an intelligent race, with their own religion and art and customs, and they . . ."

Wyatt looked at him. "They have no soul. Only the children of Bakkalon have souls, only the seed of Earth. What mind they may have is relevant only to you, and perhaps them. Soulless, they are beasts."

"Arik has shown me the worship pyramids they build," Ryther said. "Surely creatures that build such shrines must have souls."

The Proctor shook his head. "You are in error in your belief. It is written clearly in the Book. We, the seed of Earth, are truly the children of Bakkalon, and no others. The rest are animals, and in Bakkalon's name we must assert our dominion over them."

"Very well," Ryther said. "But you will have to assert your dominion without aid from the *Lights of Jolostar,* I'm afraid. And I must inform you, Proctor, that I find your actions seriously disturbing, and intend to report them when I return to Jamison's World."

"I expected no less," Wyatt said. "Perhaps by next year you will burn with love of Bakkalon, and we may talk again. Until then, the world of Corlos will survive." He saluted her, and walked briskly from the field, followed by the four Steel Angels.

"What good will it do to report them?" neKrol said bitterly, after they had gone.

"None," Ryther said, looking off toward the forest. The wind was kicking up the dust around her, and her shoulders slumped, as if she were very tired. "The

Jamies won't care, and if they did, what could they do?"

NeKrol remembered the heavy red-bound book that Wyatt had given him months ago. "And Bakkalon the pale child fashioned his children out of steel," he quoted, "for the stars will break those of softer flesh. And in the hand of each new-made infant He placed a beaten sword, telling them, 'This is the Truth and the Way.'" He spat in disgust. "That is their very creed. And we can do nothing?"

Her face was empty of expression now. "I will leave you two lasers. In a year, make sure the Jaenshi know how to use them. I believe I know what sort of trade goods I should bring."

The Jaenshi lived in clans (as neKrol thought of them) of twenty to thirty, each clan divided equally between adults and children, each having its own home-forest and worship pyramid. They did not build; they slept curled up in trees around their pyramid. For food, they foraged; juicy blue-black fruits grew everywhere, and there were three varieties of edible berries, a hallucinogenic leaf, and a soapy yellow root the Jaenshi dug for. NeKrol had found them to be hunters as well, though infrequently. A clan would go for months without meat, while the snuffling brown bushogs multiplied all around them, digging up roots and playing with the children. Then suddenly, when the bushog population had reached some critical point, the Jaenshi spearmen would walk among them calmly, killing two out of every three, and that week great hog roasts would be held each night around the pyramid. Similar patterns could be discerned with the white-bodied tree slugs that sometimes covered the fruit trees like a plague, until the Jaenshi gathered them for a stew, and with the fruit-stealing pseudomonks that haunted the higher limbs.

So far as neKrol could tell, there were no predators in the forests of the Jaenshi. In his early months on their world, he had worn a long force-knife and a hand-laser as he walked from pyramid to pyramid on his trade route. But he had never encountered anything even remotely hostile, and now the knife lay broken in his kitchen, while the laser was long lost.

The day after the *Lights of Jolostar* departed, neKrol went armed into the forest again, with one of Ryther's hunting lasers slung over his shoulder.

Less than two kilometers from his base, neKrol found the camp of the Jaenshi he called the waterfall folk. They lived up against the side of a heavily-wooded hill, where a stream of tumbling blue-white water came sliding and bouncing down, dividing and rejoining itself over and over, so the whole hillside was an intricate glittering web of waterfalls and rapids and shallow pools and spraying wet curtains. The clan's worship pyramid sat in the bottommost pool, on a flat gray stone in the middle of the eddies; taller than most Jaenshi, coming up to neKrol's chin, looking infinitely heavy and solid and immovable, a three-sided block of dark, dark red.

NeKrol was not fooled; he had seen other pyramids sliced to pieces by the lasers of the Steel Angels and shattered by the flames of their blasters; whatever powers the pyramids might have in Jaenshi myth, whatever mysteries might lie behind their origin, it was not enough to stay the swords of Bakkalon.

The glade around the pyramid-pool was alive with sunlight when neKrol entered, and the long grasses swayed in the light breeze, but most of the waterfall folk were elsewhere. In the trees perhaps, climbing and coupling and pulling down fruits, or ranging through the forests on their hill. The trader found only a few small children riding on a bushog in the clearing when he arrived. He sat down to wait, warm in the sunlight.

Soon the old talker appeared.

He sat down next to neKrol, a tiny shriveled Jaenshi with only a few patches of dirty gray-white fur left to hide the wrinkles in his skin. He was toothless, clawless, feeble; but his eyes, wide and golden and pupilless as those of any Jaenshi, were still alert, alive. He was the talker of the waterfall folk, the one in closest communion with the worship pyramid. Every clan had a talker.

"I have something new to trade," neKrol said, in the soft slurred speech of the Jaenshi. He had learned the tongue before coming here, back on Avalon. Tomas Chung, the legendary Avalonian linguesp, had broken it centuries before, when the Kleronomas Survey brushed by this world. No other human had visited the Jaenshi since, but the maps of Kleronomas and Chung's language-pattern analysis both remained alive in the computers at the Avalon Institute for the Study of Non-Human Intelligence.

"We have made you more statues, have fashioned new woods," the old talker said. "What have you brought? Salt?"

NeKrol undid his knapsack, laid it out, and opened it. He took out one of the bricks of salt he carried, and laid it before the old talker. "Salt," he said. "And more." He laid the hunting rifle before the Jaenshi.

"What is this?" the old talker asked.

"Do you know of the Steel Angels?" neKrol asked.

The other nodded, a gesture neKrol had taught him. "The godless who run from the dead valley speak of them. They are the ones who make the gods grow silent, the pyramid breakers."

"This is a tool like the Steel Angels use to break your pyramids," neKrol said. "I am offering it to you in trade."

The old talker sat very still. "But we do not wish to break pyramids," he said.

"This tool can be used for other things," neKrol said. "In time, the Steel Angels may come here, to break the pyramid of the waterfall folk. If by then you have tools like this, you can stop them. The people of the pyramid in the ring-of-stone tried to stop the Steel Angels with spears and knives, and now they are scattered and wild and their children hang dead from the walls of the City of the Steel Angels. Other clans of the Jaenshi were unresisting, yet now they too are godless and landless. The time will come when the waterfall folk will need this tool, old talker."

The Jaenshi elder lifted the laser and turned it curiously in his small withered hands. "We must pray on this," he said. "Stay, Arik. Tonight we shall tell you, when the god looks down on us. Until then, we shall trade." He rose abruptly, gave a swift glance at the pyramid across the pool, and faded into the forest, still holding the laser.

NeKrol sighed. He had a long wait before him; the prayer assemblies never came until sundown. He moved to the edge of the pool and unlaced his heavy boots to soak his sweaty, calloused feet in the crisp cold waters.

When he looked up, the first of the carvers had arrived; a lithe young Jaenshi female with a touch of auburn in her body fur. Silent (they were all silent in neKrol's presence, all save the talker), she offered him her work.

It was a statuette no larger than his fist, a heavy-breasted fertility goddess fashioned out of the fragrant, thin-veined blue wood of the fruit trees. She sat cross-legged on a triangular base, and three thin slivers of bone rose from each corner of the triangle to meet above her head in a blob of clay.

NeKrol took the carving, turned it this way and that, and nodded his approval. The Jaenshi smiled and vanished, taking the salt brick with her. Long after she was gone, neKrol continued to admire his acquisition. He had traded all his life, spending ten years among the squid-faced gethsoids of Aath and four with the stick-thin Fyndii, traveling a trader's circuit to a half-dozen stone age planets that had once been slaveworlds of the broken Hrangan Empire; but nowhere had he found artists like the Jaenshi. Not for the first time, he wondered why neither Kleronomas nor Chung had mentioned the native carvings. He was glad they hadn't, though, and fairly certain that once the dealers saw the crates of wooden gods he had sent back with Ryther, the world would be overrun by traders. As it was, he had been sent here entirely on speculation, in hopes of finding a Jaenshi drug or herb or liquor that might move well in stellar trade. Instead he'd found the art, like an answer to a prayer.

Other workmen came and went as the morning turned to afternoon and the afternoon to dusk, setting their craft before him. He looked over each piece carefully, taking some and declining others, paying for what he took in salt. Before full darkness had descended, a small pile of goods sat by his right hand; a matched set of redstone knives, a gray deathcloth woven from the fur of an elderly Jaenshi by his widow and friends (with his face wrought upon it in the silky golden hairs of a pseudomonk), a bone spear with tracings that reminded neKrol of the runes of Old Earth legend; and statues. The statues were his favorites, always; so often alien art was alien beyond comprehension, but the Jaenshi workmen touched emotional chords in him. The gods they carved, each sitting in a bone pyramid, wore Jaenshi faces, yet at the same time seemed archetypically human: stern-faced war gods, things that looked oddly like satyrs, fertility goddesses like the one he had bought, almost-manlike warriors and nymphs. Often neKrol had wished that he had a formal education in extee anthropology, so that he might write a book on the universals of myth. The Jaenshi surely had a rich mythology, though the talkers never spoke of it: nothing else could explain the carvings. Perhaps the old gods were no longer worshipped, but they were still remembered.

By the time the Heart of Bakkalon went down and the last reddish rays ceased to filter through the looming trees, neKrol had gathered as much as he could carry, and his salt was all but exhausted. He laced up his boots again, packed his acquisitions with painstaking care, and sat patiently in the poolside grass, waiting. One by one, the waterfall folk joined him. Finally the old talker returned.

The prayers began.

The old talker, with the laser still in his hand, waded carefully across the night-dark waters, to squat by the black bulk of the pyramid. The others, adults and children together, now some forty strong, chose spots in the grass near the banks, behind neKrol and around him. Like him, they looked out over the pool, at the pyramid and the talker outlined clearly in the light of a new-risen, oversized moon. Setting the laser down on the stone, the old talker pressed both palms flat against the side of the pyramid, and his body seemed to go stiff, while all the other Jaenshi also tensed and grew very quiet.

NeKrol shifted restlessly and fought a yawn. It was not the first time he'd sat through a prayer ritual, and he knew the routine. A good hour of boredom lay before him; the Jaenshi did silent worship, and there was nothing to be heard but their steady breathing, nothing to be seen but forty impassive faces. Sighing, the trader tried to relax, closing his eyes and concentrating on the soft grass beneath him and the warm breeze that tossed his wild mane of hair. Here, briefly, he found peace. How long would it last, he mused, should the Steel Angels leave their valley . . .

The hour passed, but neKrol, lost in meditation, scarce felt the flow of time. Until suddenly he heard the rustlings and chatter around him, as the waterfall folk rose and went back into the forest. And then the old talker stood in front of him, and laid the laser at his feet.

"No," he said simply.

NeKrol started. "What? But you *must*. Let me show you what it can do . . ."

"I have had a vision, Arik. The god has shown me. But also he has shown me that it would not be a good thing to take this in trade."

"Old talker, the Steel Angels will come . . ."

"If they come, our god shall speak to them," the Jaenshi elder said, in his purring speech, but there was finality in the gentle voice, and no appeal in the vast liquid eyes.

"For our food, we thank ourselves, none other. It is ours because we worked for it, ours because we fought for it, ours by the only right that is: the right of the strong. But for that strength—for the might of our arms and the steel of our swords and the fire in our hearts—we thank Bakkalon, the pale child, who gave us life and taught us how to keep it."

The Proctor stood stiffly at the centermost of the five

long wooden tables that stretched the length of the great mess hall, pronouncing each word of the grace with solemn dignity. His large veined hands pressed tightly together as he spoke, against the flat of the upward-jutting sword, and the dim lights had faded his uniform to an almost-black. Around him, the Steel Angels sat at attention, their food untouched before them; fat boiled tubers, steaming chunks of bushog meat, black bread, bowls of crunchy green neograss. Children below the fighting age of ten, in smocks of starchy white and the omnipresent mesh-steel belts, filled the two outermost tables beneath the slit-like windows; toddlers struggled to sit still under the watchful eyes of stern nine-year-old houseparents with hardwood batons in their belts. Further in, the fighting brotherhood sat, fully armed, at two equally long tables, men and women alternating, leather-skinned veterans sitting next to ten-year-olds who had barely moved from the children's dorm to the barracks. All of them wore the same chameleon cloth as Wyatt, though without his collar, and a few had buttons of rank. The center table, less than half the length of the others, held the cadre of the Steel Angels; the squadfathers and squadmothers, the weaponsmasters, the healers, the four fieldbishops, all those who wore the high, stiff crimson collar. And the Proctor, at its head.

"Let us eat," Wyatt said at last. His sword moved above his table with a whoosh, describing the slash of blessing, and he sat to his meal. The Proctor, like all the others, had stood single-file in the line that wound past the kitchen to the mess hall, and his portions were no larger than the least of the brotherhood.

There was a clink of knives and forks, and the infrequent clatter of a plate, and from time to time the thwack of a baton, as a houseparent punished some transgression of discipline by one of his charges; other than that, the hall was silent. The Steel Angels did not speak at meals, but rather meditated on the lessons of the day as they consumed their spartan fare.

Afterwards, the children still silent—marched out of the hall, back to their dormitory. The fighting brotherhood followed, some to chapel, most to the barracks, a few to guard duty on the walls. The men they were relieving would find late meals still warm in the kitchen.

The officer core remained; after the plates were cleared away, the meal became a staff meeting.

"At ease," Wyatt said, but the figures along the table relaxed little, if at all. Relaxation had been bred out of them by now. The Proctor found one of them with his eyes. "Dhallis," he said, "you have the report I requested?"

Fieldbishop Dhallis nodded. She was a husky middle-aged woman with thick muscles and skin the color of brown leather. On her collar was a small steel insignia, an ornamental memory-chip that meant Computer Services. "Yes, Proctor," she said, in a hard, precise voice. "Jamison's World is a fourth-generation colony, settled mostly from Old Poseidon. One large continent, almost entirely unexplored, and more than twelve thousand islands of various sizes. The human population is concentrated on the islands, and makes its living by farming sea and land, aquatic husbandry, and heavy industry. The oceans are rich in food and metal. The total population is about seventy-nine million. There are two large cities, both with spaceports: Port Jamison and Jolostar." She looked down at the computer print-out on the table. "Jamison's World was not even charted at the time of the Double War. It has never known military action, and the only Jamie armed forces are their planetary police. It has no colonial program and has never attempted to claim political jurisdiction beyond its own atmosphere."

The Proctor nodded. "Excellent. Then the trader's threat to report us is essentially an empty one. We can proceed. Squadfather Walman?"

"Four Jaenshi were taken today, Proctor, and are now on the walls," Walman reported. He was a ruddy young man with a blond crewcut and large ears. "If I might, sir, I would request discussion of possible termination of the campaign. Each day we search harder for less. We have virtually wiped out every Jaenshi youngling of the clans who originally inhabited Sword Valley."

Wyatt nodded. "Other opinions?"

Fieldbishop Lyon, blue-eyed and gaunt, indicated dissent. "The adults remain alive. The mature beast is more dangerous than the youngling, Squadfather."

"Not in this case," Weaponsmaster C'ara DaHan said. DaHan was a giant of a man, bald and bronze-colored, the chief of Psychological Weaponry and Enemy Intelligence. "Our studies show that, once the pyramid is destroyed, neither full-grown Jaenshi nor the immature pose any threat whatsoever to the children of Bakkalon. Their social structure virtually disintegrates. The adults either flee, hoping to join some other clan, or revert to near-animal savagery. They abandon the younglings, most of whom fend for themselves in a confused sort of way and offer no resistance when we take them. Considering the number of Jaenshi on our walls, and those reported slain by predators or each other, I strongly feel that Sword Valley is virtually clean of the animals. Winter is coming, Proctor, and much must be done. Squadfather Walman and his men should be set to other tasks."

There was more discussion, but the tone had been set; most of the speakers backed DaHan. Wyatt listened carefully, and all the while prayed to Bakkalon for guidance. Finally he motioned for quiet.

"Squadfather," he said to Walman, "tomorrow collect all the Jaenshi—both adults and children—that you can, but do not hang them if they are unresisting. Instead, take them to the city, and show them their clanmates on our walls. Then cast them from the valley, one in each direction of the compass." He bowed his head. "It is my hope that they will carry a message, to all the Jaenshi, of the price that must be paid when a beast raises hand or claw or blade against the seed of Earth. Then, when the spring comes and the children of Bakkalon move beyond Sword Valley, the Jaenshi will peacefully abandon their pyramids and quit whatever lands men may require, so the glory of the pale child might be spread."

Lyon and DaHan both nodded, among others. "Speak wisdom to us," Fieldbishop Dhallis said then.

Proctor Wyatt agreed. One of the lesser-ranking squadmothers brought him the Book, and he opened it to the Chapter of Teachings.

"In those days much evil had come upon the seed of Earth," the Proctor read, "for the children of Bakkalon had abandoned Him to bow to softer gods. So their skies grew dark and upon them from above came the Sons of Hranga with red eyes and demon teeth, and upon them from below came the vast Horde of Fyndii like a cloud of locusts that blotted out the stars. And the worlds flamed, and the children cried out, 'Save us! Save us!'

"And the pale child came and stood before them, with His great sword in His hand, and in a voice like thunder He rebuked them. 'You have been weak children,' He told them, 'for you have disobeyed. Where are your swords? Did I not set swords in your hands?'

"And the children cried out, 'We have beaten them into plowshares, oh Bakkalon!'

"And He was sore angry. 'With plowshares, then, shall you face the Sons of Hranga! With plowshares shall you slay the Horde of Fyndii!" And He left them, and heard no more their weeping, for the Heart of Bakkalon is a Heart of Fire.

"But then one among the seed of Earth dried his tears, for the skies did burn so bright that they ran scalding on his cheeks. And the bloodlust rose in him and he beat his plowshare back into a sword, and charged the Sons of Hranga, slaying as he went. Then others saw, and followed, and a great battle-cry rang across the worlds.

"And the pale child heard, and came again, for the sound of battle is more pleasing to his ears than the sound of wails. And when He saw, He smiled. 'Now you are my children again,' He said to the seed of Earth. 'For you had turned against me to worship a god who calls himself a lamb, but did you not know that lambs go only to the slaughter? Yet now your eyes have cleared, and again you are the Wolves of God!'

"And Bakkalon gave them all swords again, all His children and all the seed of Earth, and He lifted his great black blade, the Demon-Reaver that slays the soulless, and swung it. And the Sons of Hranga fell before His might, and the great Horde that was the Fyndii burned beneath His gaze. And the children of Bakkalon swept across the worlds."

The Proctor lifted his eyes. "Go, my brothers-in-arms, and think on the Teachings of Bakkalon as you sleep. May the pale child grant you visions!"

They were dismissed.

The trees on the hill were bare and glazed with ice, and the snow—unbroken except for their footsteps and the stirrings of the bitter-sharp north wind—gleamed a blinding white in the noon sun. In the valley beneath, the City of the Steel Angels looked preternaturally clean and still. Great snowdrifts had piled against the eastern walls, climbing halfway up the stark scarlet stone; the gates had not opened in months. Long ago, the children of Bakkalon had taken their harvest and fallen back inside the city, to huddle around their fires. But for the blue lights that burned late into the cold black night, and the occasional guard pacing atop the walls, neKrol would hardly have known that the Angels still lived.

The Jaenshi that neKrol had come to think of as the bitter speaker looked at him out of eyes curiously darker than the soft gold of her brothers. "Below the snow, the god lies broken," she said, and even the soothing tones of the Jaenshi tongue could not hide the hardness in her voice. They stood at the very spot where neKrol had once taken Ryther, the spot where the pyramid of the people of the ring-of-stone once stood. NeKrol was sheathed head to foot in a white thermosuit that clung too tightly, accenting every unsightly bulge. He looked out on Sword Valley from behind a dark blue plastifilm in the suit's cowl. But the Jaenshi, the bitter speaker, was nude, covered only by the thick gray fur of her winter coat. The strap of the hunting laser ran down between her breasts.

"Other gods beside yours will break unless the Steel Angels are stopped," neKrol said, shivering despite his thermosuit.

The bitter speaker seemed hardly to hear. "I was a child when they came, Arik. If they had left our god, I might be a child still. Afterwards, when the light went out and the glow inside me died, I wandered far from the ring-of-stone, beyond our own home forest, knowing nothing, eating where I could. Things are not the same in the dark valley. Bushogs honked at my passing, and charged me with their tusks, other Jaenshi threatened me and each other. I did not understand and I could not pray. Even when the Steel Angels found me, I did not understand, and I went with them to their city, knowing nothing of their speech. I remember the walls, and the children, many so much younger than me. Then I screamed and struggled; when I saw those on the ropes, something wild and godless stirred to life inside me." Her eyes regarded him, her eyes like burnished bronze. She shifted in the ankle-deep snow, curling a clawed hand around the strap of her laser.

NeKrol had taught her well since the day she had joined him, in the late summer when the Steel Angels had cast her from Sword Valley. The bitter speaker was by far the best shot of his six, the godless exiles he had gathered to him and trained. It was the only way; he had offered the lasers in trade to clan after clan, and each had refused. The Jaenshi were certain that their gods would protect them. Only the godless listened, and not all of them; many—the young children, the quiet ones, the first to flee—many had been accepted into other clans. But others, like the bitter speaker, had grown too savage, had seen too much; they fit no longer. She had been the first to take the weapon, after the old talker had sent her away from the waterfall folk.

"It is often better to be without gods," neKrol told her. "Those below us have a god, and it has made them what they are. And so the Jaenshi have gods, and because they trust, they die. You godless are their only hope."

The bitter speaker did not answer. She only looked down on the silent city, besieged by snow, and her eyes smoldered.

And neKrol watched her, and wondered. He and his six were the hope of the Jaenshi, he had said; if so, was there hope at all? The bitter speaker, and all his exiles, had a madness about them, a rage that made him tremble. Even if Ryther came with the lasers, even if so small a group could stop the Angels' march, even if all that came to pass—what then? Should all the Angels die tomorrow, where would his godless find a place?

They stood, all quiet, while the snow stirred under their feet and the north wind bit at them.

The chapel was dark and quiet. Flameglobes burned a dim, eerie red in either corner, and the rows of plain wooden benches were empty. Above the heavy altar, a slab of rough black stone, Bakkalon stood in holograph, so real he almost breathed; a boy, a mere boy, naked and milky white, with the wide eyes and blond hair of innocent youth. In His hand, half again taller than Himself, was the great black sword.

Wyatt knelt before the projection, head bowed and very still. All through the winter his dreams had been dark and troubled, so each day he would kneel and pray for guidance. There was none else to seek but Bakkalon; he, Wyatt, was the Proctor, who led in battle and in faith. He alone must riddle his visions.

So daily he wrestled with his thoughts, until the snows began to melt and the knees of his uniform had nearly worn through from long scraping on the floor. Finally, he had decided, and this day he had called upon the senior collars to join him in the chapel.

Alone they entered, while the Proctor knelt unmoving, and chose seats on the benches behind him, each apart from his fellows. Wyatt took no notice; he prayed only that his words would be correct, his vision true. When they were all there, he stood and turned to face them.

"Many are the worlds on which the children of Bakkalon have lived," he told them, "but none so blessed as this, our Corlos. A great time is on us, my brothers-in-arms. The pale child has come to me in my sleep, as once he came to the first Proctors in the years when the brotherhood was forged. He has given me visions."

They were quiet, all of them, their eyes humble and obedient; he was their Proctor, after all. There could be no questioning when one of higher rank spoke wisdom or gave orders. That was one of the precepts of Bakkalon, that the chain of command was sacred and never to be doubted. So all of them kept silence.

"Bakkalon Himself has walked upon this world. He has walked among the soulless and the beasts of the field and told them our dominion, and this he has said to me: that when the spring comes and the seed of Earth moves from Sword Valley to take new land, all the animals shall know their place and retire before us. This I do prophesy!

"More, we shall see miracles. That too the pale child has promised me, signs by which we will know His truth, signs that shall bolster our faith with new revelation. But so too shall our faith be tested, for it will be a time of sacrifices, and Bakkalon will call upon us more than once to show our trust in Him. We must remember His Teachings and be true, and each of us must obey Him as a child obeys the parent and a fighting man his officer: that is, swiftly and without question. For the pale child knows best.

"These are the visions He has granted me, these are the dreams that I have dreamed. Brothers, pray with me."

And Wyatt turned again and knelt, and the rest knelt with him, and all the heads were bowed in prayer save one. In the shadows at the rear of the chapel where the flameglobes flickered but dimly, C'ara DaHan stared at his Proctor from beneath a heavy beetled brow.

That night, after a silent meal in the mess hall and a short staff meeting, the Weaponsmaster called upon Wyatt to go walking on the walls. "Proctor, my soul is troubled," he told him. "I must have counsel from he who is closest to Bakkalon." Wyatt nodded, and both donned heavy nightcloaks of black fur and oil-dark metal cloth, and together they walked the redstone parapets beneath the stars.

Near the guardhouse that stood above the city gates, DaHan paused and leaned out over the ledge, his eyes searching the slow-melting snow for long moments before he turned them on the Proctor. "Wyatt," he said at last, "my faith is weak."

The Proctor said nothing, merely watched the other, his face concealed by the hood of his nightcloak. Confession was not a part of the rites of the Steel Angels; Bakkalon had said that a fighting man's faith ought never to waver.

"In the old days," C'ara DaHan was saying, "many weapons were used against the children of Bakkalon. Some, today, exist only in tales. Perhaps they never existed. Perhaps they are empty things, like the gods the soft men worship. I am only a Weaponsmaster; such knowledge is not mine.

"Yet there is a tale, my Proctor—one that troubles me. Once, it is said, in the long centuries of war, the Sons of Hranga loosed upon the seed of Earth foul vampires of the mind, the creatures men called soulsucks. Their touch was invisible, but it crept across kilometers, farther than a man could see, farther than a laser could fire, and it brought madness. Visions, my Proctor, visions! False gods and foolish plans were put in the minds of men, and ..."

"Silence," Wyatt said. His voice was hard, as cold as the night air that crackled around them and turned breath to steam.

There was a long pause. Then, in a softer voice, the Proctor continued. "All winter I have prayed, DaHan, and struggled with my visions. I am the Proctor of the Children of Bakkalon on the World of Corlos, not some new-armed child to be lied to by false gods. I spoke only after I was sure. I spoke as your Proctor, as your father in faith and your commanding officer. That you would question me, Weaponsmaster, that you would doubt—this disturbs me greatly. Next will you stop to argue with me on the field of battle, to dispute some fine point of my orders?"

"Never, Proctor," DaHan said, kneeling in penance in the packed snow atop the walkway.

"I hope not. But, before I dismiss you, because you are my brother in Bakkalon, I will answer you, though I need not and it was wrong of you to expect it. I will tell you this; the Proctor Wyatt is a good officer as well as a devout man. The pale child has made prophecies to me, and has predicted that miracles will come to pass. All these things we shall see with our very eyes. But if the prophecies should fail us, and if no signs appear, well, our eyes will see that too. And then I will know that it was not Bakkalon who sent the visions, but only a false god, perhaps a soul-suck of Hranga. Or do you think a Hrangan can work miracles?"

"No," DaHan said, still on his knees, his great bald head downcast. "That would be heresy."

"Indeed," said Wyatt. The Proctor glanced briefly beyond the walls. The night was crisp and cold and there was no moon. He felt transfigured, and even the stars seemed to cry the glory of the pale child, for the constellation of the Sword was high upon the zenith, the Soldier reaching up toward it from where he stood on the horizon.

"Tonight you will walk guard without your cloak," the Proctor told DaHan when he looked down again. "And should the north wind blow and the cold bite at you, you will rejoice in the pain, for it will be a sign that you submit to your Proctor and your god. As your flesh grows bitter numb, the flame in your heart must burn hotter."

"Yes, my Proctor," DaHan said. He stood and removed his nightcloak, handing it to the other. Wyatt gave him the slash of blessing.

On the wallscreen in his darkened living quarters the taped drama went through its familiar measured paces, but neKrol, slouched in a large cushioned recliner with his eyes half-closed, hardly noticed. The bitter speaker and two of the other Jaenshi exiles sat on the floor, golden eyes rapt on the spectacle of humans chasing and shooting each other amid the vaulting tower cities of ai-Emerel; increasingly they had begun to grow curious about other worlds and other ways of life. It was all very strange, neKrol thought; the waterfall folk and the other clanned Jaenshi had never shown any such interest. He remembered the early days, before the coming of the Steel Angels in their ancient and soon-to-be-dismantled warship, when he had set all kinds of trade goods before the Jaenshi talkers; bright bolts of glittersilk from Avalon, glowstone jewelry from High Kavalaan, duralloy knives and solar generators and steel powerbows, books from a dozen worlds, medicines and wines—he had come with a little of everything. The talkers took some of it, from time to time, but never with any enthusiasm; the only offering that excited them was salt.

It was not until the spring rains came and the bitter speaker began to question him that neKrol realized, with a start, how seldom any of the Jaenshi clans had ever asked him *anything*. Perhaps their social structure and their religion stifled their natural intellectual curiosity. The exiles were certainly eager enough, especially the bitter speaker. NeKrol could answer only a small portion of her questions of late, and even then she always had new ones to puzzle him with. He had begun to grow appalled with the extent of his own ignorance.

But then, so had the bitter speaker; unlike the clanned Jaenshi—did the religion make *that* much difference?—she would answer questions as well, and neKrol had tried quizzing her on many things that he'd wondered at. But most of the time she would only blink in bafflement, and begin to question herself.

"There are no stories about our gods," she said to him once, when he'd tried to learn a little of Jaenshi myth. "What sort of stories could there be? The gods live in the worship pyramids, Arik, and we pray to them and they watch over us and light our lives. They do not bounce around and fight and break each other like your gods seem to do."

"But you had other gods once, before you came to worship the pyramids," neKrol objected. "The very ones your carvers did for me." He had even gone so far as to unpack a crate and show her, though surely she remembered, since the people of the pyramid in the ring-of-stone had been among the finest craftsmen.

Yet the bitter speaker only smoothed her fur, and shook her head. "I was too young to be a carver, so perhaps I was not told," she said. "We all know that which we need to know, but only the carvers need to do these things, so perhaps only they know the stories of these old gods."

Another time he had asked her about the pyramids, and had gotten even less. "Build them?" she had said. "We did not build them, Arik. They have always been, like the rocks and the trees." But then she blinked. "But they are not like the rocks and the trees, are they?" And, puzzled, she went away to talk to the others.

But if the godless Jaenshi were more thoughtful than their brothers in the clans, they were also more difficult, and each day neKrol realized more and more the futility of their enterprise. He had eight of the exiles with him now—they had found two more, half dead from starvation, in the height of winter—and they all took turns training with two lasers and spying on the Angels. But even should Ryther return with the weaponry, their force was a joke against the might the Proctor could put in the field. The *Lights of Jolostar* would be carrying a full arms shipment in the expectation that every clan for a hundred kilometers would now be roused and angry, ready to resist the Steel Angels and overwhelm them by sheer force of numbers; Jannis would be blank-faced when only neKrol and his ragged band appeared to greet her.

If in fact they did. Even that was problematical; he was having much difficulty keeping his guerrillas together. Their hatred of the Steel Angels still bordered on madness, but they were far from a cohesive unit. None of them liked to take orders very well, and they fought constantly, going at each other with bared claws in struggles for social dominance. If neKrol had not warned them, he suspected they might even duel with the lasers. As for staying in good fighting shape, that too was a joke. Of the three females in the band, the bitter speaker was the only one who had not allowed herself to be impregnated. Since the Jaenshi usually gave birth in litters of four to eight, neKrol calculated that late summer would present them with an exile population explosion. And there would be more after that, he knew; the godless seemed to copulate almost hourly, and there was no such thing as Jaenshi birth control. He wondered how the clans kept their population so stable, but his charges didn't know that either.

"I suppose we sexed less," the bitter speaker said when he asked her, "but I was a child, so I would not really know. Before I came here, there was never the urge. I was just young, I would think." But when she said it, she scratched herself and seemed very unsure.

Sighing, neKrol eased himself back in the recliner and tried to shut out the noise of the wallscreen. It was all going to be very difficult. Already the Steel Angels had emerged from behind their walls, and the powerwagons rolled up and down Sword Valley turning forest into farmland. He had gone up into the hills himself, and it was easy to see that the spring planting would soon be done. Then, he suspected, the children of Bakkalon would try to expand. Just last week one of them —a giant "with no head fur," as his scout had described him—was seen up in the ring-of-stone, gathering shards from the broken pyramid. Whatever that meant, it could not be for the good.

Sometimes he felt sick at the forces he had set in motion, and almost wished that Ryther would forget the lasers. The bitter speaker was determined to strike as soon as they were armed, no matter what the odds. Frightened, neKrol reminded her of the hard Angel lesson the last time a Jaenshi had killed a man; in his dreams he still saw children on the walls.

But she only looked at him, with the bronze tinge

of madness in her eyes, and said, "Yes, Arik. I remember."

Silent and efficient, the white-smocked kitchen boys cleared away the last of the evening's dishes and vanished. "At ease," Wyatt said to his officers. Then: "The time of miracles is upon us, as the pale child foretold.

"This morning I sent three squads into the hills to the southeast of Sword Valley, to disperse the Jaenshi clans on lands that we require. They reported back to me in early afternoon, and now I wish to share their reports with you. Squadmother Jolip, will you relate the events that transpired when you carried out your orders?"

"Yes, Proctor." Jolip stood, a white-skinned blond with a pinched face, her uniform hanging slightly loose on a lean body. "I was assigned a squad of ten to clear out the so-called cliff clan, whose pyramid lies near the foot of a low granite cliff in the wilder part of the hills. The information provided by our intelligence indicated that they were one of the smaller clans, with only twenty-odd adults, so I dispensed with heavy armor. We did take a class five blastcannon, since the destruction of the Jaenshi pyramids is slow work with sidearms alone, but other than that our armament was strictly standard issue.

"We expected no resistance, but recalling the incident at the ring-of-stone, I was cautious. After a march of some twelve kilometers through the hills to the vicinity of the cliff, we fanned out in a semi-circle and moved in slowly, with screechguns drawn. A few Jaenshi were encountered in the forest, and these we took prisoner and marched before us, for use as shields in the event of an ambush or attack. That, of course, proved unnecessary.

"When we reached the pyramid by the cliff, they were waiting for us. At least twelve of the beasts, sir. One of them sat near the base of the pyramid with his hands pressed against its side, while the others surrounded him in a sort of a circle. They all looked up at us, but made no other move."

She paused a minute, and rubbed a thoughtful finger up against the side of her nose. "As I told the Proctor, it was all very odd from that point forward. Last summer, I twice led squads against the Jaenshi clans. The first time, having no idea of our intentions, none of the soulless were there; we simply destroyed the artifact and left. The second time, a crowd of the creatures milled around, hampering us with their bodies while not being actively hostile. They did not disperse until I had one of them screeched down. And, of course, I studied the reports of Squadfather Allor's difficulties at the ring-of-stone.

"This time, it was all quite different. I ordered two of my men to set the blastcannon on its tripod, and gave the beasts to understand that they must get out of the way. With hand signals, of course, since I know none of their ungodly tongue. They complied at once, splitting into two groups and, well, lining up, on either side of the line-of-fire. We kept them covered with our screechguns, of course, but everything seemed very peaceful.

"And so it was. The blaster took the pyramid out neatly, a big ball of flame and then sort of a thunder as the thing exploded. A few shards were scattered, but no one was injured, as we had all taken cover and the Jaenshi seemed unconcerned. After the pyramid broke, there was a sharp ozone smell, and for an instant a lingering bluish fire—perhaps an afterimage. I hardly had time to notice them, however, since that was when the Jaenshi all fell to their knees before us. All at once, sirs. And then they pressed their heads against the ground, prostrating themselves. I thought for a moment that they were trying to hail us as gods, because we had shattered their god, and I tried to tell them that we wanted none of their animal worship, and required only that they leave these lands at once. But then I saw that I had misunderstood, because that was when the other four clan members came forward from the trees atop the cliff, and climbed down, and gave us the statue. Then the rest got up. The last I saw, the entire clan was walking due east, away from Sword

Valley and the outlying hills. I took the statue and brought it back to the Proctor." She fell silent but remained standing, waiting for questions.

"I have the statuette here," Wyatt said. He reached down beside his chair and set it on the table, then pulled off the white cloth covering he had wrapped around it.

The base was a triangle of rock-hard blackbark, and three long splinters of bone rose from the corners to make a pyramid-frame. Within, exquisitely carved in every detail from soft blue wood, Bakkalon the pale child stood, holding a painted sword.

"What does this mean?" Fieldbishop Lyon asked, obviously startled.

"Sacrilege!" Fieldbishop Dhallis said.

"Nothing so serious," said Gorman, Fieldbishop for Heavy Armor. "The beasts are simply trying to ingratiate themselves, perhaps in the hope that we will stay our swords."

"None but the seed of Earth may bow to Bakkalon," Dhallis said. "It is written in the Book! The pale child will not look with favor on the soulless!"

"Silence, my brothers-in-arms!" the Proctor said, and the long table abruptly grew quiet again. Wyatt smiled a thin smile. "This is the first of the miracles of which I spoke this winter in the chapel, the first of the strange happenings that Bakkalon told me. For truly he has walked this world, our Corlos, so even the beasts of the fields know his likeness! Think on it, my brothers. Think on this carving. Ask yourselves a few simple questions. Have any of the Jaenshi animals ever been permitted to set foot in this holy city?"

"No, of course not," someone said.

"Then clearly none of them have seen the holograph that stands above our altar. Nor have I often walked among the beasts, as my duties keep me here within the walls. So none could have seen the pale child's likeness on the chain of office that I wear, for the few Jaenshi who have seen my visage have not lived to speak of it—they were those I judged, who hung upon our city walls. The animals do not speak the language of the Earthseed, nor have any among us learned their simple beastly tongue. Lastly, they have not read the Book. Remember all this, and wonder; how did their carvers know what face and form to carve?"

Quiet; the leaders of the children of Bakkalon looked back and forth among themselves in wonderment.

Wyatt quietly folded his hands. "A miracle. We shall have no more trouble with the Jaenshi, for the pale child has come to them."

To the Proctor's right, Fieldbishop Dhallis sat rigidly. "My Proctor, my leader in faith," she said, with some difficulty, each word coming slowly, "surely, *surely*, you do not mean to tell us that these, these *animals*—that they can worship the pale child, that he accepts their worship!"

Wyatt seemed calm, benevolent; he only smiled. "You need not trouble your soul, Dhallis. You wonder whether I commit the First Fallacy, remembering perhaps the Sacrilege of G'hra when a captive Hrangan bowed to Bakkalon to save himself from an animal's death, and the False Proctor Gibrone proclaimed that all who worship the pale child must have souls." He shook his head. "You see, I read the Book. But no, Fieldbishop, no sacrilege has transpired. Bakkalon *has* walked among the Jaenshi, but surely has given them only truth. They have seen him in all his armed dark glory, and heard him proclaim that they are animals, without souls, as surely he would proclaim. Accordingly, they accept their place in the order of the universe, and retire before us. They will never kill a man again. Recall that they did not bow to the statue they carved, but rather gave the statue to *us*, the seed of Earth, who alone can rightfully worship it. When they did prostrate themselves, it was at *our* feet, as animals to men, and that is as it should be. You see? They have been given truth."

Dhallis was nodding. "Yes, my Proctor. I am enlightened. Forgive my moment of weakness."

But halfway down the table, C'ara DaHan leaned forward and knotted his great knuckled hands, frowning all the while. "My Proctor," he said heavily.

"Weaponsmaster?" Wyatt returned. His face grew stern.

"Like the Fieldbishop, my soul has flickered briefly with worry, and I too would be enlightened, if I might?"

Wyatt smiled. "Proceed," he said, in a voice without humor.

"A miracle this thing may be indeed," DaHan said, "but first we must question ourselves, to ascertain that it is not the trick of a soulless enemy. I do not fathom their stratagem, or their reasons for acting as they have, but I do know of one way that the Jaenshi might have learned the features of our Bakkalon."

"Oh?"

"I speak of the Jamish trading base, and the red-haired trader Arik neKrol. He is an Earthseed, an Emereli by his looks, and we have given him the Book. But he remains without a burning love of Bakkalon, and goes without arms like a godless man. Since our landing he has opposed us, and he grew most hostile after the lesson we were forced to give the Jaenshi. Perhaps he put the cliff clan up to it, told them to do the carving, to some strange ends of his own. I believe that he *did* trade with them."

"I believe you speak truth, Weaponsmaster. In the early months after landing, I tried hard to convert neKrol. To no avail, but I did learn much of the Jaenshi beasts and of the trading he did with them." The Proctor still smiled. "He traded with one of the clans here in Sword Valley, with the people of ring-of-stone, with the cliff clan and that of the far fruit tangle, with the waterfall folk, and sundry clans farther east."

"Then it is his doing," DaHan said. "A trick!"

All eyes moved to Wyatt. "I did not say that. NeKrol, whatever intentions he might have, is but a single man. He did not trade with all the Jaenshi, nor even know them all." The Proctor's smile grew briefly wider. "Those of you who have seen the Emereli know him for a man of flab and weakness; he could hardly walk as far as might be required, and he has neither aircar nor power sled."

"But he *did* have contact with the cliff clan," DaHan said. The deep-graven lines on his bronze forehead were set stubbornly.

"Yes, he did," Wyatt answered. "But Squadmother Jolip did not go forth alone this morning. I also sent out Squadfather Walman and Squadfather Allor, to cross the waters of the White Knife. The land there is dark and fertile, better than that to the east. The cliff clan, who are southeast, were between Sword Valley and the White Knife, so they had to go. But the other pyramids we moved against belonged to far-river clans, more than thirty kilometers south. They have never seen the trader Arik neKrol, unless he has grown wings this winter."

Then Wyatt bent again, and set two more statues on the table, and pulled away their coverings. One was set on a base of slate, and the figure was carved in a clumsy broad manner; the other was finely detailed soaproot, even to the struts of the pyramid. But except for the materials and the workmanship, the later statues were identical to the first.

"Do you see a trick, Weaponsmaster?" Wyatt asked.

DaHan looked, and said nothing, for Fieldbishop Lyon rose suddenly and said, "I see a miracle," and others echoed him. After the hubbub had finally quieted, the brawny Weaponsmaster lowered his head and said, very softly, "My Proctor. Read wisdom to us."

"The lasers, speaker, the *lasers!*" There was a tinge of hysterical desperation in neKrol's tone. "Ryther is not back yet, and that is the very point. We must wait."

He stood outside the bubble of the trading base, bare-chested and sweating in the hot morning sun, with the thick wind tugging at his tangled hair. The clamor had pulled him from a troubled sleep. He had stopped them just on the edge of the forest, and now the bitter speaker had turned to face him, looking fierce and hard and most unJaenshi-like with the laser slung across her shoulders, a bright blue glittersilk scarf knotted around her neck, and fat glowstone rings on all eight of her fingers. The other exiles, but for the two that were heavy with child, stood around her. One of them held the other laser, the rest carried quivers and powerbows. That had been the speaker's idea. Her newly-chosen mate was down on one knee, panting; he had run all the way from the ring-of-stone.

"No, Arik," the speaker said, eyes bronze-angry. "Your lasers are now a month overdue, by your own count of time. Each day we wait, and the Steel Angels smash more pyramids. Soon they may hang children again."

"Very soon," neKrol said. "Very soon, if you attack them. Where is your very hope of victory? Your watcher says they go with two squads and a powerwagon—can you stop them with a pair of lasers and four powerbows? Have you learned to think here, or not?"

"Yes," the speaker said, but she bared her teeth at him as she said it. "Yes, but that cannot matter. The clans do not resist, so we must."

From one knee, her mate looked up at neKrol. "They . . . they march on the waterfall," he said, still breathing heavily.

"The waterfall!" the bitter speaker repeated. "Since the death of winter, they have broken more than twenty pyramids, Arik, and their powerwagons have crushed the forest and now a great dusty road scars the soil from their valley to the riverlands. But they had hurt no Jaenshi yet this season, they had let them go. And all those clans-without-a-god have gone to the waterfall, until the home forest of the waterfall folk is bare and eaten clean. Their talkers sit with the old talker and perhaps the waterfall god takes them in, perhaps he is a very great god. I do not know these things. But I *do* know that now the bald Angel has learned of the twenty clans together, of a grouping of half-a-thousand Jaenshi adults, and he leads a powerwagon against them. Will he let them go so easy this time, happy with a carved statue? Will *they* go, Arik, will they give up a second god as easily as a first?" The speaker blinked. "I fear they will resist with their silly claws. I fear the bald Angel will hang them even if they do not resist, because so many in union throws suspicion in him. I fear many things and know little, but I know *we* must be there. You will not stop us, Arik, and we cannot wait for your long-late lasers."

And she turned to the others and said, "Come, we must run," and they had faded into the forest before neKrol could even shout for them to stay. Swearing, he turned back to the bubble.

The two female exiles were leaving just as he entered. Both were close to the end of their term, but they had powerbows in their hands. NeKrol stopped short. "You too!" he said furiously, glaring at them. "Madness, it is the very stuff of madness!" They only looked at him with silent golden eyes, and moved past him toward the trees.

Inside, he swiftly braided his long red hair so it would not catch on the branches, slipped into a shirt, and darted toward the door. Then he stopped. A weapon, he must have a weapon! He glanced around frantically and ran heavily for his storeroom. The powerbows were all gone, he saw. What then, what? He began to rummage, and finally settled for a duralloy machete. It felt strange in his hand and he must have looked most unmartial and ridiculous, but somehow he felt he must take something.

Then he was off, toward the place of the waterfall folk.

NeKrol was overweight and soft, hardly used to running, and the way was nearly two kilometers through lush summer forest. He had to stop three times to rest, and quiet the pains in his chest, and it seemed an eternity before he arrived. But still he beat the Steel Angels; a powerwagon is ponderous and slow, and the road from Sword Valley was longer and more hilly.

Jaenshi were everywhere. The glade was bare of grass and twice as large as neKrol remembered it from his last trading trip, early that spring. Still the Jaenshi filled all of it, sitting on the ground, staring at the pool and the waterfull, all silent, packed together so there was scarcely room to walk among them. More sat above, a dozen in every fruit tree, some of the children even ascending to the higher limbs where the pseudomonks usually ruled alone.

On the rock at the center of the pool, with the waterfall behind them as a backdrop, the talkers pressed around the pyramid of the waterfall folk. They were closer together than even those in the grass, and each had his palms flat against the sides. One, thin and frail, sat on the shoulders of another so that he too might touch. NeKrol tried to count them and gave up; the group was too dense, a blurred mass of gray-furred arms and golden eyes, the pyramid at their center, dark and unmovable as ever.

The bitter speaker stood in the pool, the waters ankle-deep around her. She was facing the crowd and screeching at them, her voice strangely unlike the usual Jaenshi purr; in her scarf and rings, she looked absurdly out of place. As she talked, she waved the laser rifle she was holding in one hand. Wildly, passionately, hysterically, she was telling the gathered Jaenshi that the Steel Angels were coming, that they must leave at once, that they should break up and go into the forest and regroup at the trading base. Over and over again she said it.

But the clans were stiff and silent. No one answered, no one listened, no one heard. In full daylight, they were praying.

NeKrol pushed his way through them, stepping on a hand here and a foot there, hardly able to set down a boot without crunching Jaenshi flesh. He was standing next to the bitter speaker, who still gestured wildly, before her bronze eyes seemed to see him. Then she stopped. "Arik," she said, "the Angels are coming, and *they will not listen.*"

"The others," he panted, still short on breath. "Where are they?"

"The trees," the bitter speaker replied, with a vague

gesture. "I sent them up in the trees. Snipers, Arik, such as we saw upon your wall."

"Please," he said. "Come back with me. Leave them, leave them. You told them. I told them. Whatever happens, it is their doing, it is the fault of their fool religion."

"I cannot leave," the bitter speaker said. She seemed confused, as so often when neKrol had questioned her back at the base. "It seems I should, but somehow I know I must stay here. And the others will *never* go, even if I did. They feel it much more strongly. We must be here. To fight, to talk." She blinked. "I do not know *why,* Arik, but we must."

And before the trader could reply, the Steel Angels came out of the forest.

There were five of them at first, widely spaced; then shortly five more. All afoot, in uniforms whose mottled dark greens blended with the leaves, so that only the glitter of the mesh-steel belts and matching battle helmets stood out. One of them, a gaunt pale woman, wore a high red collar; all of them had hand-lasers drawn.

"You!" the blond woman shouted, her eyes finding Arik at once, as he stood with his braid flying in the wind and the machete dangling uselessly in his hand. "Speak to these animals! Tell them they must leave! Tell them that no Jaenshi gathering of this size is permitted east of the mountains, by order of the Proctor Wyatt, and the pale child Bakkalon. Tell them!" And then she saw the bitter speaker, and started. "And take the laser from the hand of that animal before we burn both of you down!"

Trembling, neKrol dropped the machete from limp fingers into the water. "Speaker, drop the gun," he said in Jaenshi, *"please.* If you ever hope to see the far stars. Let loose the laser, my friend, my child, this very now. And I will take you, when Ryther comes, with me to ai-Emerel and farther places." The trader's voice was full of fear; the Steel Angels held their lasers steady, and not for a moment did he think the speaker would obey him.

But strangely, meekly, she threw the laser rifle into the pool. NeKrol could not see to read her eyes.

The Squadmother relaxed visibly. "Good," she said. "Now, talk to them in their beastly talk, tell them to leave. If not, we shall crush them. A powerwagon is on its way!" And now, over the roar and tumble of the nearby waters, neKrol could hear it; a heavy crunching as it rolled over trees, rending them into splinters beneath wide duramesh treads. Perhaps they were using the blastcannon and the turret lasers to clear away boulders and other obstacles.

"We have told them," neKrol said desperately. "Many times we have told them, but they do not hear!" He gestured all about him; the glade was still hot and close with Jaenshi bodies and none among the clans had taken the slightest notice of the Steel Angels or the confrontation. Behind him, the clustered talkers still pressed small hands against their god.

"Then we shall bare the sword of Bakkalon to them," the Squadmother said, "and perhaps they will hear their own wailing!" She holstered her laser and drew a screechgun, and neKrol, shuddering, knew her intent. The screechers used concentrated high-intensity sound to break down cell walls and liquefy flesh. Its effects were psychological as much as anything; there was no more horrible death.

But then a second squad of the Angels were among them, and there was a creak of wood straining and snapping, and from behind a final grove of fruit trees, dimly, neKrol could see the black flanks of the powerwagon, its blastcannon seemingly trained right at him. Two of the newcomers wore the scarlet collar—a redfaced youth with large ears who barked orders to his squad, and a huge, muscular man with a bald head and lined bronze skin. NeKrol recognized him; the Weaponsmaster C'ara DaHan. It was DaHan who laid a heavy hand on the Squadmother's arm as she raised her screechgun. "No," he said. "It is not the way."

She holstered the weapon at once. "I hear and obey."

DaHan looked at neKrol. "Trader," he boomed, "is this your doing?"

"No," neKrol said.

"They will not disperse," the Squadmother added.

"It would take us a day and a night to screech them down," DaHan said, his eyes sweeping over the glade and the trees, and following the rocky twisted path of the waterwall up to its summit. "There is an easier way. Break the pyramid and they go at once." He stopped then, about to say something else; his eyes were on the bitter speaker.

"A Jaenshi in rings and cloth," he said. "They have woven nothing but deathcloth up to now. This alarms me."

"She is one of the people of the ring-of-stone," neKrol said quickly. "She has lived with me."

Dattan nodded. "I understand. You are truly a godless man, neKrol, to consort so with soulless animals, to teach them to ape the ways of the seed of Earth. But it does not matter." He raised his arm in signal; behind him, among the trees, the blastcannon of the powerwagon moved slightly to the right. "You and your pet should move at once," DaHan told neKrol. "When I lower my arm, the Jaenshi god will burn and if you stand in the way, you will never move again."

"The *talkers!*" neKrol protested, "the blast will—" and he started to turn to show them. But the talkers were crawling away from the pyramid, one by one.

Behind him, the Angels were muttering. "A miracle!" one said hoarsely. "Our child! Our Lord!" cried another.

NeKrol stood paralyzed. The pyramid on the rock was no longer a reddish slab. Now it sparkled in the sunlight, a canopy of transparent crystal. And below that canopy, perfect in every detail, the pale child Bakkalon stood smiling, with his Demon-Reaver in his hand.

The Jaenshi talkers were scrambling from it now, tripping in the water in their haste to be away. NeKrol glimpsed the old talker, running faster than any despite his age. Even he seemed not to understand. The bitter speaker stood open-mouthed.

The trader turned. Half of the Steel Angels were on their knees, the rest had absent-mindedly lowered their arms and they froze in gaping wonder. The Squadmother turned to DaHan. "It *is* a miracle," she said. "As Proctor Wyatt has foreseen. The pale child walks upon this world."

But the Weaponsmaster was unmoved. "The Proctor is not here and this is no miracle," he said in a steely voice. "It is a trick of some enemy, and I will not be tricked. We will burn the blasphemous thing from the soil of Corlos." His arm flashed down.

The Angels in the powerwagon must have been lax with awe; the blastcannon did not fire. DaHan turned in irritation. "It is no miracle!" he shouted. He began to raise his arm again.

Next to neKrol, the bitter speaker suddenly cried out. He looked over with alarm, and saw her eyes flash a brilliant yellow-gold. "The god!" she muttered softly. "The light returns to me!"

And the whine of powerbows sounded from the trees around them, and two long bolts shuddered almost simultaneously in the broad back of C'ara DaHan. The force of the shots drove the Weaponsmaster to his knees, smashed him against the ground.

"*RUN!*" neKrol screamed, and he shoved the bitter speaker with all his strength, and she stumbled and looked back at him briefly, her eyes dark bronze again and flickering with fear. Then, swiftly, she was running, her scarf aflutter behind her as she dodged toward the nearest green.

"Kill her!" the Squadmother shouted. "Kill them all!" And her words woke Jaenshi and Steel Angels both; the children of Bakkalon lifted their lasers against the suddenly-surging crowd, and the slaughter began. NeKrol knelt and scrabbled on the moss-slick rocks until he had the laser rifle in his hands, then brought it to his shoulder and commenced to fire. Light stabbed out in angry bursts; once, twice, a third time. He held the trigger down and the bursts became a beam, and he sheared through the waist of a silver-helmeted Angel before the fire flared in his stomach and he fell heavily into the pool.

For a long time he saw nothing; there was only pain and noise, the water gently slapping against his face, the sounds of high-pitched Jaenshi screaming, running all around him. Twice he heard the roar and crackle of the blastcannon, and more than twice he was stepped on. It all seemed unimportant. He struggled to keep his head on the rocks, half out of the water, but even that seemed none too vital after a while. The only thing that counted was the burning in his gut.

Then, somehow, the pain went away, and there was a lot of smoke and horrible smells but not so much noise, and neKrol lay quietly and listened to the voices.

"The pyramid, Squadmother?" someone asked.

"It *is* a miracle," a woman's voice replied. "Look, Bakkalon stands there yet. And see how he smiles! We have done right here today!"

"What should we do with it?"

"Lift it aboard the powerwagon. We shall bring it back to Proctor Wyatt."

Soon after the voices went away, and neKrol heard only the sound of the water, rushing down endlessly, falling and tumbling. It was a very restful sound. He decided he would sleep.

The crewman shoved the crowbar down between the slats and lifted. The thin wood hardly protested at all before it gave. "More statues, Jannis," he reported, after reaching inside the crate and tugging loose some of the packing material.

"Worthless," Ryther said, with a brief sigh. She stood in the broken ruins of neKrol's trading base. The Angels had ransacked it, searching for armed Jaenshi, and debris lay everywhere. But they had not touched the crates.

The crewman took his crowbar and moved on to the next stack of crated artifacts. Ryther looked wistfully at the three Jaenshi who clustered around her, wishing they could communicate a little better. One of them, a sleek female who wore a trailing scarf and a lot of jewelry and seemed always to be leaning on a powerbow, knew a smattering of Terran, but hardly enough. She picked up things quickly, but so far the only thing of substance she had said was, "Jamson' World. Arik take us. Angels kill." That she had repeated endlessly until Ryther had finally made her understand that, yes, they would take them. The other two Jaenshi, the pregnant female and the male with the laser, never seemed to talk at all.

"Statues again," the crewman said, having pulled a crate from atop the stack in the ruptured storeroom and pried it open.

Ryther shrugged; the crewman moved on. She turned her back on him and wandered slowly outside, to the edge of the spacefield where the *Lights of Jolostar* rested, its open ports bright with yellow light in the gathering gloom of dusk. The Jaenshi followed her, as they had followed her since she arrived; afraid, no doubt, that she would go away and leave them if they took their great bronze eyes off her for an instant.

"Statues," Ryther muttered, half to herself and half to the Jaenshi. She shook her head. "Why did he do it?" she asked them, knowing they could not understand. "A trader of his experience? You could tell me, maybe, if you knew what I was saying. Instead of concentrating on deathcloths and such, on real Jaenshi art, why did Arik train you people to carve alien versions of human gods? He should have known no dealer would accept such obvious frauds. Alien art is *alien*." She sighed. "My fault, I suppose. We should have opened the crates." She laughed.

The bitter speaker stared at her. "Arik deathcloth. Gave."

Ryther nodded, abstractly. She had it now, hanging just above her bunk; a strange small thing, woven partly from Jaenshi fur and mostly from long silken strands of flame red hair. On it, gray against the red, was a crude but recognizable caricature of Arik neKrol. She had wondered at that, too. The tribute of a widow? A child? Or just a friend? What *had* happened to Arik during the year the *Lights* had been away? If only she had been back on time, then . . . but she'd lost three months on Jamison's World, checking dealer after dealer in an effort to unload the worthless statuettes. It had been middle autumn before the *Lights of Jolostar* returned to Corlos, to find neKrol's base in ruins, the Angels already gathering in their harvests.

And the Angels—when she'd gone to them, offering the hold of unwanted lasers, offering to trade, the sight on those blood-red city walls had sickened even her. She had thought she'd gone prepared, but the obscenity she encountered was beyond any preparation. A squad of Steel Angels found her, vomiting, beyond the tall rusty gates, and had escorted her inside, before the Proctor.

Wyatt was twice as skeletal as she remembered him. He had been standing outdoors, near the foot of a huge platform-altar that had been erected in the middle of the city. A startlingly lifelike statue of Bakkalon, encased in a glass pyramid and set atop a high redstone plinth, threw a long shadow over the wooden altar. Beneath it, the squads of Angels were piling the newly-harvested neograss and wheat and the frozen carcasses of bushogs.

"We do not need your trade," the Proctor told her. "The World of Corlos is many-times-blessed, my child, and Bakkalon lives among us now. He has worked vast miracles, and shall work more. Our faith is in Him." Wyatt gestured toward the altar with a thin hand. "See? In tribute we burn our winter stores, for the pale child has promised that this year winter will not come. And He has taught us to cull ourselves in peace as once we were culled in war, so the seed of Earth grows ever stronger. It is a time of great new revelation!" His eyes had burned as he spoke to her; eyes darting and fanatic, vast and dark yet strangely flecked with gold.

As quickly as she could, Ryther had left the City of the Steel Angels, trying hard not to look back at the walls. But when she had climbed the hills, back toward the trading base, she had come to the ring-of-stone, to the broken pyramid where Arik had taken her. Then

Ryther found that she could not resist, and powerless she had turned for a final glance out over Sword Valley. The sight had stayed with her.

Outside the walls the Angel children hung, a row of small white-smocked bodies still and motionless at the end of long ropes. They had gone peacefully, all of them, but death is seldom peaceful; the older ones, at least, died quickly, necks broken with a sudden snap. But the small pale infants had the nooses round their waists, and it had seemed clear to Ryther that most of them had simply hung there till they starved.

As she stood, remembering, the crewman came from inside neKrol's broken bubble. "Nothing," he reported. "All statues." Ryther nodded.

"Go?" the bitter speaker said. "Jamson World?"

"Yes," she replied, her eyes staring past the waiting *Lights of Jolostar,* out toward the black primal forest. The Heart of Bakkalon was sunk forever. In a thousand thousand woods and a single city, the clans had begun to pray.

—Chicago, October 1974